PARADISE GIRLS

PARADISE GIRLS

A Novel

Sandy Gingras

ST. MARTIN'S GRIFFIN
NEW YORK

This is a work of fiction. All of the characters, organizations, and events portrayed in this novel are either products of the author's imagination or are used fictitiously.

First published in the United States by St. Martin's Griffin, an imprint of St. Martin's Publishing Group

Printed in the United States of America. For information, address St. Martin's Publishing Group, 120 Broadway, New York, NY 10271.

www.stmartins.com

Designed by Gabriel Guma

Library of Congress Cataloging-in-Publication Data

Names: Gingras, Sandy, 1958– author.
Title: Paradise Girls: A Novel / Sandy Gingras.
Description: First edition. | New York: St. Martin's Griffin, 2022.
Identifiers: LCCN 2022003287 | ISBN 9781250816719 (trade paperback) | ISBN 9781250816726 (ebook)
Subjects: LCGFT: Novels.
Classification: LCC PS3607.I458 P37 2022 | DDC 813/.6—dc23/eng/20220211
LC record available at https://lccn.loc.gov/2022003287

First Edition: 2022

10 9 8 7 6 5 4 3 2 1

PARADISE GIRLS

BEFORE

Mary hummed carols as she draped strands of tinsel on her desktop tree. She rubbed a pine needle between her fingers and breathed deep. What a transporting smell—so forest-rich, so secret. She imagined herself in a sleigh with Ron under a snuggly blanket, whooshing through snow-laden trees, the smell of horses' oaty breaths clouding the air, the heavy, hollow clunking of bells, flurries drifting down all around them.

Maybe she and Ron could find a place that offered sleigh rides.

Right. In Manhattan.

She looked out the window. She was on the eighteenth floor of Ron's New York offices, and she was watching people in nearby buildings sitting at their desks in other eighteenth-floor windows. It was a week before Christmas. No snow was in the forecast. The dusky sky was laden with clouds. It was supposed to rain later tonight.

Oh well, she thought. Ron wouldn't have gone for it anyway. He was afraid of horses.

"Twelve hmm-hmms leaping, eleven somethings um-ing," she sang.

She'd put the tree in a concrete urn that took up most of her desk. A wooden snowman stood next to it, staring at her with black eyes and a wavery smile as if he were watching over her. She stepped back. Her desk looked tacky and cluttered and jolly, and there was absolutely no room left to work. Oh well. She wasn't a desk kind of person anyway. Most of the time, she ended up working sitting cross-legged on the floor on her orange shag rug that Ron called "the yak-hair mat" with piles all around her, crookedly writing her articles on a sketch pad. Ron didn't know she did that, though. It was her little secret. He'd told her that he liked her to compose on a computer, told her that her thoughts "lined up better that way." Well, they were *her* thoughts—let them get out of line if they wanted to.

She looked around her office. Strands of garlands and twinkle lights swooped and wove everywhere. It was like a Christmas spider had gone crazy.

"Face it, Mary. You have decorating issues," she said to herself. Which was ironic, she knew. She wrote for Ron's five home magazines. Her life was décor. Ron told her she was a "guru of tasteful," that she could do tasteful in her sleep. But, it was weird, in the past year or so, when it came to her own work space and her own home, Mary was a decorating mess.

She'd started to overdo everything. Not one inspirational sign on her wall, but six of them. Not two throw pillows on her couch, but a lumpy mountain range of them. She used to pride herself on the simplicity of her life, but now it was as if she couldn't get enough belongings surrounding her. She kept buying more and more cute trinkets. Her home and office were turning into higgledy-piggledy muddles. Her therapist, Zelda, said that Mary was looking to "fill a kind of hole inside," that she was "trying in vain to make home homier."

Mary didn't like that "in vain" part. But she knew that Zelda was right on some level. What Mary was doing was compulsive and unhealthy.

At least she hadn't turned into a hoarder—but she watched that show sometimes as a cautionary tale. And she wasn't a collector. Thank goodness she hadn't taken up amassing frog statuettes or hundreds of different salt and pepper shakers. But sometimes she opened the door to her office or her condo in Brooklyn and thought, *Where am I in all of this stuff?*

Now she looked around her office and thought, *I've gone overboard with Christmas too.*

She said aloud, "Don't beat yourself up. You're doing okay. You still manage to get things done. A lot done." That was true. She'd just completed another assignment. Somehow, out of her personal chaos, a totally together article about somebody else's beautiful house always emerged. How she managed to pull it off, she didn't know. Some days she felt like a total fraud.

She sighed. Twinkle lights blinked on and off around her. A garland above her head proclaimed, BELIEVE! Old-fashioned statues of Santa heads lined her shelf, and a pair of angel wings hung on the wall next to a picture of her daughter and granddaughter—CC looking like an imp with her ragged cap of brown hair and big blue eyes and Larkin looking like a miniature longer-haired version of her mother, with her serious expression and black glasses. She tried not to look at their faces. That way was sadness. She hadn't seen them in months.

"Six somebodies doing something, five golden rings . . ." she sang quietly. *One golden ring would be enough,* she thought. Well, it was finally going to happen. She and Ron were getting married. They'd been semi-engaged for four years. Or at least that's what Mary called it. Although he hadn't given her an engagement ring. Well, who needed an engagement ring these days? She wasn't a diamond lover anyway. They had a plan this time. Not like the other three times when Ron had postponed their wedding. This time it was real. They were getting married January third. Justice of the peace at ten a.m., then brunch with a few friends at a new restaurant that had just opened in a converted brownstone. Mary had a reservation for the private dining room. She'd decided on the menu (a medley of all different kinds of crepes, from quinoa lemon curd to ham, asparagus, and Swiss—so fun) and the flowers (bunches of miniature daisies), and although Ron wanted to use someone from his staff to be the photographer, she'd gone ahead and booked a young guy who was just starting out instead. He'd shot his share of indie bands and skateboarders, but never a wedding. Yet he was so sweet, so vulnerable when she interviewed him, and his photos, especially the portraits, had such sensitivity she couldn't resist hiring him. It was only candid shots she wanted anyway. She'd put a deposit down on it all. There was no going back now.

After the wedding, she was moving in with Ron. She'd already sold her condo. The closing was in three weeks. Then they were going to buy their own house together. She'd have a chance to start over then. Make a homey home. So there, Zelda!

She was looking forward to that. So forward. She felt a hopeful blippy rise in her chest every time she thought of it. It was going to be perfect—two home-décor addicts uniting! She could almost see their kitchen—a walk-in pantry so big you could do a little dance in it, an island with storage for every shaped pot and pan, a farm sink with a faucet as big as a swan's neck. She was so lost in her thoughts that she flinched when her phone dinged with a text from Ron.

C u in my office?

She brushed her glittery hands off on her pants and hurried down the hall. She was excited to hear what Ron was going to say.

She'd emailed him earlier with an idea about starting a monthly DIY feature in one of his magazines where she showed how to redo a living room for under five hundred dollars. Snap! She knew it would be a hit. Lately she'd been longing to use her decorating skills again, besides just writing about décor.

"What did you think of my idea?" she asked him the minute she walked in the door. That was Mary. She found it hard to contain herself. It was a constant struggle around Ron because he'd become such a model of restraint. Everything was a thoughtful "maybe" or a "perhaps" these days. Never a "YES!" anymore. Mary could throttle him sometimes.

He said, "I have another project I want you on."

He was so elegant. His pants draped beautifully as he stood up from behind his desk. Why didn't he ever wrinkle? He looked British somehow with that aristocratic nose, those long fingers. Like a Ralph Lauren model. When Mary met him, he was always in ripped jeans and a pair of paint-splattered sneakers. Now he was rich. Imagine! And Mary had helped him get there.

She could see the perfect posture of his body reflected in the sheen on his desk, the one made out of that exotic wood from a tree that was endangered in the rain forest, only one stand of them left in the whole world, but Ron had managed to get some of it anyway when they moved into these new offices, had it made into this huge "statement" of a desk. It made Mary sad to look at it. So she looked at him instead—gorgeous, brilliant, successful him.

He said, "I'm starting a new magazine."

Ron was always starting new home magazines these days. He knew people couldn't get enough of home—buying, restoring, expanding, renovating—and he was making a killing off it. Ron was aware that the home craze had to do with people's longing to change their lives but their being unable or unwilling to do that—

too much emotional work! So they knocked down a wall in their foyer instead or installed some French doors in their bedroom or changed out their laminate countertops for granite, and they managed to feel okay about themselves again. At least for a moment. Home reno was the new drug, and he was pushing it hard. His business was juggernauting, higher, higher, higher. Mary was typing her heart out just to keep up.

He said, "It'll be called *Home Tweet Home*. Just photos with captions. And we'd keep it down to the Twitter two-hundred-and-eighty-character limit. People's attention spans are so short. It's such a great concept. And you're perfect to write the captions!"

"Perfect to write captions," she said, her heart sinking.

She could see herself in the reflection of his floor-to-ceiling window. It was getting dark so early now. Her hair stuck out of its ponytail—why wouldn't it ever stay put? Was that glitter reflecting on her nose? Probably. She tugged at her sweater, which was slumping off one shoulder. No matter how hard she tried to knife-edge her eyeliner, no matter how many black outfits she bought, she was never going to be a sleek New Yorker. Her Midwestern genes always won out. Her eyes were too soft for New York, her cheeks too round; her corn-blond curly hair, no matter how she tried to tame it, was always slipping its bounds. And her heart? Well, that too was well-meaning but clumsy. Sometimes around Ron these days, she felt like a puppy let loose in Tiffany's.

"What about my idea?" she said.

When she'd first started working for him, they'd thrown ideas at each other all the time. It was such a creative, playful period. She was Ron's only employee. He had had one home décor magazine basically running out of his garage. It was called *Make Yourself a Home*. Mary was constantly writing articles titled "How to Create

Shelving out of Salvage!" or "Decorate with Living Branches!" or "Make Friends with Your Glue Gun!" Her use of exclamation points was rampant back then. It was so much exuberant fun. And the magazine was a hit. She and Ron had laughed together working long hours side by side in his garage office, which still had a concrete floor and a lawn mower in it and smelled like gasoline. They thought it was endlessly entertaining that they were churning out a successful home décor magazine from there.

Mary missed those days.

Now she said, "We could call the first article 'Put the Life Back in Your Living Room!'" She rarely said things like this anymore. Now she just yielded to his direction. He was the boss. And there was no doubt he knew what he was doing. *But it's such a good idea.*

She said, "I can show people how to make spaces that are rich with personality, not just money. I mean, Ron, last week I wrote an article about a twenty-million-dollar house that had a moat! Don't you think we're getting out of touch?"

He stared at her.

Over the years, as Ron became more and more successful, his magazines had gotten progressively more upscale too. Now they were mostly glossy showcases for mansions. Ron had even "rebranded" *Make Yourself a Home* a few months ago. Now it was simply called *Coveted.*

Why are his eyes so distant? "Alexandra called me," Ron said.

"What?" Mary said.

She noticed that he was holding his odd snow globe of the Swiss village that he took out of the closet every Christmas and put on his desk. Alexandra was Ron's ex, and she'd given the globe to him for their first Christmas together. It was the only thing he decorated his office with at Christmastime. Mary had always hated it. He shook it now. She could tell he didn't even realize he was doing it, making it snow and snow and snow, burying all the little Swiss people in a blizzard.

"She's back in town," he told her.

"Now?" Mary couldn't get her mouth to move right.

"She wants to see Joanna for Christmas."

"But . . ."

"She says she turned her life around."

"So?" Well, that wasn't the right thing to say. Mary could see Ron's mouth tug down on one edge the way it did when she slipped up, when she said anything that suggested that there might be anything wrong with him or his family. But Alexandra? Why was she back? She couldn't say that either.

"I called Joanna. She's coming home tomorrow," Ron said.

"But I thought Joanna hated Alexandra." Mary had only heard tales of Joanna's mother—the exotic and screwed-up Alexandra. Alexandra evidently had an alcohol issue and, when Joanna was two, had taken off to live in a commune. She lived in California now. Ron called her a "mermaid artist." As far as Mary could tell, what she did for a living was dress up in a blue sequined outfit and weave tinsel into people's hair at craft shows. Alexandra "traveled a lot for business," which meant she was often popping in and out of Ron and Joanna's life, leaving a wake of emotional chaos. And Ron let her.

"Joanna wants to see her mother for Christmas." Ron's voice had that cold, even tone that meant he'd made up his mind.

Joanna was eighteen and had had chronic fatigue syndrome since childhood. So, in Ron's mind, she was fragile and always needed accommodating. But was she really? Mary and Ron had set three dates in the past year alone to get married, and Ron had postponed each one because "something was going on with Joanna."

Pale, fragile Joanna, whose IQ was off the charts. Mary barely knew her—well, she really hadn't had a chance to know her. Joanna had gone to a private school and to a science camp during the summers, and it seemed like she had always been cached in her room reading or studying. Ron had a live-in French housekeeper, Arles, who took care of all of Joanna's "needs" when she was home. Arles was so humorless Mary secretly called her the Anti-Poppins.

In Mary's mind, Joanna was just a wounded kid, lost and shattered by Alexandra's continuous abandonment of her. Mary thought Joanna needed her father to stop making excuses for her and to draw the line with Alexandra. And the whole family needed to lose the Anti-Poppins. But nobody asked what Mary thought.

Once, when she and Ron first started going out, Mary took Joanna "on an adventure" when Ron was working on the weekend. Joanna was fourteen. They went to a street fair, and Joanna learned how to juggle from a clown. She was instantly good at it too. Mary bought her a set of squishy balls at that stall to bring home and practice with. Then she'd bought them big felt hats—one shaped like a hot dog (for Mary) and the other, a hamburger (for Joanna)—and they made faces at themselves in fun-house mirrors. Then they'd eaten fried dough with powdered sugar from a food truck. When they got home, Joanna had gotten really sick. She was in bed for a week. That had been that. Ron never let her go out with Mary again. One day not so long ago, Mary found one of the juggling balls stuffed away in the back of Ron's kitchen drawer.

But Joanna had gone away to college in September, and she'd been doing just fine there. She finally got a chance to be herself, Mary thought. She seemed healthy and happy. She was going to spend Christmas away—with her friend Evie at Evie's house in Vermont. Evie had snowmobiles! So Mary was going to be able to spend her first Christmas alone with Ron. She'd been so looking forward to it.

Now this.

Ron said, "Xanny's staying in a hotel for a week, so I asked her to come spend Christmas Eve and Christmas Day with me and Joanna. I can't ask Joanna to spend her Christmas in a hotel room, can I?"

"Xanny?" Mary had never heard Ron refer to Alexandra that way. And here Mary was, excluded from Christmas. Again. Every year it was something. Ron said that Joanna "needs her father to herself." Or Ron said that it would be "too foreign" to invite Mary. Now it was Xanny getting included and Mary kicked out? This couldn't be happening.

Ron looked down.

"But we have plans to spend Christmas together," Mary said.

Ron said, "We'll have the rest of our lives together."

Mary thought about buying herself another Cornish game hen for Christmas dinner instead of a turkey. She'd had to use her pinky last Christmas to stuff the tiny bird. Or she could go over to her friend Joelle's house for Christmas dinner. She was always invited there, and she could watch Joelle's uncle Guido throw up in the ice bucket again.

She couldn't. She just couldn't.

"It's not a big deal, so don't make it into one," he told her. "You know how you do."

Sure, she thought, *it's just another short-term delay*. But her life had been like this for years. One delay after another, none of which had seemed like much in and of itself. But all together? They added up to something. Mary knew it. She'd felt this stone of truth in her belly for a long time now, a hardness that made her shudder. It wasn't Joanna who was the problem. It was Ron. Why couldn't he commit? Why was there always another roadblock, another excuse not to be with her? And now Xanny?

"Why can't we *all* be together like every other extended, screwed-up American family on Christmas?" she said. Truth was she was interested in finally meeting Alexandra. Who knew? Maybe she could get Alexandra to weave those mermaid thingies into her hair.

Ron's eyes shifted quickly as if he was considering it.

Maybe he'll change his mind, Mary thought. Hope flickered in her for a second. *Choose to be with me!* Her stupid heart leaped around in her chest. But that was the power of Ron. He was like a firefly beckoning, lighting up, appearing, but when Mary reached for him, he flitted away and disappeared, and Mary was left holding nothing but darkness. She should have learned by now not to grasp at him.

Ron said, "No. Joanna needs this time to sort things out with her mother."

Mary felt the weight of his words settle over her. For a second, she almost couldn't breathe.

"Did Joanna say that?" Mary said. She knew it was useless to argue with him, but she couldn't help herself.

"I said that," he said, and his face changed as though an automatic garage door came sliding down inside of him. A door with no windows. Not even little ones.

She looked at Ron's desk, his closed laptop, his two matching gold photo frames sitting side by side—one holding a picture of Mary, one of Joanna. She watched Ron put the globe down on his desk and start walking toward her, his arms out like he was going to hug her. *No*, she thought, *not that*. Mary shot her hand straight out, her palm facing him. *Like Diana Ross and the Supremes. Stop. In the name of love.* He halted in his tracks.

She walked toward his desk. Her legs felt like wobbly sticks. Was she going to fall over? *No. Stand up, girl*, she told herself. She took a deep breath. She forced herself not to focus on his soft navy blue cashmere sweater that she'd bought for him, his crisp white shirt underneath, the way his chest hair ever so slightly peeked over the edge of it.

He smiled at her, but she could see uncertainty in his eyes. "Babe," he said evenly. "I know you're angry, but just think about next year, think about all our plans."

"You won't ever . . ." she said. She tried to make her voice even too. But she heard it quaver. She stopped, felt a burning in her chest. What was that feeling? *Shame,* she thought, as she felt her face flush. How odd. She felt naked standing there. Helpless. *I'll never be able to get him to love me. Not enough.*

He said, "Christmas is just a day like any other day."

Was he right? Why did he make her doubt herself? *Not this time*, she thought. She said, "This is important. This is now. This is what we have. It might be all we have. It's Christmas!"

"It'll be over before you know it," he said, and looked down.

She wanted to cry and yell and beat on his chest. *This matters to me!* But she'd done all that before. So many times. She'd expressed every one of her feelings to him the way you're supposed to if you want someone to know who you are, but nothing had ever changed.

"You don't understand the situation I'm in," he said.

She held herself very still, and her voice came out calm although she was boiling inside. "Yes, I do, Ron. I actually endlessly understand your situation. How could I not? It's *all* about you and your situation. *All* the time."

Her eyes lit on the snow globe. She picked it up. She wasn't sure why. She saw him look up at her and his eyes widen. His precious snow globe. She'd never touched it before. She thought it was going to be heavy, but it wasn't. She looked at the little world. She felt so far outside it—the cozy, brightly lit windows of the homes, the people gathered together. Her breath heaved in her chest, and before she could think about it, she reared back and threw the snow globe toward his wall—all her hopes and dreams and rage and sadness in one flinging, awkward gesture.

There. There goes your situation.

She watched it wobble in an arc across the room.

There was one very silent moment. Then it slammed into the wall and shattered. The pieces went everywhere. The little people flew in all different directions. Mary watched as some landed headfirst in the wall-to-wall carpeting. *Goodbye, Swiss village*, she thought.

Her heart was pounding.

Ron walked over to where what was left of the globe had fallen. The water had already disappeared into the carpet. He picked up the base of it. One house still stood, but it was leaning and its roof was gone. He held it in his palm, staring at it. Then he looked at his wall.

"You dented it," he said. Disbelieving.

Mary was shaking. "Good," she said.

He shook his head at her. *Bad Mary. Very, very bad Mary*, she could almost hear him saying. Although she didn't feel bad. She felt elated. She knew it was a high and it would fade, but still she felt exultant in the moment. That damn snow globe.

"Good?" he said.

"I'm gone," she said. Her arms were wrapped around herself. Was she holding herself up? She could feel her whole body shaking.

"What?"

"I quit. You can find someone else to write your captions."

"But what the hell, Mary? I don't understand you at all." He shook his head at her again.

"And you and Xanny can have a merry Christmas without me. You can have a whole lifetime of Christmases without me." She turned and started walking away.

He said, "You can't."

She kept walking.

~

Mary was sitting on Joelle's couch. She'd come straight here from Ron's office and had been raving for half an hour, all her held-in emotions spewing. She was gulping wine. Joelle had been quiet up to this point, filling her glass, listening. But Mary was starting to wind down from her high, starting to feel the weight of what she'd thrown away—Ron, the wedding, her job.

Joelle said, "So what are you going to do now, après snow globe?"

"Do?" Mary said.

"Besides fill my couch with negative energy."

"I love your couch."

It was green velvet. Mary had helped Joelle pick it out when Joelle bought this condo two years ago. Mary had helped her furnish the whole place, which was gorgeous and seemed to hover like a spacecraft over Central Park. Joelle knew everything about real estate—she owned her own Manhattan brokerage—but she knew nothing about décor. She was going to hire someone to do the space, but Mary insisted they could do it themselves. And Mary was right. With Joelle's brashness and bigger-than-life personality added to Mary's vision, they'd created a truly lovely space of mustard leather and earthy textures and olive accents and pink softness. It was not quite mod, not quite boho. It was, according to Mary, "Joelle chic."

Joelle said, "I love my couch too, but you're messing with its positive vibes. It's Christmas. We're supposed to be joy-to-the-worlding."

"I know. I know," she said. "But I feel . . ." She threw up her hands, looked out Joelle's windows at the vast blackness of Central Park. "Ugh. He was my whole future, my whole life!"

"No, he wasn't."

"He was my heart, then."

"Your heart has lots of rooms in it. It's like an apartment building. He was just squatting in one of the rooms."

"My heart is an apartment building?"

"Yes. So it's time to open another door and see what's inside. It's high time you slept with someone else."

"What?"

"You heard me. He has you voodooed. You need to break the spell."

Mary knew it was true. He did have her under some kind of spell. She couldn't get free of him. She'd tried. She'd broken up with him many times before. She'd said, "This is the line in the sand" after he did one of his, as Mary called them, "push-Mary-aways." But then she'd cave and erase that line when he came back to her with his promises. Because they were such wonderful promises she had to believe him. "You belong with me," he'd whisper to her while he was making love to her, and she'd collapse right back into the relationship.

Joelle said, "I'm serious."

"You can't be."

"I am."

"I think I'll join a nunnery. Do they still have those? With very high walls and those layers of robes that make you look like you don't even have a body? I could eat as many Twinkies as I wanted for the rest of my life."

"You like Twinkies?"

"I could develop a taste for them."

"No, I mean it. You can't let him get to you. You can't just mope around. What's your plan?"

"Are you kidding? I have no plan. I'm not ready to do anything."

"Ready is overrated. You have to throw yourself into something new. You should sleep with the next man you see."

"You mean like the Uber driver? The guy at the deli?"

"The guy at the deli could work. Think Genoa salami."

"Oh Lord."

"This is a total sorbet opportunity."

"What?"

"Some men are just meant to be palate cleansers, not main courses. In-between-distraction things. They don't have to have a lot of flavor necessarily in and of themselves, maybe just some fresh mint leaves stuck on the top . . ."

Joelle knew a lot about in-between distracting men. Since her divorce, Joelle had dated serially, flitting la-di-da from one man to the next and never really getting involved. She looked like Cher, and men were mostly scared of touching her, never mind holding her. But a month ago, Joelle had met a carpenter, Frank Markowski, who was redoing her kitchen pantry, and, well, Mary thought things might be different with him. Frank didn't seem at all put off by Joelle's everything-is-a-joke persona. In fact, he saw right through her. And Joelle seemed changed around him—more open. Mary liked Frank. He carried himself like he had a tool belt on his hips, even when he didn't.

Mary said, "So you want me to find some guy emotionally garnished with mint leaves?"

"Exactly."

Mary laughed. "But I think I'm already falling in love with the salami guy."

"And that's understandable."

A gust of wind slashed rain against Joelle's windows. The horizon line of the city was lit up and blurry. Mary shivered.

"What is wrong with me?" she asked Joelle. "Why am I stuck in the middle of a bad love story again?"

"It's his issue, not yours. He's got Bubble Wrap around his heart. You'll never pop your way through it."

"That's what Zelda keeps telling me, but it's my issue that I keep falling for Bubble Wrapped men."

"But it's so satisfying in the moments when the bubbles pop," Joelle said.

"Don't I know it," Mary said. She leaned toward Joelle and asked, "He and I were once close, weren't we? He used to be different, didn't he?"

"I think he wanted to be different. That's what lured you in."

"It wasn't all a lie, was it?"

"Not all of it."

Mary said, "I wish I lived on another planet, light-years away from him, so I'd never have to see him again, never even breathe the same air as him. So far away he could never get to me."

"You're not going to let him get to you again, are you? I mean, every time you withdraw, he pursues you. Are you really done with him?"

Mary nodded once. "He's never going to change. If I keep waiting for him, I'll waste my life until there's nothing left of me."

"You, Mary Valley, will always have a lot to you."

Mary smiled sadly at her. "Oh God, I just threw away my job. What am I going to do? And where am I going to live?"

"I'll find you a place, and you may be unemployed, but you're not alone. Don't panic."

Mary said, "But it's Christmas."

Joelle said, "Yes, it is."

Mary put her head in her hands and said, "I just want to totally disconnect from my heart. It's nothing but trouble." She set an invisible package on Joelle's coffee table. "Here. You can have it. I don't want it anymore."

Joelle said, "But your heart is what makes you, you."

"It's killing me," Mary insisted.

"We have to get you out of here, change your perspective," Joelle said.

"What?"

"Let's send you away for Christmas—somewhere sunny and tropical."

"But I can't leave. What about CC and Larkin?" Mary said. Although she knew she'd barely get to see them over Christmas week, maybe only for a few hours. Things were so fritzy with CC these days. But still, Mary felt she couldn't just abandon them and cut out of town.

"Take them with you," Joelle said.

"They won't come."

"Give CC the trip as a gift. Then they'll have to come."

A hopeful spark sputtered inside of Mary. *Larkin*, she thought. Her granddaughter was a love. *If I could only be with Larkin for Christmas.*

"But I'll miss Christmas—all the hoopla, the tree, the everything," Mary said. "It won't be Christmas without all the trimmings."

"Yes it will."

"I don't know," Mary said, and peeked over Joelle's shoulder as Joelle pulled her laptop out and scrolled through the Internet. Joelle's fingernails tapped away at the keys like she was playing a jaunty Christmas carol on the piano—ho, ho, ho.

"This is ideal," Joelle said. "You can pick up a young bartender when you're down there. Bartenders are perfect. They have hands like lightning."

"We're back to the sorbet thing? I don't even like sorbet."

"You have to throw yourself into the present moment. Push the pulse button on the blender of your heart, whip up a sex-colada."

"I thought my heart was an apartment building. Now it's a blender?"

"Well, you're going somewhere tropical," Joelle said. As if that made sense.

"But won't I be busy being a grandmother?"

"You're a grandmother who's still got what it takes."

"I'm forty-two, though. You think I still have it?" It was a genuine question.

Joelle put her arm around Mary and hugged her. "Grandma, *you* are buried treasure."

Mary smiled sadly.

There wasn't much left to choose from in the way of hotels because Mary wasn't sure CC or Larkin had passports, and most places in Florida were booked for Christmas. It was between one hotel, the Low-Key Inn, and a much fancier all-inclusive resort on Captiva.

In the Low-Key Inn's "About Us" section was a story about the hotel's Freedom Fountain, which was a dolphin spouting water out of its mouth in the center of the pool. Evidently, the owner of the hotel—some kind of maverick type back in the seventies—had rescued a dolphin from a place called Sugar Bob's Backyard Aquarium and returned it to the wild. The dolphin stayed the rest of her life in the waters near the hotel, patrolling along the beach.

Mary's eyes stung reading the story. "That one." She pointed to the screen.

"You're basing your vacation on a hokey concrete fountain?" Joelle asked her. "But this other place has poolside pedicures!"

"I know."

On the website, the hotel looked like a little iced cake plopped down on a white beach. Mary got a great deal of satisfaction knowing that Ron would have hated it.

MARY

"An igloo?" Mary said.

"Yeah. They're, like, these little houses shaped like igloos all around the property." The teenage girl behind the counter made a mounding motion with one hand.

It sounded dreadful.

Mary said, "But I know I booked a suite with a balcony. It overlooked the beach."

The girl yawned and said the hotel was full. They'd overbooked. And if Mary had booked through them directly and not through Hotels-4-U, they could have guaranteed the lovely oceanfront balcony room, but since she didn't, she was stuck with the igloo overlooking nothing.

Mary almost turned around and went back to the airport. There *had* to be an airport motel they could stay at, and they could fly home in the morning, bake gingerbread in her kitchen, try to salvage Christmas.

But just then an old lady came into the lobby and said she was the owner and asked if she could help. She pressed two poker chips hand-painted to look like daisies into Mary's palm and told her they were good for two free drinks at the tiki bar. Mary shook her head, but the old lady turned to Larkin and stooped down.

"I'm Ollie. What's your name?" she said, and offered to shake Larkin's hand.

Larkin put out her limp hand but didn't open her mouth, so Mary told her both of their names. "Ah, Larkin. That's a beautiful name. It sounds like a bird. Do you know what sound a lark makes?"

Larkin shook her head.

Ollie made a bird noise then. The sound whistled in the room, clear and beautiful. Larkin's eyes got wide.

"We have no larks here on Terns' Island, but we do have ruby-throated hummingbirds. Have you ever seen a hummingbird?" Ollie asked.

Larkin shook her head.

"I'll show you one tomorrow. Their wings beat one hundred times every second. Can you count to one hundred?"

Larkin nodded. Her mouth was open.

"They go so fast that they make a humming noise. Like this." And Ollie hummed. "See if you can make a hummingbird noise."

Larkin mmmed.

"Excellent!" Ollie said, smiling. "I'll see you tomorrow, then. And I'll teach you how to feed the iguana. He eats hibiscus flowers. He loves the red ones best. I don't quite know why."

Larkin looked up at Mary then, a little glimmer in her eyes. Mary thought, *I'll just try this for one night.*

So she and Larkin dragged their bags through a dizzying maze of narrow leafy paths to the two-bedroom "mound." When Mary opened the door and flipped on the light, Larkin said, "Oh, Gramma! We're in a rainbow."

And it seemed they were. The door was aqua. The walls were arched concrete painted lime green with orange trim. A vase with fresh purple flowers was on the table. Big vibrant images of palm trees and sunshine hung over the couch. Larkin ran into the kitchen to explore. Mary heard her squeal with excitement. A pink refrigerator!

Mary felt a wash of relief. Maybe it would be all right.

She'd had second thoughts about the place after she and Joelle booked it. Well, she had been in a daze that night. When she woke up the next morning, she thought, *What have I done?* But there was no going back. She'd gone to her office and cleared it out. A whole career in a cardboard box, a couple hugs from co-workers with promises to stay in touch, and it was over. Ron's office door had remained closed.

Now Mary checked in the hotel's closets and bathroom for snakes, geckos, giant palmetto bugs. Who knew what could get in down here? But there was nothing. She bent down to smell the sheets. Clean, at least. Clorox, and maybe lavender? Nice.

Larkin followed Mary around the tour of the rooms, wide-eyed. Mary chose to look on the cheery side of the place, keeping up a constant monologue. "Oooh, look at the pretty blue flowers on the chenille bedspread; feel how soft and nubby that is!" She knew she was overdoing it. But she was trying her best to make Larkin feel better about being in a strange place without her mother.

Mary still couldn't quite believe that CC had backed out of the whole vacation. At the last minute too. But that was so CC. She decided, the night before they were all due to fly to Florida, to go on a cruise instead with her new boyfriend, James-Walter. He'd supposedly gotten a great deal on it.

As far as Mary could tell, the cruise didn't even go anywhere! It just chugged around in circles in the ocean. It was a "couples cruise," whatever that meant. Mary supposed they'd be doing couples massages and couples yoga and couples whatevers. It was good for CC to have a guy. Finally. But did she have to do this now? And with James-Walter, of all people?

James-Walter was a caffeine scientist at a giant coffee company where CC had recently gotten a job. Mary had only met him once at CC's place. He'd sat on the couch reading a science magazine through most of Mary's visit. He actually reminded Mary a bit of a couch—one of those rigidly upholstered ones with the softness sewn in so tightly you could never sit back and relax on it. God forbid you try to take a nap. He had a tattoo on his arm of the periodic table all in black. Mary couldn't stop staring at the little boxes with the symbols of the elements stacked up in rows. She kept thinking about tenth-grade chemistry class when she had to memorize that stupid table. She'd been a good student, but she never could understand chemistry.

CC told Mary that she and James-Walter could really use some "away time." Mary kind of understood. Since Larkin was born five years ago, CC had thrown herself full force into a single-mom independence kick—raising Larkin with little help from Mary, insisting on doing everything herself, her own way. CC never went out on a date for the whole first five years of Larkin's life. With anyone. Until she met James-Walter a few months ago.

Now, it seemed, she'd gotten swept up in him. Lately, Larkin was always being babysat by that woman next door—Mary forgot her last name. Douflaut? Doonaught? Mrs. Donut, Mary called her—which drove CC crazy. Mary kept forgetting her name purposely, truth be told. She was jealous of Mrs. Donut, who saw Larkin way more than she ever did. She could count all the times she'd seen her granddaughter in the last four years on her fingers.

"Please, let me come babysit for you," Mary had been pleading for years. But CC had a hard time accepting any help from Mary, and it was tearing Mary's heart out. CC thought Mary's grandmothering style was "too loosey-goosey." CC told her that she didn't want Mary "to ruin Larkin by spoiling her."

Ruin? Mary had thought.

CC and Larkin had lived with Mary for the first year of Larkin's life. Mary had instantly bonded with Larkin. Well, that was an understatement. Mary had been the second parent to Larkin. Mary adored that baby, wanted to breathe her in, and Larkin loved her back. Larkin's face was like a little sun breaking out when she saw her grandmother peek over the bassinet. When Larkin stretched her arms out to Mary, Mary felt a tug of yearning to pick her up and hold her, a feeling so deep she thought she'd swoon. Mary kept reminding herself that she was just the grandmother, but it didn't matter. She was in love. She wanted to spend every second with that child. But when Larkin was a year old, CC had moved out of Mary's condo to Paramus, New Jersey, a good hour away.

"I have to establish my own rules," CC had told her. "You have none."

Mary had to admit that CC was kind of right. Mary had raised CC with no rules, really, except "Be kind" and "Be you" and "Do the best you can." Mary had learned along the way that rules were all well and good, but love was a messy thing. It made its own rules. You couldn't love by the book. What book? As a parent, every time you thought you knew what you were doing and tried to take a stand, your kid would balk and want to do it their way. Or no way at all. CC would figure out eventually that you couldn't control childhood. It wasn't a board game where you moved your kid like a token from one square to the next, heading toward the winner's circle. It was more like Twister. You put your left foot on green, your kid put her right hand on red, then you spun the wheel and rearranged yourself again, and tried not to turn yourselves into tangled-up pretzels in the process. Tried not to fall down. And if you fell down, what the hell? Wasn't it okay if you landed with your kid in a giggly pile?

But CC had to work it out for herself, Mary knew. Although it had been like Mary's arms were amputated when CC took that baby away. She'd sobbed for days, then thrown herself into her work, into Ron.

They'd only seen each other on special occasions since then. CC told Mary to respect her boundaries. Boundaries? They might as well be the Great Wall of China for how insurmountable they were. Mary felt like she was forever scrabbling at the other side of CC's rules with her bare fingers. *Let me in, let me in.*

Mary got teary just thinking about how stark CC was making Larkin's childhood. Larkin's gray-and-white bedroom looked more like an insurance office than a kid's room—abstract art on the walls instead of pastel pictures of elephants, Mozart CDs instead of Raffi's "Baby Beluga" playing ambient music, a chrome and white leather midcentury modern chair instead of a rocker. Every toy was made of organic cotton or sustainable bamboo. No plastic allowed! When Mary bought Larkin Mr. Potato Head last Christmas, CC almost had a nervous breakdown. This year, when Mary asked, "What does Larkin want for Christmas?" CC gave Mary a list of "appropriate gifts." One was a bamboo doll with door compartments that held wooden organs—a wood liver, a wood brain behind a door in the head, even wood intestines.

"But I can't give her a wooden-hearted toy!" Mary said.

"It's educational," CC insisted.

When CC left Larkin at the airport with Mary, Larkin had what Mary thought of as a silent tantrum. She looked as if she'd been suddenly frozen—refusing to talk, shaking her head no, no, no at everything Mary asked during the airport wait. She clutched a little doll in one fist. It was one of those nesting dolls—the innermost one, the size of a clothespin. She absently chewed on its head.

Mary had packed coloring books and crayons in her carry-on. When she brought them out, Larkin shook her head. No. Etch A Sketch? No. Just the doll, which Larkin held like a lollipop.

"Is that your friend, honey?" Mary had asked.

Larkin looked at the floor. CC had warned Mary that Larkin had recently "gotten quieter." CC said, "She doesn't pipe up the way she used to about everything. She thinks first. Sometimes she doesn't say anything at all. It's like she shut the door on herself. And when she does talk, her words are all garbled or made-up. So I signed her up for singing lessons."

"What?" Mary said.

"People who stutter, and Alzheimer's patients, they've found, can vocalize things better with music."

"But . . ." Mary said.

CC admitted, "She won't sing. The voice coach says she just sits and stares out the window. I'm thinking of taking her to a speech therapist."

Mary sighed and bit her tongue. She was determined to try her own way of opening up Larkin.

When Mary and Larkin got seated on the plane, Mary brought out a green-haired troll and a purple stuffed horse she'd bought for Larkin. *Forbidden fruit*, Mary thought.

Larkin's eyes got huge.

"They have no names, so they need you to give them names," Mary told her, leaning down close to her. Larkin pulled away sharply.

Mary winced and forced herself to sit back and wait.

Larkin unzipped her little black patent leather purse and put the wooden doll inside. She stared at the troll and horse for a long time, considering. She finally said "Tutu," to the troll and "Blanket," to the horse, in her pinched voice.

Mary reached out and put down Larkin's tray table, and Larkin stood the troll on it and galloped the horse around, making little gurgling, whooshing, and clicking noises to it. She waved the horse through the air. *Fly, Blanket, fly*, Mary thought.

Now when Mary started unpacking, Larkin unzipped her suitcase like a little grown-up and started unpacking her own bag.

"I'll do that for you, honey," Mary said.

Larkin shook her head.

It almost broke Mary's heart to see how neat she was trying to be, piling one flowered pair of underwear on top of the next in the drawer, adjusting the big black glasses that kept slipping down her nose, struggling to wiggle the drawer shut.

Mary gaped at the clothes Larkin unpacked. Where did her mother think they were going on vacation—a Victorian tea party? Ruffled dresses with buttons and tight little collars. Some of the fabrics seemed like, what, canvas? Mary helped Larkin hang them in the closet. Where were the kid's cotton shorts and tee shirts? They'd definitely have to go shopping.

Mary had brought some storybooks, so after Larkin got in her jammies—a scratchy lace nightgown—Mary started reading to her about Trouble the Whale and how he kept getting himself in pickles, saying and doing the wrong things. Larkin's head drooped right away, and she fell asleep on page 3.

Mary tucked her in and walked out onto the little front porch. Their igloo was on two-foot concrete pilings, and below her were lights shining up into the rubbery plants and palm trees. Around her, other igloos glowed in the moonlight—like they were in an Eskimo village! Curving pathways wound around them. The pool was in the middle of it all like a giant aqua alien kidney. And she could see the shadowy tiki hut where colored lights were strung and a steel band was playing off-key. Beyond that was the beach where the moon threw a silver bolt of light on the water. The night was vast and black. Scurrying noises came out of the bushes around her. She took a shaky breath. She didn't want to admit it, but she was scared to be here alone with Larkin. What if she did everything wrong? Mary imagined one of those resort tee shirts—one that said I WENT ON VACATION WITH MY GRANDMOTHER, AND I WAS SCARRED FOR LIFE!

Oh, CC. Mary wished again, for the hundredth time, that CC had come on this trip. That CC had given Mary—no, both of them—this chance to heal things. She sighed and sat down on the wicker chair. It creaked and wobbled beneath her.

She took a deep breath of damp air that smelled, almost tasted, like flowers. She thought of what a creative, funny child CC had been. Mary had stayed home with CC until she went to first grade. Then Mary started helping CC's father, Charles, in his work. Charles was an architect, but he also did house flipping on the side. Mary was the design crew for the house flips, and she learned to do demo and some construction too. She worked hands-on with Luigi the foreman while Charles was on the phone or directing—being the general contractor. After school each day, CC pitched right in working with Mary. She sorted fabrics and chose her own scraps to make little pillows. Mary bought CC her own sewing machine. CC helped Mary lay tile and, once, even painted some tiles that Mary was doing for a kitchen backsplash. She was a little decorator herself! She used to collect branches and leaves and flowers and rocks and construct fairy houses with them in her bedroom. Emulating Mary and Charles.

Mary thought CC would grow up to be her friend. She imagined them going shopping together, cooking dinners together, talking to each other every day on the phone, helping each other out. She even had a fantasy that they'd go into business together one day. But it didn't work out that way.

Mary blamed herself.

She should have never married Charles. But she didn't feel like she had much of a choice. Her first year of college, before she even had time to declare a major, and after a stupid frat party, of all things, she was pregnant. She never loved Charles. He was just a guy she thought it would be interesting to sleep with. If she admitted it to herself, she'd slept with him because he was so unlikeable.

That actually had made sense to her at the time.

Charles came from a very religious family, and he was hell-bent on doing the right thing by Mary. Mary had no family to help her through anything, so she kind of fell into Charles's plan. They would get married, and Charles would stay in school, and she would quit school. Charles would work, and she would stay home with the baby. It was all settled, and life started to steamroll over her.

Mary knew now that she should have never stayed married to Charles, but she thought she was doing the right thing at the time, providing stability, giving CC at least the idea of family. Or maybe it was that she was giving *herself* the idea of family? But it couldn't have been good for CC to grow up in a loveless house, a house where Charles and Mary slept in separate rooms and barely interacted. What did it teach CC to be in a home where there were no parents boogeying in the kitchen, smooching in the hallway, calling each other "sweetheart"? They were just two business partners discussing countertop options.

Charles was never much of a dad to CC. He was such a workaholic. He provided well, but CC almost never saw him for the fifteen years of the marriage. He was like an architect and general contractor even when it came to fatherhood. He'd draw up his plans from a distance, and Mary would do her best to make them work. Then he died in his sleep when CC was in high school.

And Mary herself? What kind of role model had she been for CC growing up?

The way Mary figured it back then, feeling emotions was a luxury she couldn't afford. She didn't have time, and when she did have time, she was too exhausted. When she wasn't redoing houses, she was being PTA secretary, class mother almost every year, driving endless miles back and forth to soccer practice and ballet class. One time she stayed up all night long making flowers out of tissue paper for CC's third-grade class when they had "Spring Fling Day." She wired them on long green stick "stems" and carted them all to school in her car the next day. CC told her later that the whole class got in trouble because they had flower fights with them, bashing each other over the head, smashing the paper blossoms. Did she really think CC would appreciate her for being supermom? For being a mother who abandoned her own heart?

Of course, CC turned out to be a handful in her teens. Who wouldn't have issues growing up with Charles in absentia and Mary trying to overcompensate for him? In tenth grade, after Charles died, CC started skipping school to go drinking. Her grades plummeted. By senior year, she was barely passing, hanging around with a guy named Zoomer who'd quit school and worked in a record store. Mary read every book about adolescent rebellion that existed. She took CC to counselors right and left, CC complaining with each one that "nothing worked," until CC said she was "just not into it" and refused to go anymore. Then CC went off to that college in upstate New York where Mary thought CC might be okay, but it didn't work out like that. She was pregnant just like Mary had been at eighteen. All that Mary had done trying to prevent CC from making the same mistakes as Mary did, didn't work.

Mary took a deep breath of night air. Zelda wouldn't want her to beat herself up over mistakes she'd made in the past. Zelda was a big advocate of the present tense—letting the past go, not wasting anxiety on the future. Mary had been seeing her for six months.

Zelda was a brittle-looking woman with spiked shoes, an almost-shaved head, and slippery pink leather chairs. She scared the hell out of Mary initially. With a name like Zelda, Mary thought she was going to try to convince Mary to become a warrior princess, or make Mary do I-am-woman-hear-me-roar therapy, or start calling Mary "Sister Goddess Mary" or something. But she didn't. She was brusque, though, and no-nonsense—no doubt about that. But Mary had grown to really like her.

Joelle had recommended her. "She can whip your life right into shape," Joelle said.

"She doesn't know what she's up against," Mary said.

Mary had gone to her initially because she'd started walking in her sleep. It was so strange. She'd wake up and find herself in the kitchen, opening the pantry door. Or in the bathroom, looking in the medicine cabinet. Always looking for something. But what? Zelda told Mary she didn't have an answer, that Mary would have to discover the answer on her own.

She told Mary that the sleepwalking was not really the issue. It was the "presenting problem," and that they weren't going to work specifically on "curing it," since Mary wasn't going far or doing anything dangerous or weird in her sleep—"You're not driving a car, are you? You're not peeing in the closet?" Mary shook her head vehemently. *Oh, please don't let me start peeing in the closet.* She was just anxious, Zelda said. And she was looking for something.

"What if I don't find it?" Mary asked.

"Oh, we'll find it," Zelda said, smiling.

Mary liked the sound of "we." She'd come to trust Zelda, to think, *What would Zelda think of this?* She'd seen Zelda right after she broke up with Ron, and Zelda had nodded once when Mary told her about the snow globe. "Indeed," Zelda said. And Mary felt it like a little pat on the back.

Zelda approved of Mary going on vacation too. Said that Mary needed to keep going on "the journey to herself." Said "I believe in you" to Mary. Which filled Mary with a kind of pride.

When Zelda said goodbye to Mary that day, she raised her fist and said, "Onward with your life!"

Mary thought about it now. That was all well and good and quest-like and everything, but how could Mary go forward with CC if CC kept running away from her?

Zelda had told Mary that CC needed to find her own way, but that "there will be a time when your life paths will cross again."

Not on this vacation, Zelda, Mary thought now.

Well, Mary had Larkin, at least, for a week. She'd do her best with Larkin. She adored that child. And maybe by loving Larkin, Mary could find a way to "cross CC's life path" again.

Mary just hoped she didn't sleepwalk while she was here. She looked around at the darkness. What if her life path ended her up in the pool?

~~~

It was early morning, and the sun was streaming into the dining room. It smelled like melted butter and bacon. Larkin pointed
~~~

at the pile of "Mr. Chip" pancakes that the kids at the next table were eating and nodded her head.

"Are you sure?" Mary said.

Larkin nodded harder.

Mary read the description on the menu. Mr. Chip pancakes sounded more like a bunch of Reese's Peanut Butter Cups piled on top of each other than an actual meal. Plus, CC had given her a whole list of what Larkin was and was not allowed to eat. Mary was sure none of these pancake ingredients would meet CC's requirements. CC had an associate's degree in nutrition, a Nutritious Life Certification, and worked as a health coach at the coffee company—whatever a health coach was. Mary didn't really understand it. So CC was always on some new sort of food kick. Lately, everything she ate had to be green. Or couldn't have a mother. Or something like that. CC had looked terrible when she'd seen her at the airport—taut and angular, not a carbohydratey spot on her.

Mary rustled around in her purse, but she'd left CC's list back in the room. Oh well. She looked over at Larkin.

Larkin looked at her grandmother over the top of her glasses.

Truth was Mary was trying, but she had no idea how to be CC's kind of grandmother. What would Mrs. Donut do in this situation?

Mary ordered the pancakes for Larkin. She ordered the papaya and some oatmeal with raisins for herself—trying to set a good example, even though she didn't really like oatmeal.

"Do you want to try the papaya?" Mary asked.

Larkin furrowed her brow and shook her head. No.

"A vacation should be a world of newness opening up," Mary said. That was what Mary kept telling herself, anyway.

Larkin chewed her pancake.

"Are you looking forward to going fishing today?" Mary asked.

Larkin stared at her.

When Joelle had helped Mary set up the trip, they'd booked a backwater fishing adventure for them their first day.

"Can't we just relax?" Mary had said. "Do nothing?"

But Joelle had said, "Little kids need family activities." She'd told Mary, "This is not the time to hold back. Throw yourself into the experience!"

"I know, I know," Mary said, but she was dubious. Fishing? She hoped they didn't get seasick.

Now Mary assured Larkin, "It will be fun. Just you wait and see." She didn't even like the sound of her own voice. Overly cheery and, well, grandmotherly. *Just you wait and see?* When had she ever said *that* before?

"Tutu doesn't want to go, and neither does Blanket," Larkin said.

"Well, tell them we are going on an adventure." She kind of drew out the word and put a lot of emphasis on the end syllable. Ad-ven-*ture*. What the heck was the matter with her?

"Why?"

"Because that's what life is," Mary insisted.

Her heart was pounding. She knew she was talking to herself. She'd just gutted her whole life, hadn't she? There was really nothing left but the studs. She knew she had to resee herself, revamp—all the home-improvement things she'd been doing for others and writing about. What a project. *I'm like a forty-two-year-old house that needs a top-to-bottom redo.*

Ugh. It was scary. But wasn't it actually kind of exciting too? Like when you tore into a house and saw through what were once walls, created new sight lines, smelled raw wood, saw all the possibility. But you also didn't know what you were getting into. If you'd find rot in the walls or bad wiring. And there was no blueprint to follow.

Enough, she thought. *Stop worrying. Just be in the present tense.*

Larkin had chocolate smeared on one cheek, and her pancakes had turned into a mushy island in a pond of syrup on her plate. She'd pulled the pancakes apart with her fork and eaten as many chips as she could find. The AC evidently was broken in the restaurant, so it was hot. Really hot. There had been a wait for an outdoor table, so they were sitting in a sweltering pink room. THIS IS OUR HAPPY PLACE! a sign insisted.

A scraggly Christmas tree was in the middle of the room, blinking with white lights. A motley assortment of shiny balls and tinsel shot tiny laser beams around the room. Sweat beaded on Mary's chest and trickled down toward her belly.

"Hurry up, now, and finish up so we can be off," she said. She made a blasting-off motion with one hand. Larkin stared at Mary's hand hovering in the air. Mary let it drop back, *plunk*, to the sticky table.

DANIEL

Daniel waited with Tripod on the dock. They were late. He hoped they wouldn't show up at all. Then he could go back to painting his houseboat. He'd started painting it black the other day. He'd picked out the color Rain Cloud in the Sherwin-Williams.

"Are you sure?" the clerk had asked.

He really wasn't. Next to all the other jaunty pastel houseboats bobbing like party balloons along the dock, his was beginning to look like Darth Vader. He knew he'd lost touch with what normal was. Perhaps, as Addie told him, he'd turned eccentric in his early forties instead of waiting until he was eighty like other people did. Well, so be it.

A couple of charters had already gone out. Another fisherman on the dock, Sal, had a crew of guys going offshore who were already drunk, and it was only nine a.m. They'd brought a cooler on board the size of a couch. He'd been on those kinds of trips before. This wouldn't be that, at least. He'd never had a group of women book—it was always just guys or fathers with their sons.

"I hope they're not those talky kinds of women," Daniel said to Tripod. Tripod looked up at him and whomped his tail once on the dock.

Daniel didn't think he could deal with a million questions today. *How does it feel to do nothing but sit around and fish all day? What's it like to live in paradise?* Not after last night, not after how Addie knocked down all his carefully constructed defenses in one phone call like they were nothing. This morning, he felt like a sandcastle washed out by the tide.

A car pulled up into the marina parking lot, its tires crunching shells. A woman got out, leaned into the back seat, and stayed there for quite some time. Arguing, it seemed.

"Please," he heard her say. "Please?" again, like a question.

A stuffed animal flew out of the car. Uh-oh. Should he go over there, try to help? But kids seemed like aliens to him now. He had no idea how to communicate with them. Hand gestures? A smile? *I come in peace . . .*

He had been great with Timmy when Timmy was young because, well, it was easy. It was natural to get down on the grass and look at bugs and dig in the dirt. He couldn't think about that. It was a long time ago.

Now the child was emerging. What was she wearing? A dress? Black shiny shoes? Oh no. She'd have to take those off. There would be scuff marks all over his skiff. What was wrong with the mother? Why didn't she have flip-flops for that kid, shorts, a tee shirt? Neither one of them had hats. They would hopefully have sunscreen.

They scuttled toward him, and he walked to meet them. The woman was laden down with a big flowered beach bag, the little girl half dragged along with a stuffed animal clutched in her hand. Was that the mother or the grandmother? She looked to be some indeterminate age—maybe in her forties? Why were there only two of them?

"Oh shit," she said as a water bottle, then a towel, fell out of her bag. "Shoot, I mean." Her blond hair was a corkscrew mop popping out of its ponytail in escapist spirals.

He bent to help her gather things up.

"Thank you. Are you Dayes's Charters?" she asked.

He nodded. "Daniel Dayes."

"I'm Mary Valley. And this is my granddaughter, Larkin." She pulled the little girl out from behind her. "Her mother isn't here. I mean, she didn't come with us."

"She didn't want to have an adventure," the little girl said.

"True," Mary said. "She's on a couples cruise. She needed to get away."

"Ah, away," he said. *Good luck looking for that.*

"I'm so sorry we're late," the woman continued. "I hate to be late for anything, but, well, we had issues getting dressed."

"Mommy packed in a poopy way," Larkin said.

"Inappropriately," Mary said. A smile crossed her face. Then it was gone.

"She can't wear those on board." He pointed to Larkin's shoes. "You don't have sneakers for her?"

Mary shook her head.

"Then she'll have to go barefoot." It sounded gruffer than he intended. "Boat rules. And she'll have to wear a life vest."

"Why does your dog have three legs?" Larkin asked, staring at Tripod.

"Bomb," he said.

The woman seemed to freeze, and the little girl blinked. Maybe he shouldn't have said it so harsh. But it was what he always said when anyone asked. He couldn't go into it. It was too, well, everything.

He looked off toward the blue sky and the puffy clouds. People forgot they were at war, because it was all happening so far away.

Who could blame them? War was better not to think about. A year ago, he could get away with that. Now it was as if bombs went off randomly all day long in his head. The other day in the Winn-Dixie, he'd flinched, actually cringed, as a little kid reached for a cereal box on a high shelf and he'd watched the box tip and fall. Did he really yell "Run!"? Maybe that was just a bad dream. He had those too. But no, he remembered the kid's face crumpling into tears. A box of Cap'n Crunch, it was.

"Sorry," he'd said, pushing his cart quickly down the aisle.

He'd had to leave the store, he was sweating so badly. He'd left his cart parked right there next to the hot dogs with the single roll of paper towels, the six-pack of English muffins still in it.

"Come this way," he said now, and turned and walked toward his boat.

"Aye, aye, Skipper," the grandmother muttered behind him.

Tripod hopped along beside him. He didn't need a leash, wasn't going anywhere. He did all right on his three legs, but sometimes Daniel wondered if Tripod was ashamed of his own gait—it gave him a jaunty look, a flippy-floppiness to his ears that was almost comical it was so cute. People instantly adored him. "Aw, what kind of dog is that?" they'd ask, bending down to pat his head. Daniel didn't know quite how to answer—maybe a Jack Russell mixed with basset hound but with longer legs? Tripod endured the attention. He wasn't much for being petted. He was one of those one-man dogs. He'd been Timmy's dog.

Now Tripod was stuck with Daniel.

"You deserve better," he told the dog every day.

The boat was in the fifth slip down, a long blue flat-bottomed fishing skiff that Daniel had bought a year ago off a family trying to unload it because the grandfather had to go into a nursing home. He'd bought it to try a new profession. He'd bought it to make a whole new life. But it was just a boat, he was finding, not an answer to anything.

It had a name: *Everyt'ing Cool*. Daniel wanted to paint over it, but he knew that was bad luck. And he didn't need any more bad luck.

"I don't want to go," he heard the little girl say behind him. "No, no, no." Her voice was rising.

Daniel kept on walking. He had devised a system to get Tripod on the boat so that Tripod didn't have to be carried. He hated being carried. Daniel had made a portable trampoline the size of a bath mat that he kept on board. Now he stepped in the boat and placed it back on the dock.

Tripod had caught on right away to the concept. Even seemed to like it. He scurried onto the trampoline, gave it a few bounces, and *BOING*, he sailed up into the air and onto the deck of the boat. Nailed the landing. Well, he always did. The dog was a natural.

He heard the little girl gasp. "He flew in the air!"

He gave the woman a hand on board and she smiled at him. Then he lifted the kid. She was light as a little cloud, and her feet kicked up in the air. He couldn't help himself. He said, "You're flying too," as he swooped her onto his boat.

He turned on the engine, let it idle loudly right away so they didn't talk to him, but he didn't have to worry. They sat quietly. He drove looking purposefully at the GPS, although he could have driven these waters blindfolded. They both just stared ahead, their hair blowing into tangles.

He took them to the best spot he knew and baited a pole for each of them.

Now the little girl was sitting on the starboard bow with her stuffed animal and troll lined up on either side of her, keeping her company. She seemed to be over her grumpiness. Daniel had forgotten the way kids could click themselves on and off like this as if they had a switch inside of them. He wished he had one of those switches. What a great invention that would be. A heart switch or a brain switch. Maybe on a dimmer. You could control your own inner self with a flip of your finger.

The grandmother took the stupid dress off the little girl, and she sat in her flowered underwear and the life vest, her black glasses perched on her nose. She hummed a meandering song as she talked to her troll and horse.

"This is how we fish," she said to them, rearranging them next to her. "Your turn next." She dipped her fishing pole tip into the water and jerked it this way and that, tapping and swirling it on the top of the water.

He said, "Try to hold the pole up. Keep the line tight." But her lip started to tremble, so he stopped talking and let her do it her way.

The grandmother sat on the port side. She was terrible at casting. He showed her a couple of times, but she couldn't get the hang of flicking it with her wrist and letting the line flow simultaneously. Every cast was a plop into the water right below her. He said he'd do it for her, but she was stubborn.

She kept insisting, "I have really good hand-eye coordination."

Every thirty seconds, she'd reel in, do a big swoopy motion with her arms, and her line would go nowhere. Daniel couldn't watch.

They were catching nothing. Not a bite. He cast his line under the mangrove roots, skimming it expertly into the shady protected shallows. He wanted to hook something. Anything. Let the little girl reel it in.

It mattered to him if people caught a fish, even though he got paid no matter what. He'd gotten twenty reviews so far on Rate-Ur-Adventure. His star rating was a three out of five. Most people caught fish with him but found him lacking in some way. "Unfriendly" they called him. "Silent as a fish himself," another said. His favorite was "Boring. Enough said." That had actually made him smile. He didn't smile much these days. It felt unnatural now to stretch his face that far. It was ironic, because his whole life he'd been a smiler, a laugher.

Addie used to despair of him. "Life is serious," she'd insist.

He'd tell her, "Yes, I know. But I'm happy." And he was.

That was back then.

Now the woman swept her hand around. "There's really *nothing* out here! Just miles and miles of nothing." Her pole wobbled with her gesture, and it almost fell in.

He looked around. It looked like a world to him, but he didn't say anything.

"Do you live on this island?" she asked him. *Here we go with the questions*, he thought.

"In a houseboat," he told her.

"What's that like to live on the water? Doesn't it go up and down all the time?"

"Up and down? Well, yes."

"I bet I would be seasick constantly."

"You get used to it."

"I think I'd need to feel a foundation under me."

"Ah."

"To make me feel safe," she insisted.

"Safe is an illusion," he said. He looked at the clouds skimming along across the sky. The breeze was fresh.

"I guess you're right," she said. She seemed to go into a world of her own then.

The sun climbed slowly in the sky. Insects rose out of the mangroves in little clouds. Far in the distance, he heard Jet Skis revving.

This cove was his secret spot. He'd found it one day puttering along exploring. Sometimes he did that without looking at the GPS at all—to see if he could find his way. The mangrove islands, which at first all looked the same to him, now had more personality. This cove he called Pinky Cove, for when he saw a pair of roseate spoonbills fly over him and found one of their pink feathers afterward on the floor of his boat. He'd seen them a bunch of times now, knew they had a nest around here somewhere, but he hadn't found it yet.

"Look there," he pointed.

A mother dolphin and her baby glided side by side across the middle of the cove.

"Oh," Mary gasped. "See that, Larkin?"

Larkin shaded her eyes.

"There's the mommy and the baby!" Mary said.

"Mommy," Larkin said, and her lip quivered.

Mary bit her lip.

Daniel said, "All the dolphins around here have names. The marine mammal center keeps track of where they live and how many new babies are born each year. They identify them by their dorsal fin. You see that?" He pointed to the fins plowing through the water.

Larkin nodded.

He said, "There's a dolphin that I usually see around here that had his fin cut almost in half by a boat, and it kind of flaps when he swims. They call him 'Boo-Boo.'"

"Aw," Mary said.

"He gets along just fine," Daniel said, suddenly feeling defensive.

"What are those dolphins' names?" Larkin asked, looking at the mother and baby.

He said, "I don't know. Maybe it's a new baby. If you see a new baby, you get to name it."

Just then, the baby jumped clear out of the water.

Larkin said, "That baby is Sky."

"Good name," Daniel told her. He rummaged in his console. He pulled out a sheet of stickers. They were a little stained from bait and being in his knife drawer, but they were big blue round stickers that proclaimed I AM A DOLPHIN EXPLORER! He'd gotten them from a friend of his who took people out on dolphin-watching ecotours. He held the sheet out to Larkin.

"Here, take one," he said.

She looked at Mary, and Mary smiled. Larkin peeled one off and put it right on her forehead. A piece of her hair was stuck in it and the sticker was crooked, but Larkin was grinning big. Mary didn't do anything to fix it. She just let it be, nodded at Daniel, and he nodded back.

"Let's reel in," he said. He knew they'd never catch anything now. The dolphins would spook the fish.

"But I haven't caught anything yet!" Mary said.

"We'll start again somewhere else," he told her. Really, he didn't have any intention of starting again anywhere. He'd take them to the little island he found with the sandy beach, tell them they discovered it, let the little girl name that too. People loved things like that. They'd find the big ship's beam that washed up from who knows where. He'd get them shell collecting, distract them for another hour or so. Then it would be over.

"Aye, aye, Kipper," the little girl said. "We don't want to hurt the fish anyway," she said, and yanked in her line. "Come here," she said to Tripod, patting the seat next to her troll doll. "Tutu wants to talk to you."

Tripod looked up at Daniel. Tripod was keeping his distance from everyone. The little girl had tried to pet him, but he'd ducked and scampered away to sit in the shade under the console at Daniel's feet.

Larkin called to him again. "Come here. Come here, Try-Hard."

"He doesn't really like people," Daniel told her, kind of apologizing. But, as if to spite him, Tripod hopped over to Larkin. He sat down and looked over his shoulder at Daniel.

"Just one more chance," Mary pleaded. "One more cast. Please." She looked at him. "Kipper," she said.

What is with this Kipper thing? He nodded.

She swung the pole back.

He cringed and closed his eyes.

At first, he thought it was a bug landing on his eyebrow. Before he could brush it away, the pain tore into him, and he thought, *So that's what being hooked feels like.* Then he felt the blood rush into his eyes, and everything was red, and he fell back. And he thought, *I'm falling.* The deck was hard under him, and his head bounced. And he thought, *That's not good.* But nothing cracked, and he thought, *That's good.*

He heard the little girl say, "Gramma, you killed-ed Kipper."

MARY

"Don't take the hook out." Kipper's voice emerged muffled from the wad of white towel Mary was pressing to his head.

"I had no intention of doing that," she said, making a face at the towel.

"Just in case."

"What do you think I am?"

He didn't answer that.

"A bad caster," Larkin said. She was next to Mary, looking at the puddle of blood growing under Kipper's head.

Mary was kneeling. She leaned against Tripod, his hard-packed body, his short, bristly pinprick hairs.

"I'm sorry," she said again. How many times had she said it? "We have to get you to a doctor."

She looked around at the solid green wall of mangroves surrounding the cove. *All this nothing.* The water rippled in streams going in all directions. *How are we going to get out of here?* It looked like there were, at once, a million ways to go.

"I'm fine," he said.

She lifted the towel a bit and the blood gushed out of his head. She pushed the towel back on.

"Ow. Jesus."

"Well, the hook . . ."

"There's a scissor in my tackle box." He pointed.

Mary hurried over to it, returned with the scissors, and snipped the line close to the hook. "There," she said.

He sat up, and the towel wobbled. Mary steadied it. His skin looked blue. "Give me a minute," he said. His voice was wispy. He held his hand to his head and struggled to his feet. Then he sat down hard on the bench.

"You can't think you're going to drive," Mary said.

"I have to get you back . . ." he said.

"Just tell me how to do it. Here," she said as she wrapped the towel carefully around his head like a turban and clamped it with her own barrette. His hair was thinning on his forehead, and he had a sprinkling of gray. She hadn't been this close to a man in years, except Ron, and it made her feel all wobbly to see the pulse near his temple. She stood back and looked at him. He'd missed a spot shaving his sideburn, and it gave him an off-kilter look.

"You look like the Cat in the Hat," she said. And he did—with his bloodred-and-white turban and his wide mouth strung like a clothesline across his long face.

"I want to be Thing One," Larkin said. "Gramma, you can be Thing Two."

Mary said, "You probably have a concussion. How many fingers do I have up?" she said, sticking her hand in his face.

"Three," Larkin piped up. Then she said in a small voice, "The blood is very . . ." She took one step and threw up into her shiny black shoes, which were neatly lined up on the deck.

Mary hurried over to her while pointing at Daniel. "Don't move." She wrapped Larkin in a towel and sat her down on the bench in the bow. "There, there—you're just fine."

Larkin said, “I want to go home,” and kicked at the seat. Tripod hopped up next to her and watched her warily.

Mary climbed back behind the wheel. “I can do this,” she said, looking at the instrument panel. Kipper hadn’t moved, but he was looking worse. The turban on his head was listing hard to the left.

He said, “You ever drive a boat before?”

“How much different could it be than a car?”

“Um,” he said.

He told her what to do, measuring out his words evenly—key, anchor, gear shift. “Now ease the throttle.”

“The what?” she said.

He pointed.

“Okay,” she kept saying, trying to follow.

The boat jolted forward, then stalled.

“Whoa.” He clutched the console. “Thing Two.”

She clenched the steering wheel and tried again and stalled.

His mouth opened, then shut.

She did it again. “I know. You don’t have to tell me. I know.”

“I didn’t say a word.”

Her hands were shaking. The sun blazed in the sky. Sweat ran down her cheek. *Where are we? How far away are we from anywhere? Why did I come on this vacation? Why, why, why?*

Larkin said again, her voice wavering, “I want to go home . . .”

A huge gray bird spooked and clattered through the trees.

“We’re heading back now,” Mary yelled to her. Although they weren’t moving an inch.

“Home-home,” Larkin said, a quiet sob shaking her. “I want to go home-home.”

Mary wished suddenly that she had thought to bring Mrs. Donut along on the vacation. She could have taken CC’s place.

She'd probably be multitasking her ass off right now—soothing Larkin, piloting the boat; maybe she even had some EMT training.

He said, "Maybe I should . . ."

"Go ahead, then. Knock yourself out." She folded her arms over her chest.

He looked really pale. He didn't move an inch.

"You think I can't do it, don't you?" Her voice screeched higher. She winced at herself. This was no time for an insecurity fit.

"I didn't say that."

Her heart was pounding. She tried to settle herself down. Take a deep breath.

He started to say something.

"I can!" Mary yelled. She didn't know if she was talking to herself or to him, but the silence afterward was abrupt. Even the air seemed startled. Larkin was looking at her, blinking rapidly. Tripod's head was cocked and his face wrinkled up with interest. Kipper was looking down. A drop of blood fell on his shoe.

Mary took a deep breath. "I'm sorry," she said. "I'm just . . . It's not you," she said.

"Okay," he said. Their eyes met. His black mirrored sunglasses had broken when he fell, and he looked different without them. Before, when she had looked at him, all she saw was herself, all jittery-looking. She'd kept trying to smooth down her hair. Now she saw his eyes were as green as seaweed.

"Try again," he said. She turned the key, and this time, the engine revved, and she slid it into gear.

He said, "Follow the path on the GPS. If I pass out, just follow that line. It will lead you home."

"You're not going to pass out, are you?"

"I'm trying not to."

"Where are the channel thingies to go between?"

"There aren't any. Not here."

She steered the boat into a narrow tunnel through the mangroves. The engine growled and churned up mud behind them. The boat slowed and wiffle-waffled, and she held her breath. Were they stuck? Then the boat swung a little and jerked forward. The air smelled dank and rotting and ancient but somehow sweet. She took a deep breath of it. Held it in her lungs. Could it make her high, this air? It felt like it could.

She concentrated hard, trying to follow the GPS and still look ahead. His hands clutched the console, but his fingers kept tapping. Was he counting down the seconds until he could get rid of her?

"I'm getting the hang of this now," Mary told him.

"Uh-huh," he said. His eyes were shut.

What is it that they say about concussions? Don't let them go to sleep.

"So, have you always been a fishing charter guide guy, Kipper?"

"Um, nope."

"Try to form complete sentences. It will keep you conscious."

"Is that true, Thing Two?" He opened his eyes.

"I just made that up."

"Ah."

"Just talk," she said. "I need to focus on something else besides the blood gushing out of your head and your potential concussion and us being lost in the Everglades and . . ."

She looked over at Larkin, but Larkin had somehow fallen asleep. Tripod was lying right next to her, staring at her, his stiff little body unmoving.

"Tell me something about your life." She pointed to the GPS. "Enough to get us to the end of this line."

He readjusted the towel on his head. The towel was full of blood. How much had he lost? How much could a person lose without dying?

"Did you always want to be this?" she asked, looking out over the water.

"I used to be a landscaper. I had my own business." The words came out oddly creaky, like they were rusted over.

Mary was peering ahead, squinting. She turned toward him. "Oh," she said, surprised. He seemed to her somehow to belong at sea. "Go on, then. Tell me why you became a landscaper." She turned to look ahead, but kept glancing back at him. Just to check.

"Why? Well, it was a while ago."

"In a country far, far away?"

"New Jersey."

"Far enough."

"I think it was that I used to believe in buffer zones."

"From what?"

"I don't know. Reality?" he said. "Like a protective layer in between a person and the street."

"Where no hook could get in?" She looked at him to see if he would smile, but his eyes were elsewhere.

"Do you have a yard?" he asked.

"I live in Brooklyn. There are a couple of trees on my street, though." The trees grew out of small squares of fenced-in dirt. When they got leafy in the spring, the street looked like an arched pathway into a secret garden.

"Oh," he said. "You probably have herbs, at least, on your kitchen windowsill?"

"I don't cook much."

"A spider plant?"

She shook her head.

"Plastic flowers in a wreath on your door?"

She smiled. "Just a number: 2C. Mrs. Engleson, in the house on the corner, has a hedge. Does that count?"

"Is it square trimmed?"

"Yes."

"Then no."

"I bet you were a good landscaper."

"Not really. I wanted to do native plants only. I called my business Wild Gardens, but nobody wanted that. I should have called it Tamed or Mowed Down or Paved Over." He shook his head. "Addie would tell me, 'Give people what they want.' But there was a part of me that couldn't work for those people who wanted their flowers in tight, straight lines or wanted one of those look-at-me-I've-conquered-nature yards. What people want . . ." He shook his head.

"Addie?"

"My wife."

Mary looked straight ahead. They were entering another mangrove tunnel, and thc shade felt cool and secret. She slowed the engine, and they putted through. The only sound was the engine and little wavelets burbling through the roots of the mangroves from the wake of the boat. It smelled like mud again and vaguely, mysteriously, like flowers.

"Easy," he told her. His voice was low and soft and rumbly, like an engine itself.

I wish we could stay in here forever, she wanted to say. *It's so peaceful.* But that was crazy. They had to get out of here. They had to get home. The tunnel opened, and the sun blazed again. She pushed the engine into a higher gear, and the boat surged forward.

"Keep the pressure on," Mary told him, glancing at him. "Keep talking. Tell me a story—a landscaping story."

He got quiet. She thought he wasn't going to say anything.

"A guy hired me to cut down his weeping willow tree," he said. "Claimed the tree was 'messing up' his lawn. He wanted to put a pool in. He had this frail ghost of a wife in a ruffled apron who just stood by his side, twisting the apron around in her hands, saying nothing.

"When I came the next day with my crew and my chain saws, he wasn't there, and she told me she was going out shopping, that she couldn't watch. 'How I love that tree,' she told me.

"That's the way she said it. 'How I love . . .'—kind of old-fashioned and longing.

"That tree was I don't know how old. It was beautiful." His voice hitched, and Mary glanced at him.

He said, "It had such a wide trunk, I couldn't put my arms around it, branches sweeping down all around like a woman's hair shook loose. I could imagine the reach of the roots."

Mary could see it too—the tangled web of roots below the surface, searching for water.

"The woman told me she liked to go out there under it in the morning and lean against the trunk. She'd write in her journal. She called it her dreamy time."

Of course she did, Mary thought. Mary could almost feel what it would be like to lean against a solid alive thing like that, the nub of the bark, the sense of a life force pulsing within it, the sheer hardness of it. *Oh*, she thought. *I'm getting all stirred up thinking about, what, a tree?* She hoped he wasn't looking at her, but no, he was staring at the channel ahead. She looked at his worn jeans and tee shirt with a hole in the sleeve big enough she could put her finger through it.

He was listing to the left, his eyes slitted. She reached out and touched his arm where the little hole was. "Don't keel over on me now," she said.

Was that her imagination, or did she feel that tiny touch of hot skin?

He straightened up, readjusted his turban.

She wished suddenly she were that woman under the tree in the safe protected canopy with the light sifting through the green leaves. Her eyes met his, and she blushed. Could he see her thoughts? She looked down at the GPS, realigned her course. She thought, *That woman didn't have safety, anyway. She just had an illusion of safety. You can't lean against something and expect it to hold you up. You have to hold your own self up in life.* She got this image of herself leaning up against Ron and knocking him over, both of them falling in a heap. *See? Leaning up against someone gets you nowhere!* She could almost hear Joelle's voice: *Chickie, you just picked the wrong tree to lean against.*

"So, what happened?" Mary asked Kipper.

"Nothing. I made a bench for her instead under the tree, so she'd have a place to sit and write. When she came home from shopping, I led her in through the curtain of branches, and she sat down and sobbed like her heart was going to break out of her chest." He said his words carefully, as if he were placing one foot in front of the next on a tightrope. Was that just who he was, or was it his injury?

He said, "She just needed a place where she could be. Anyone could see that."

Mary looked at him. "Not just anyone," she said.

"It probably was a stupid thing to do," he said. "The husband probably took it out on her."

"You don't know that."

He shrugged. "It was just another job I didn't get paid for."

"And did the tree get cut down?" Mary asked.

"I don't know."

"But aren't you curious? Didn't you ever drive by to see if it was still there?"

"That was my last job. After that, I took off for Florida."

"And how did you end up here?" she said.

"I was heading for a town called Sunshine. I saw the name of the town on the map. It seemed like a good enough place to aim my truck. But I made a wrong turn in the middle of the night, and suddenly I was going over a bridge. I ended up on this island. It's actually just south of Sunshine."

She wanted to hear more, but the boat rounded the bend, and there, suddenly, fast approaching, was the dock with the little bay beach next to it. They'd made it. Why didn't she feel relieved?

"You'll want to pull back . . ." he started to say. "Stay to the starboard."

She turned the boat left, and he said, "No, stay . . . stay . . ." He gestured urgently right with his hand.

She pushed the lever instead of pulling, and the engine revved, and the front of the boat rose up, and they went roaring into the sand.

DANIEL

"These head wounds bleed like drama queens," the doctor told Daniel. He was an older doctor, and he thought it all was a big joke. "Don't you know you're supposed to use minnows instead of your face for bait?"

He was a disheveled sort who inspired no confidence at all. He charged into the exam room like a natural disaster, knocking into a cart, pens and little packets tumbling out of his pockets the whole time he was working on Daniel. But he was deft with his hands, and he stitched up Daniel in no time.

"I'm good," the doctor said, "but eyebrows are tough. It may heal a little off. You may have a kind of quizzical look to you from now on, a what-the-hell expression. But what harm could that do? And you're not entering any beauty contests anytime soon, are you now?"

"Do I have a concussion?" Daniel asked.

"Nah. It just knocked some stuffing out of you. No harm in that. Ha ha."

And it was over. Daniel was back out in the waiting room, and Larkin and Tripod were looking up at him. Tripod had his red service-dog vest on—Daniel always carried it with him so he could take Tripod anywhere. Tripod had an issue about being left alone. The little girl had the dog lying down with her stuffed animals piled on top of him. She was galloping the purple horse across his back while she was singing a song. Tripod held himself very still. His tail thumped once when he saw Daniel, but he didn't move otherwise.

"Do you have a concussion?" Thing Two, as he was starting to think of her, asked. "Why do you only have a Band-Aid? How many stitches did you get?"

"I'm fine. Let's go," he said. He couldn't wait to get home, pop open a beer, put his feet up on his houseboat railing. He'd lived alone for a year, and he'd forgotten what relentless questioners women could be. He could do with some quiet.

They got in her car.

"Where do you live? I'll drive you home," she said.

"Take me back to the boat."

"But you should go home and rest."

"I can't leave the boat where it is." He didn't say, *Where you drove it, where you screwed up my engine, where we had to leave it like a beached whale.* He thought he deserved points for restraint.

"I feel so bad about all of this."

She should feel bad. His prop was probably bent all to hell, and he'd have to get someone to tow him off the sand. It was a wonder they all didn't fly to the moon when she hit the beach. But nope, Tripod and the little girl just rolled in a ball together. And he ended up in a tangled pile with Mary half on top of him. She was all body and clothes and words. Endless words. "I'm sorry" and "Oh my God" and on and on until he wanted to just dive deep into the water and stay under there.

It was weird, though. This was the first time he'd touched another person's skin in a year, except to shake some stranger's hand. He'd forgotten how warm a person could be. Maybe it was just the sun that made her skin feel so hot. And her hair had smelled like lemon cookies. After he got his footing and helped her up, he felt suddenly, achingly hungry.

Once they got back to his boat, she wrote down her cell phone number on a scrap from her bag, told him where they were staying. "So you can give me the bill for your doctor and your boat."

He nodded, stuffed the paper in his pocket, but he had no intention of calling her or seeing her ever again. What a nightmare. Insurance would cover his head. And he'd have Donnie over at the marina to look at the prop. He probably wouldn't charge him much.

"Good riddance," he said as he watched them drive away moments later.

The little girl hung out the back seat window. "Try-Hard!" she yelled, all gap-toothy, her sticker still stuck to her forehead. Her glasses seemed more crooked after the crash. Something in him lurched as he listened to her voice crack and fade as they drove away. Tripod's tail hit against Daniel's leg. He whimpered. Daniel had never heard him do that before.

After they disappeared down the road, Daniel said, "Come on."

Tripod stared at him. Daniel had to almost drag him away from the parking lot.

Daniel's friend Sleep and Donnie, who owned the marina, helped him tow his boat off the sand. It took them an hour, and by the end of it, Daniel's head was pounding, and he wanted to go back to his houseboat and take a nap. But he needed to hose the boat down, so Sleep stayed to help him.

Sleep lived in the houseboat next to Daniel. He was a retired high school English teacher from some nowhere town in North Carolina, never married, now just "floating out" his retirement. He and Daniel avoided meeting each other's eyes for the first few months after Daniel moved in, but then it seemed silly, both of them sitting six feet away from each other on their separate boats, looking at the same sunset, drinking their beers alone. So Sleep started coming over to Daniel's boat, and they sat together and talked about baseball, weather, books they were reading—nothing, really. Just guy talk every evening. Daniel did most of the talking. Sometimes Daniel thought Sleep wasn't listening at all. A few times Sleep nodded off in the middle of one of Daniel's sentences. Daniel didn't know whether to envy him or be frustrated by him. How could he be so relaxed about the world?

While they were cleaning the boat, Sleep held up a wallet he found under the boat's console. "This yours?" It was aqua with pink flowers.

"Oh shit," Daniel said.

"Does it belong to the boat driver from hell?" Daniel had told Sleep the story.

Daniel sighed.

"You have her number? Where's she staying? Tell her to come pick it up," Sleep said.

Daniel hesitated. Did he want her anywhere near him and his boat again? He looked down. The water was so clear he could see the ripples of sand on the bottom. He saw a school of fish moving. *Mullet,* he thought. Sun sparkled on the surface of the glassy harbor. Across the cove, the mangroves pulsed with heat. He knew crabs were scuttling in the mud in and out of the roots, geckos were racing along the branches, banana spiders were weaving webs. It gave him a comforting feeling to be in the midst of so much busy life going on around him, ignoring him. A tern flew overhead, tucked its wings and dove. Came up with a fish. Daniel nodded. *Good for you, bird.*

Daniel wound up the hose slowly, neatly. He handed Sleep a beer from his cooler and they sat down on the dock. Tripod lay down next to him. Daniel dangled his legs off the dock, which made him feel like a kid. He took a sip of beer. It was very cold. He licked his lips and tasted beer and the sting of the can and salt. It was good to taste all the different flavors at once. This probably wouldn't do his head any good, but he didn't care.

"She's staying in the Low-Key Inn," he told Sleep.

"That place is in a time warp."

"You been there?"

"I played guitar there a few times. Happy hour at the tiki bar. Back when the old man was alive. He was a stingy guy. Paid me once, then wanted me to play just for tips. I did a few times. But nobody there had any money. Now it's just the wife, Ollie, running the place. She was kind of mowed down by him. I felt bad for her. She used to sneak me a sandwich and a few free drinks when I played."

"I met her once," Daniel said. He hadn't been near there in a while, though. He mostly kept to the other end of the island where his houseboat was moored in the marina. The Back End, as the locals called it—the hokey mobile home park with all the colorful trailers flying their flags; the fishing piers where the shrimpers and stone crabbers came in; the bar that was a converted old bait shack and was called The Bait Shack; the little restaurant, Channel Marker 8.5, where he ate breakfast every morning. He swore that place was sliding into the bay another inch with each passing day. "It was when I first came down here. She was advertising for a landscaper. I went and talked to her."

"You're a landscaper?"

He never talked about his past to Sleep. He just stuck to the present. It struck Daniel now how little Sleep knew about him.

"I was," Daniel said. "Ollie was looking to hire someone after her husband died. The husband had a landscaping service do the work for years, but Ollie wanted to see if she could find someone with 'more imagination.' She was looking to drum up business with the ecoclients—birders and nature buffs. Plus, she said, she wanted it to be the way she wanted, not the way her husband wanted . . ."

"She's an interesting lady," Sleep said.

"We hit it off. She offered me the job right then and there." Daniel thought of that job interview. They'd sat out by the pool and had iced tea with lemon, slices of oranges, and cookies. Birds flitted everywhere. He'd thought the place was run-down and odd but beautiful in its own way. Like Ollie herself. She'd given him a tour, and his heart had galloped around in his chest while he walked with her as she pointed—here she wanted a butterfly garden, there a raised walkway through the bit of wetland. If he could have gotten his hands on someplace like that! It was an oasis, a little dollop of paradise.

"But you didn't take the job?"

Daniel shook his head. He had gone home and thought about it, and The Big No kicked in. That's the way he thought of his heart these days, as The Big No. *Don't care about anything; don't love anything. No, no, no.* It was like having a cement block in his center. Ever since Timmy died. So, Daniel had called Ollie up the next day and told her, "I can't. I just . . . can't."

He told Sleep, "I started fishing."

Sleep looked hard at him. "The Low-Key Inn is a strange place. You know that people around town say that Ollie's a witch?"

"Her? A witch?"

"That she has powers. That her place is . . . Well, there's something not quite right there."

"What do you mean? It's a run-down hotel."

"She has a garden. You're not supposed to eat anything from it."

Daniel said, "That's ridiculous. I ate an orange she grew. She told me it was straight from her tree's hands to mine."

"Yeah, and look at you now."

Their eyes met, and they both chuckled.

Daniel said, "People love to talk."

"Maybe, man. Maybe. Just watch out for that place. They say it changes people."

"You still thinking of heading up north tomorrow?" Sleep had told him that his mom was sick, that he might fly back to see her.

"Got to." Sleep took a long sip of beer. "Maybe sooner, if I can get a flight out. She took a turn."

"Sorry."

"What can you do?"

Sleep had put the wallet down on the dock. It sat there between them. Daniel's eyes kept going to it. He'd better check and make sure it was hers. Although, who else could it belong to? He picked it up and unzipped it. He thought he smelled that lemon scent of her, but then it was gone. There was her driver's license. Her picture smiled up at them vaguely.

"Pretty," Sleep said, leaning over to look.

"Mmm," Daniel said. He was surprised at how organized the wallet looked, the bills aligned, the credit cards each to a slot. He would have guessed it would be a mess. He zipped it back up quickly. The sound made him feel embarrassed. Like he'd glimpsed something really private. But it wasn't. It was just a wallet.

"Why don't you take it to her?" Sleep said.

"I don't know." He definitely didn't want to see Ollie, have to face her. He didn't know why, but he felt ashamed.

But a little while later, when Sleep walked away, Daniel decided.

"Let's get this over with," he said to Tripod.

They walked to the truck, and Daniel helped him in.

"We'll just leave it at the desk for them," he said, getting in the driver's side. Tripod stared at Daniel, then turned to look out the window.

It didn't work out the way Daniel planned. He asked the receptionist at the desk to take the wallet.

"Oh, I don't think I could take that," she said, shaking her head at the wallet. She was a teenager. "You'll have to deliver it in person."

"But why?"

"It won't be a problem. She's right there," she said, and pointed out toward the pool.

He grimaced. There she was, Thing Two, floating around on a raft—like it was just another day in paradise.

OLLIE

Ollie was sitting on the shaded patio at one of the round tables by the hotel pool. The guests were all busy having happy hour—such a quaint phrase. A boisterous group of women next to her were using an inordinate number of plates and glasses. Lipstick-stained napkins kept drifting down to Ollie's feet like crayoned paper airplanes.

She'd been sitting there for an hour, sketching idly. Ollie watched her "new arrivals," as she called them, Mary and Larkin, her hand moving across the page, drawing them. Both of them had thrown themselves into the pool as if the pool were the last bed on earth. Larkin was in her one-piece red bathing suit that had a tube attached to the middle of it. She floated around quite safely—like a bobber. She reminded Ollie of a baby duck as she followed a little old man in a white bucket hat who was walking laps in the shallow end, back and forth, back and forth. But oh, what strain on that little face.

Mary looked as if she'd spent a couple of hours in a clothes dryer. She had an I've-been-flipped-around-and-turned-inside-out glaze to her eyes, and she floated inert as a board on an ice-cream-cone-shaped raft with her skirted black suit splayed out around her hips. Why ever did she dress so conservatively with that nice shape and that sweet smile that went clear up to her eyes?

Having a pencil in her hand helped Ollie to think these days. She'd been going to an art group that met once a week for a year now. Ever since Wilson died. Mostly, Ollie drew birds. But the group did portraits, still lifes, sometimes went "on location" and did landscapes. Just a group of old folks. Then they'd go out and have lunch together.

It was the first social thing she'd done in years. Not counting the hotel. But the hotel was about other people's social lives. Not hers. While the art class was all about her. It was a luxury, and she really couldn't afford to be doing it, timewise. She should be working instead, trying to figure something out. Anything. To save the hotel.

She wished Frances were here now to talk to. She and Frances had met at the art group, and Frances was the only one who knew about the problems at the hotel. Wilson had often accused her of "not being able to open up." But he didn't really want her to open up, did he? A nitpicker, he was. Well, that was a nice word for it. A faultfinder. She became a person who closed up to him and spent her days only chitchatting with strangers at the hotel or spending time with her birds. Often, she didn't speak to him for entire days at a time, and he barely noticed.

But with Frances, she'd started to trust again.

Frances lived in a trailer, one of those jaunty ones in the Back End with cutout wooden flowers stuck in among the actual flowers, a hand-painted sign tacked to her set of steps—SURRENDER THE BOOTY!—and cheery strawberry-strewn curtains in all the windows. Her paintings were framed and hung not one here and there, but all clumped together covering a wall. "Like wallpaper, but better," Frances said. Frances did very bright acrylic paintings.

"Might as well use all the colors I bought!" They were mostly portraits of people doing ordinary things—reading, knitting, sitting on a bench with a grocery bag. Just people pausing in their day. There was a freedom to her work that Ollie admired, a looseness that Ollie didn't have in her own careful lines.

Frances saw not only the good in people, but the inherent specialness of them—the happy, crooked tilt of an old man's smile; the knobby, tender wornness of a woman's hand placing a bookmark in between pages; the hopeful back of a man bending to push his son on his bicycle (and somehow you could tell—oh, you could just tell—this was the first push without the training wheels). Maybe that's why Frances and Ollie liked each other. Because each had work that was uncompromisingly themselves. Frances worked lickety-split fast, Ollie more deliberately. But lately, Ollie found herself looking at something, then looking away and drawing it without looking back again. Those were her best drawings. Something happened in the space between looking and drawing, some magical transformation that made the bird not out there and not in her but on the page, both itself and how she saw it, mixed up into something new and distinctly hers. It was exciting when it happened.

The other day, their class had done a creativity exercise together. They did what the instructor called "energy drawings," where they had to draw with their nondominant hands, making no recognizable thing or symbol, only color, texture, and line. Ollie bowed her head when she thought of it now. Frances's drawing had been a radiant ball of fire. Of course it had. Ollie's was quiet, more horizon than sun, more reflection than ray, and bound in by some tangled-up lines. "Like the cat's gotten into it," she joked. But she felt sad that her energy looked so tight. She was jealous of Frances's drawing.

"I wish I had used my whole page," Ollie told her then.

"You still can, Ollie," Frances said.

Ollie hoped that there was still time for her. She was seventy-two. Could she really change her energy at this late date? She knew the birds that she drew were always in the corner of the picture and not front and center. Would it help if she moved them, drew them bigger, used more color? She'd try.

Ha, she said to herself now. *You internalized Wilson. You've become your own nitpicking critic. But he's gone now . . .* She looked around at the people splashing and laughing in the pool. If only she could be more like them, on vacation, carefree!

She closed her sketchbook and reached into her purse and took out the letter Mr. Emerson had sent her last week. She'd shown it to Frances yesterday. Frances had been all excited.

"Ooooh," she had said. Nothing could dampen that woman's spirit. She believed that the world was friendly. Ollie had felt a little spark of hope after talking to Frances. Frances's optimism was contagious.

The letter from Mr. Emerson was handwritten, which they both took as a good sign. And it was on nice creamy paper, the kind you just couldn't resist running your palm over. Ollie had read it twenty—no, thirty—times already. She had the thing memorized.

Until she got it last week, the future had seemed bleak.

She read it again. *I am in the investment business, and your business interests me. I'll be coming your way soon to view the property and discuss options. I look forward to meeting with you.* His signature was an incomprehensible tangle but seemed friendly, with lots of swirls. Ollie was glad it wasn't one of those cramped signatures, spiky and mean-spirited.

But wasn't the whole thing a bit presumptuous? Like he saw himself swooping down as Superman to rescue Ollie. And Ollie, although she knew she needed help, balked at the idea of being rescued. It was *her* hotel, after all. No one knew it like she did.

Frances often told her, "You hold the key, Ollie. You just misplaced it somewhere, and we have to find it."

That's how it seemed to Ollie too. Like the answer wasn't out there somewhere, but within her. Somewhere. But where?

Nonetheless. Maybe he *could* help. No matter what Ollie and Frances thought of to save the hotel—and they'd had many strategy sessions over glasses of wine in Ollie's garden—they kept coming up with one thing: cash. The hotel needed a cash infusion to turn it around. And it needed it fast.

So, Ollie kept calling Mr. Emerson to try to pin him down. When was "soon"? And what did he really mean by "your business interests me"? "Interests" sounded so *Shark Tank*-y to Ollie, so heartless. Like he was a man driven by money and used to getting his own way. But he was her only real hope. She'd tried the banks. But they looked at her like she was crazy when she said she wanted to increase the credit line. At her age? And with what collateral? The hotel was already mortgaged to the hilt. At least Mr. Emerson wasn't the Marriott. The Marriott had been after her to sell ever since Wilson died. But they only wanted the Low-Key Inn so they could knock it down and put up another Marriott. And did the world really need another Marriott?

The faded yellow-striped umbrellas fluttered around the pool, and the dolphin fountain spritzed. She loved this little hotel. She always had. From the minute Wilson won it in a poker game—of all things! What a magical thing that had been. He'd had four aces in his hand. That had never happened to him before, and Wilson had played his share of poker games. He couldn't believe his luck. He said it was all he could do to keep his hands from shaking, holding those cards.

He'd tossed the deed onto the kitchen table in front of her that morning thirty years ago and said, "This might be swampland, but it might be something else." She couldn't wait to sell their old duplex in Cleveland. She hated that dark paneling and being hemmed in on all sides by apartment buildings. She longed to pack up the station wagon right then and there and drive to go see it.

Florida! All she could think of was orange trees.

And even though the hotel *was* an outpost in the middle of nowhere back then, even though this island *was* indeed swampland, it didn't matter. There were bald eagles flying overhead and cougars prowling around in the tangled woods. There were gopher tortoises that lived in holes, along with burrowing owls. Why, it *was* magical. So many birds. Ollie couldn't get over them. The place had been as much a preserve for nature as it was a hotel, and Ollie had made sure it stayed that way over all these years.

But now Wilson was gone, and it was all on Ollie. Nobody in their right mind wanted to stay in the Low-Key Inn anymore. They hadn't for years. It was a dated seventies hotel. It needed new everything.

The hotel was booked for Christmas. That was good. But every place on the island, even the Barracuda Inn, which had a screechy karaoke happy hour and carpeting on its restaurant walls, was booked for Christmas. After that, the bookings dwindled down to a trickle.

Ollie picked up her phone, even though she knew what would happen. Talking to Mr. Emerson's secretary or personal assistant or whatever she was, was like trying to get a rise out of the stars. She was unflappable. Each time Ollie called this week, the assistant told her, "I apologize, but Mr. Emerson is indisposed." Ollie could tell she was that persnickety kind of person who always used the largest words she could think of in a sentence just to intimidate you. What did "indisposed" mean, anyway? Such an unforthcoming word! Did she mean Mr. Emerson was busy signing papers? Didn't feel like opening his mouth today? Had been in the bathroom for a half hour and she didn't know what the heck he was up to in there?

"Can you *please* ask Mr. Emerson to call me back when he can?" Ollie said into the phone this time when the secretary gave her the same old response.

She knew she shouldn't take out her frustration on the secretary, who was just trying to do her job. She could tell she was an older woman. Ollie heard the same door-creaking-open-and-catching in her voice that Ollie heard in her own. Maybe Mr. Emerson's secretary really was a wonderful person deep down inside. Maybe she had a secret love of quilting, her cupboards full of scraps of soft fabrics, her fingers callused, her eyes bleary from making all those tiny stitches. Or maybe she had a desk full of pictures of her grandchildren in an assortment of mismatched frames. You never knew about people—those little details that made them warm up in your eyes.

Ollie sighed into the phone. She gave the secretary her cell phone number for the umpteenth time. Ollie told her to have a nice day and also a merry Christmas. Even though the secretary basically had, as the young people put it, "blown her off" again. She always thought of a dandelion when she heard that phrase—a big fluffy one that was turned into nothing but a naked stem with one puff of air. *Whoosh.* There went your whole being, your whole world.

Now she was being dramatic. But her world *was* going! Quite literally too. Another tile from the hotel's roof had fallen in front of her as she was walking to work this morning, and the second "f" light had burned out on the office sign, so it now just read OF ICE. Ollie knew there'd be a stream of people knocking on her door soon, holding their little plastic buckets and scoopers, saying, "Yoo-hoo, is this where the ice machine is?" unless she got that sign fixed. But how? With what?

Wilson had gambled them into a hole. No, more like a pit. He'd had a gambling problem on and off through the years, although he called it "having a knack with cards." Well, not so much of a knack. They'd had to remortgage the hotel twice, and then, in the last two years of his life, it had gotten worse. Terrible. It was almost like he'd given up on everything, especially himself. He'd discovered online poker, and before Ollie even realized what was happening, their just-holding-their-heads-above-water finances were shattered. All the money was gone. He'd raided their retirement accounts and maxed out the credit line they had on the hotel. He'd always done the books, so Ollie didn't see how bad it had gotten until it was too late.

Or maybe she'd just closed her eyes. It was her fault too. She should have left him long ago when the gambling first started. She'd thought about it many times. But although she knew she could have lived just fine without Wilson, she couldn't abandon the hotel. The Low-Key Inn was her family.

So, she'd made a life for herself within her married life, a kind of oasis in the desert. But look where that had gotten her.

Thankfully, Ollie had started her own savings account years ago, squirreling money away. She'd been using that to pay the bills, but now that was almost gone too. The bills were piling up on Ollie's desk. Funny how when you couldn't pay on time, they started sending you bills on different colored pieces of paper. Pink and green and blue—a little rainbow of awfulness. She couldn't bear to look at them anymore.

She'd hired an accountant, Lucille, a lovely woman who looked over everything after Wilson died. She suggested bankruptcy. She recommended selling the hotel, taking what she could, and living out the rest of her days, although there wasn't much equity left. She tried to get Ollie to "be realistic." But Ollie was too stubborn for realism.

Ollie looked at Mr. Emerson's letter again. It could mean anything. And she couldn't reach him. Well, of course she couldn't. It was two days before Christmas! The man was probably busy with his family. He was "indisposed." She put her head into her hands. She wouldn't cry.

How could she live with herself if she sold out to the Marriott? She couldn't let the gopher tortoise burrows be bulldozed or the trees strung with her colorful birdhouses and feeders be chainsawed. What would happen to the people who came back here year after year—those motley families who couldn't afford the bigger hotels and condos, the people with their straw hats and crooked smiles and odd assortments of suitcases? And what would happen to her? She had to do something.

MARY

Mary saw Kipper walk toward the pool with Tripod hopping by his side. Kipper was staring at Mary, but she couldn't read his face. It was blank as cardboard. And grim. Maybe she'd totally screwed up his boat. Maybe she'd have to buy him a new one.

As she scrambled out of the pool, she hoped he wasn't watching her. She hated her stupid bathing suit. She looked like a bat in it, a spandex bat with a droopy skirt. Ron had gone shopping with her for a suit last summer—what had she been thinking inviting him? When he held that suit up for her to look at, her heart had slumped in her chest. He said it would "hide all sorts of problem spots."

Problem spots?

She'd always been pretty happy with her body. It had taken her a lot of places, given her a lot of pleasure over the years. Maybe it wasn't the body it used to be, but she didn't really want to be twenty again or even thirty. She enjoyed life more now—being good and doing good rather than just looking good. She enjoyed a glass of wine more than having six-pack abs. She enjoyed smiling more than having an unlined face. And looking perfect was not all it was cracked up to be anyway. When she thought about it, the years she probably looked her best were the years she was the most unhappy, the most self-conscious and self-critical. She didn't think she was alone in that either. Everyone knew that the prettiest women had way too much to live up to, way too much stress and pressure, way too many I-hate-myself days.

But Ron didn't see things that way. He was always after her to get in better shape. He wanted them to work out together, said it would be healthy and fun. But the couple of times they had tried linking feet and doing sit-ups or mirroring each other doing jumping jacks, Mary had collapsed in peals of laughter and Ron had gotten mad at her.

Ron had eventually convinced her to get a treadmill for her condo since she wouldn't go to gyms. They smelled like anxiety to her, and the mirrors made her dizzy. She actually had vertigo once just walking through one on a tour. She probably *should* have used that treadmill more. But why did it have as the screen image a desolate desert with a rocky brown mountain? It was endless, watching the line inch through that wasteland. She felt like Bilbo Baggins trudging reluctantly up the Lonely Mountain to meet the dragon, Smaug.

Ron was in great shape himself. He'd turned into an exercise fiend in the last few years. He had an entire ceiling-to-floor mirrored gym in his house now with one of those machines that supposedly worked every muscle at once. The Turbo-Simultron? The Power-Stimulator? No, that couldn't be it. Ron kept telling her, but the word went right through her. He was very big on it. He strapped himself into it as if it were a race car that could take him to another world, and he pushed and pedaled repetitions every single day. Of course, he'd wanted her to get one too, but she refused.

If she wouldn't exercise, Ron said, she should consider revamping her wardrobe—"emphasizing your strong points, de-emphasizing the rest." He liked the chiseled parts of her best—her shoulder blades, the arc of her breastbone. So, she'd ended up with a closet full of black clothes and V-neck tees. She'd ended up with a de-emphasized self. And where did that get you in the world? No-where.

He wasn't here now, was he? So why was she even thinking about him and his muscles and his whatchamacallit-stimulator? She'd throw away this suit tonight after she peeled herself out of it. Good riddance. She'd seen a lime-green bathing suit with an interesting crisscross pattern of straps in the gift shop window this afternoon. Maybe she'd buy that for herself. Give herself a boost.

She wrapped the towel around her waist like a sarong.

Just then, Larkin caught sight of Tripod. "Try-Hard!" She raised her arms. The dog stopped short and his tail started whirling like a little helicopter. His body looked like it was going to lift up off the ground.

Larkin had cried the whole way from the marina to the hotel, bereft about leaving Tripod. Mary had actually considered turning around at one point, asking Kipper if they could borrow Tripod for a playdate. She would even pay him. Larkin's face was different when she was with that dog, all the little-old-lady worry erased. But Mary had been afraid to ask Kipper for anything—not after everything she'd done to the man.

Kipper bent down to Larkin and said a few words, then handed Tripod's leash to her. That was sweet of him.

Larkin paddled along the edge of the pool and Tripod hopped alongside. An old man in a bucket hat who had been doing laps stopped and watched them. A puddle formed under Mary, drip, drip, drip. Mary could feel Kipper's eyes on her. He was holding something out to her. Was that her wallet? She was suddenly confused.

"You left this on the boat."

"I did?" She took it from his hand.

"It must've fallen out of your bag," he said.

"I didn't even notice it was gone," Mary said, laughing nervously. "You didn't have to come give it to me. I mean, I would have come get it if you had called."

She was opening and shutting her wallet and riffling inside like she was searching for her ID.

"It's all there. I didn't touch anything."

"I know you wouldn't. I was just . . ." What was she going to say? *I was just looking to see who I am?* As if a bunch of ID cards could define her.

They both looked at Larkin. She was beckoning to Tripod, and he was hopping down the steps into the pool. One. Two. And then he was swimming toward her.

"Uh-oh, Kipper," she said. She didn't like calling him Daniel, even thinking of him as Daniel. It was too stodgy somehow. Too sad. Kipper had more zip to it. And he looked like he needed a bit of zip. He looked like someone who'd had the center pulled out of him. As if he'd collapsed upon himself like a soufflé. Although maybe it was just that he'd had a hard day. God knew he'd had to deal with her.

"They probably don't want dogs in their pool," he said.

"No," she said.

"I better get him out," he said just as Mary said, "I better get Larkin out."

"Yes," they both said.

They looked at each other and smiled, but neither of them

moved. Tripod glided around Larkin in happy circles, his half-brown, half-white face tilted up to her. Larkin was laughing. The dolphin fountain burbled water.

"Bravo, little doggie." The old man in the hat clapped.

Mary wished that a moment was something that you really could stretch. The sun was warm on her back, and she could feel the droplets disappearing on her skin as if they were tiny champagne bubbles popping. She was aware of Kipper's clean, minty scent, like he'd just gotten out of the shower and used some tingly soap. Little hairs stood up on her arm.

Just then, the little old lady, Ollie, walked up to them.

"Ahem," Ollie said.

"It's my dog, my fault," Kipper started. "I'll get him out."

"I'll get Larkin out," Mary said too.

"There's no need," the lady said.

"No?" Mary and Kipper said.

"They look like they're having a grand time. Let them at it."

"But won't you have dog hairs in your pool?" Mary said.

"He doesn't look like much of a shedder."

"Not much," Kipper said.

They all looked at the little girl and the dog.

"Nice," the lady said. And it *was* nice. Mary felt a rush of gratitude toward her for seeing that.

"May I buy you both a drink?" Ollie said.

"I was just leaving," Kipper said.

"Without your dog?" One of Ollie's eyebrows went up. She looked hard at Kipper. "You're that landscaper fellow, aren't you? I thought I recognized you."

"Yes," he admitted. He looked down.

"Come, let's sit," she said, touching his arm. They walked to a table, and Kipper pulled out a chair and held it for her.

"I love kindness in a man." She smiled at Kipper. Her whole face upturned.

"Hello, Stephen," she said to a waiter who'd come up to their table. "We'll have three piña coladas. And make them special." She winked at Mary. "I find that an umbrella drink is the antidote to many of life's ills."

Mary stared. Ollie looked like what Mary wanted to look like when she got old. She wore no makeup, but her features were so defined she didn't need any. Her hair was cut short like a little helmet of pure white, and such eyes—so pale blue. She looked a bit like an elf.

"Do you know each other?" Mary asked Ollie and Kipper.

Ollie looked at him. Kipper kind of winced. He said, "Ollie was kind enough to offer me a job once. I needed to get out of landscaping, though."

"Well, if you ever change your mind, I would so love to have that butterfly garden we talked about."

He said, "I saw some milkweed growing by the boat ramp the other day. I could dig some out for you."

"Oh, the monarchs would love that," she said.

"It spreads, though. I have to warn you."

"I have the perfect spot for it. It can spread any way it pleases, make itself a whole world." She threw her arms out.

He said, "I could bring some parsley for the swallowtails too. I have some extra in my houseboat's herb garden. I grow herbs just to have the smell of them around me. I've seen the swallowtail caterpillars eat a whole parsley plant in one day."

"Voracious," Ollie said, her eyes glittering. "Well, they have to turn themselves into butterflies. That's got to take some doing."

Mary said, "It would be so lovely to have a butterfly garden here."

"To do a butterfly garden really right, you need some nectar plants as well as food plants," Kipper said. "If you want the butterflies to hang around, that is, and not just stop over on their migration."

"Oh, I would love for some to stay," Ollie said.

"They'd need sheltering plants too. Probably even a water source," he said.

"Another fountain!" Ollie said, clapping her hands.

"That would be great," Mary said. She could feel the energy level rising at the table and almost see the garden forming. It was contagious!

There was a pen on the next table on a bill where someone had signed the check. Kipper reached over for it and started sketching on a napkin. Ollie and Mary leaned over to watch him.

"See, you'd need both horizontal and vertical landscaping. Ideally, you'd have different blooming times and lots of different colors." He looked at Ollie. "I assume you're okay with lots of color."

She smiled at him.

He was sketching as he talked. "Some canopy trees. Some shade, some sun. And I love groupings of flowers where they're all massed together." His lines were awkward, but there was playfulness in them—his trees looked like lollipops, his flowers like they had smiling faces.

"I love that too," Ollie said.

A little blue-ink garden took shape on the napkin.

Mary watched them both wrapped up in this hypothetical world they were creating. She asked Ollie, "You'd want seating, wouldn't you? For people to come and watch the butterflies and just be." She thought of the bench that Kipper built under the weeping willow tree. She could see him building this garden, his hands dirty, pushing a red wheelbarrow. "It would be nice to have quiet places along pathways that would encourage people to meander and pause."

She reached to touch the napkin and trace a crooked path with her finger. Her heart was pounding in her chest. She would love to be a part of a project like this! To make the garden a human place as well as a butterfly place.

She watched Kipper sketching on the napkin. He was really getting into it. Ollie was leaning forward.

"Yes, that's exactly what I want," Ollie said to him. Her eyes met his and they both looked down, then at Mary.

She could sense they were held back by something. Mary wanted to wave her hand, whoosh whatever that something was away. *Let's make the garden!*

Just then, Tripod yipped. They all turned to look at him. He was still in his red vest, swimming happily in circles around Larkin.

"Is he a service dog?" Ollie asked.

"He was my son's in Afghanistan," Kipper said. "He lived with their troop. He's got a service medal and an honorary military discharge."

"He must be a very special dog."

"Timmy found Tripod in a blown-out building, half dead. Timmy saved Tripod's life. Then Tripod returned the favor and saved his life. Saved everybody's lives, really, in their tent. He woke them all up when someone set the place on fire one night with a cigarette. They all could have died."

Kipper was talking to Ollie as if Mary weren't even there. Mary found she was holding her breath as he was talking. It all felt so private. She wanted to interrupt and say, *Go on, go on. What happened to Timmy?*

Kipper's eyes went to Tripod. "My wife worked for months to get Tripod sent back to the States. She wrote letters to senators, even the vice president. Addie got very political after . . . Well, I think it was her way of dealing with things. She started a group called PACT. It's one of those acronyms—Parents Alone Can Talk. They run these support groups and try to get parents of soldiers in foreign countries connected on Facebook and other social media. She thinks that will help to stop wars—if we all just knew each other." He shook his head.

"She's a better person than I am," he added. "Always has been. She couldn't understand why I didn't want to be a part of it. Anyway, she can be real persuasive, Addie. She hounded everyone until she got results. She arranged for Tripod's transport here six months ago. We decided we'd split the time with him since we were, uh, living apart by then."

"Split the time?" Mary couldn't help interjecting, her heart jittering at the word "split."

"Well, we both wanted him. We couldn't cut the dog in half, could we? Anyway, we flipped a coin, and I got Tripod first. I went up to JFK to pick him up, flew him back down here. But now my six months are up." His voice got thin.

"What? You have to give him back?" Mary said.

"Christmas Day."

"But tomorrow's Christmas Eve," Mary said.

He nodded.

"You can't give him up," she said. She hardly knew the guy, but it seemed like he and that dog were connected by more than a leash.

Stephen came just then with the piña coladas, and Ollie's phone beeped. She looked down at it and frowned.

"Oh dear," she said. "I'm being summoned. Please enjoy the drinks on me. I insist."

Mary watched her walk away. Ollie's gait was sprightly and her feet seemed almost not to touch the ground.

A knot tightened in Mary's chest. How could this Addie woman just up and whisk Tripod away?

"But you can't allow this to happen," she said to Kipper.

"What do you mean 'allow'?"

"I don't think it will be good for Tripod. What will he do without you?"

"Ha. I'm no catch." He took the umbrella out of his drink and tossed it on the table.

"How can you let him go?"

Kipper turned to her. His eyes were like a jungle, and she suddenly thought, *He's been places I've never been.*

"I gave my word," he said. His hand was resting on his napkin, the one with the garden drawn on it, and he crumpled it up into a ball.

DANIEL

He'd missed the sunset, and he was *always* here for the sunset. That was one of his rules—sit with Tripod on the deck of his houseboat, drink a beer, and try to hold on to those last few moments of light as he watched the sun fade away. Put off the dark world, as he'd come to think of it, for as long as possible—the endless hours of emptiness and sleeplessness. How to fill those hours? Bars? No—he'd lost the knack of talking to strangers, that back-and-forth of words like a ping-pong ball being jauntily batted over a little net. Now everything he thought of to say was heavy, dense as brick. Except this evening, talking to Mary and Ollie, it had been easier. He'd gotten all worked up picturing that butterfly garden. Well, it wasn't going to happen. Ollie clearly didn't have the money for it, Mary was just here for a week's vacation, and he was a fisherman now. It was a garden that would never be. He wanted it, though. It was strange how badly he wanted it. He could see it, smell its greenness, almost taste it. He still had the napkin crumpled up in his pocket. Now he sat down at his kitchen table and opened it, smoothed it with one hand. Tripod lay down at his feet.

My blue period, he thought, smiling. Then his smile faded. It was not just a blue period. It was a blue forever.

He got up and put the napkin in the kitchen drawer on top of the folded dish towels and shut it. He felt a click inside of him, something settled. Tripod watched him.

He took out his whittling tool, got a branch from his pile, and walked out to his deck. Tripod trotted after him. Daniel had been doing this a lot lately, whittling until way past midnight, until he exhausted himself and could sleep for a few hours. *Just don't think*, he kept telling himself.

He chopped at whatever wood he picked up on the beach. Most times his carvings came out looking like squat chunks on stick legs—more like animals than people. Sometimes they came out looking like wild, skinny women, limbs akimbo, branch hair splayed. Some had open mouths like they were trying to yell something at him. He called them his "tree people." They were a bunch of odd, sometimes disturbing little folks. But they were distinctly his. They were what he was doing. So he kept at it.

Some nights, he couldn't work on the boat deck because of the mosquitoes, so he worked below, filling the whole inside of his boat with branches and tangled pieces of driftwood. He couldn't stop collecting interesting shapes. It was amazing how the world smoothed and weathered the wood. Some of the tree people he carved he tossed into an old clam bucket on the floor, and they huddled in there together. What would Addie make of all this—this forest of dead trees, this bunch of bodies and faces inside his boat? He could just imagine her shaking her head.

His dining table was often his worktable. Well, what did he need a dining room table for anyway? He always ate on the run, haphazardly—an apple or a slice of cheese folded into a hot dog bun. More and more, he'd gotten into canned foods. So easy to just open and spoon up. He didn't even need a dish. Didn't need to warm it in the microwave. Room temperature was fine with him. He'd go to the store, buy a bunch of cans—Beefaroni, asparagus spears, sliced peaches—trying to keep a kind of balance. He'd pyramid them up on his counter, then eat down the pyramid. When it was gone, he'd go back to the Piggly Wiggly, buy another pyramid.

Really, Daniel? One coffee mug, one plate? she'd probably say, tsk-tsking at him.

Well, he didn't need more. Did he? The other day he'd actually looked in his silverware drawer and thought, *Do I really* need *that one fork? Wouldn't the spoon work just as well for most things?* But then he'd stopped himself.

He probably should sweep up the wood shavings on his floor before Addie came on Christmas Day. But he liked the softness of them underfoot. It was kind of homey and carefree, like those bars where people tossed peanut shells on the floor.

Tonight he wanted to be out under the stars. To hell with the mosquitoes. First he'd check the boat lines, although he already knew they didn't need any adjusting. He'd never taken this boat anywhere—*The Dreamboat*. It was funny how he'd ended up with two boats with such hopeful names.

He could see the shadow of his little herb garden, a few stray pots he had filled with basil, parsley, rosemary, and mint. He only had that one pot of parsley. He'd told Ollie he had more. Well, he'd wanted her to have it. She was a nice woman. He'd bring it to her and she could put it in her yard. Maybe the swallowtails would find it. He could always grow more for himself.

The deck creaked under his feet. Tiny wavelets lapped at the side of the boat. He settled into his chair with his piece of wood in one hand, his knife in the other. Tripod sat on his feet. He could feel the dog's warmth, his steady breathing.

He told the dog, "Face it. Something's wrong with me. More wrong than usual." He'd been on a flat line for the past year, his life not getting any better—well, he had little hope of that—but not really getting any worse. But the last few weeks, he'd had this overwhelming desire when he was out deep in the mangroves to just throw the GPS overboard. Get lost and stay lost. "Who would care?" he asked Tripod now.

He started carving the wood. He loved the smell—earthy and salty and sweet. He never had a plan, just let what wanted to happen, happen. He sometimes didn't even look down at it. He did it by feel. Yes, there a nose, there cheekbones, there a chin. He liked to be surprised by what emerged from the wood. Like it was a visitation of sorts.

"Well, we don't have any visitors for real, do we?" he asked Tripod. He stared out at the sky. Lots of stars very far away.

His hands moved in a kind of rhythm. He lost track of time. When he looked down at the wood, a face stared back up at him. He could see it under the white twinkle lights he'd strung, a shadowy face, but young—a child's face, a boy. Something about it looked like Timmy, the tilt to the upturned nose, the wry smile. What was his son doing in the wood? His hands shook.

"Hello?" he said in spite of himself. His voice was hoarse. His heart pounded. He knew it was just a piece of wood. But nobody knew anything, really, about dead people, did they? If they came back, how they came back, how they communicated. Was his son here with him? He listened hard, but there was only the sound of the boat rustling in its slip.

Some days it felt like his whole day was spent listening. For a sign from Timmy, a clue. And Tripod was the same way. Every little noise, his ears would perk up. Sometimes he'd just put his nose high in the air and sniff like he was trying to locate Timmy's scent. Both of them stared down the houseboat dock for hours every night. Waiting, irrationally waiting.

Maybe this was because they'd never recovered Timmy's body after the explosion. It was a roadside bomb. That's all Daniel knew, and it was strapped to a dog. Timmy had tried to unstrap it. He should have waited for the bomb squad. But they were off working on something else. So Timmy didn't wait for them. Of course he didn't.

If Daniel had seen the evidence of Timmy's shattered body, maybe he wouldn't be in this state of limbo—half in the world of the living, half in the dead. But then again, maybe he would. There was something about death that left you hanging. It was essentially unbelievable. How could a person be present so strongly in life, so chock-full of personality and, well, substance and then be gone? He just couldn't take it in.

When he thought of God these days, he thought of a guy with a really big pink eraser, someone who just willy-nilly rubbed people out. But he didn't do a very good job of it, did he? There were those traces left, those faint lines indented into the paper, those eraser nubs all over the place. Who could believe in a guy who operated like that?

He got up and walked inside and put the carving in the kitchen drawer on top of the napkin. The napkin would be a soft bed. Then he shut the drawer ever so gently, leaving a little gap. So Timmy could breathe? He *was* going crazy.

Tripod was standing at the screen door, staring at him.

He went back outside and stood at the rail. All the other houseboats were empty. Everyone had gone back to visit relatives for Christmas. Daniel had seen Sleep briefly when he'd gotten back to the dock, but Sleep was hurrying to get packed. He'd gotten a flight out late tonight.

Daniel thought of his older sister, Melody, in Las Vegas. She and her husband lived in a retirement community on a golf course where the houses all looked exactly the same. He hadn't spoken to her in years. Everything was a lecture with Melody.

And his parents were both dead now. They'd died five years ago, one after the other like dominoes knocking each other down—his mother going first of a stroke, then his father two months later to a fast-moving bone cancer. They were always inseparable, those two. They had their own gluey intimacy, their own whispered secret language that excluded everyone else. He always felt like an outsider in his own family. When Daniel got married and had Timmy, he couldn't believe his good luck. It was like he'd finally found the secret password to the hidden door, and he'd entered the magical world—the world that everyone else seemed to automatically have the key to—the world of the loving.

Now he could feel the tide shifting, tugging at the boat.

He was tired. He felt his shoulders sagging. He had thought he'd never get out of the Low-Key Inn tonight. Larkin wouldn't get out of the pool even after the sun had set and the pool lights came on. Thing Two kept calling her out of the water, but she kept throwing her troll for Tripod to swim after, and Tripod kept retrieving it. The kid was shriveled and blue by the time she finally got out.

By then, he had drunk both his and Ollie's piña coladas, and they were strong. Or else he just wasn't used to anything other than beer. Or maybe Ollie *was* a witch and there was some kind of juju in the pineapple juice. His stomach was all churned up.

He and Mary didn't eat a thing, and they talked and talked about, of all things, their wedding ceremonies. What had he said? Crazy stuff. And too much, too much. His words had turned into something like hot fluid, out of control, plowing through him like lava carving its own path.

He cringed now to think he'd told her he'd wanted to do one

of those back-to-nature weddings in his own backyard garden; how he would've built the arbor himself, wound grapevine around branches, made the arch crooked and a bit tippy; how he'd wanted to have simple bouquets like leggy wildflowers in Mason jars with cherry branches; how he'd wanted to rent picnic tables, have everyone sit on benches, serve up some platters family style; how the small children could have waded into the nearby brook, caught tadpoles with colorful little nets that he would have handed out.

He'd gone on and on. Well, it was all that garden talk with Ollie that must've stirred him up. He'd told Mary how he and Addie ended up with a church wedding, because Addie wanted one, with stained glass throwing reds and blues on the floor of the church, and an organ droning on in a vibrating tone, and Addie's sister Shantelle playing a breathy flute in the loft. It was more like a funeral than a wedding. The flowers looked stiff as mummies.

He asked Tripod, "What was I thinking telling her all that?"

His mouth felt rubbery and overused. The cut on his head ached. She'd laughed at him, called him "a drifty hippie type." Well, perhaps he was.

Tripod plopped down next to him on the deck. Daniel had fluffed up his fur with one of the Low-Key Inn's towels before they left the pool. He turned his face up to Daniel, and his hair was tufted lopsidedly on the top of his head.

"You look a wreck," Daniel told him.

Tripod seemed to shrug and dropped his head down on his front paws.

"I probably look a wreck too," Daniel told him. "But who cares, eh?"

Tripod didn't move, but he could tell the dog was listening.

In the last few weeks when he and Tripod were alone in the

boat, and he was thinking about tossing the GPS, he'd swear that Tripod knew what he was thinking. Tripod would peer at him all squint-eyed.

"Don't go judgmental on me," he'd tell Tripod. And Tripod would look away. Then Daniel would turn the boat around and putter home.

But now Tripod would be leaving with Addie.

Addie was coming in Christmas morning on the noon flight, leaving that night. She said, "I don't celebrate anything anymore." He didn't either, so what did it matter?

Last Christmas, they'd still been together in the house, but they hadn't gotten a tree, hadn't decorated at all. He didn't buy Addie anything, but Addie got him a hand vacuum for his truck. She said it had really strong suction. He still had it in the box unopened on the back seat. They'd sat on their couch together and ate popcorn in separate bowls and watched Indiana Jones movies all day. *Dumpdadahdum, dumpdaDAH!* Now whenever people mentioned Christmas, that theme song would fire up in his head, trumpets blaring. He had a soft spot for Harrison Ford. Harrison got him through that day, one adventure after the next. Maybe he'd watch those movies again this year after Tripod left. He'd have to check to see if he had any microwave popcorn.

Tripod would be fine with Addie. Dogs were adaptable, and that dog was a survivor. He'd put up with Daniel and his boats. Daniel thought then of what Mary had said about going "up and down all the time." He chuckled.

"Yeah, you probably won't miss that part, will you?" he said to Tripod. "You'll appreciate some solid ground, a nice yard of your own to patrol around in."

But he wasn't sure Addie had a yard anymore. She had the

house in Boxwood up for sale now and had moved to a condo in Westchester County in New York. She'd told him, "I want a life without maintenance."

Addie had seemed to gain strength after Timmy died. She turned into a zealous advocate, like a soldier herself. That group of hers was, she said, "like a family." She talked endlessly about the beauty of the World Wide Web, how it connects everybody. But all he could think of was a giant spider weaving together the dangling bodies of strangers.

He didn't want any part of that group. Any part of her either. It was like they were suddenly strangers after Timmy died. Or maybe they'd been strangers all along, and his death just made that clear. How could people have an entire marriage and never really connect? Never really understand each other? He hadn't missed her a single day.

"We never ate from the same popcorn bowl," Daniel said to Tripod.

Tripod inched one ear up, then lowered it.

"Why did I say I'd spend the day with them tomorrow?" he asked Tripod.

Thing Two had asked him right before he left the pool if Larkin could spend some more time with the dog. She'd said, "All I know about my grandchild is that she loves your dog."

She'd been stammering when she asked him. "If you could, if you would consider . . ."

"Those drinks went to my head," he said to Tripod.

He'd agreed to it. More than just a visit too. He'd volunteered to take them kayaking for the day. Sleep had two double kayaks and always told Daniel he could use them anytime. Thing Two said she'd bring a picnic lunch.

He'd kept nodding at her like a bobblehead.

A fish jumped out of the water next to his boat, a flash of silver. Something must be chasing it. He watched the dark water. The white lights reflected in the ripples, and it looked like stars were buried deep in the sea. Daniel thought of Timmy resting on the napkin garden inside his houseboat drawer.

"Can you wish on an underwater star?" he asked Tripod. But Tripod seemed to be asleep.

MARY

Mary and Larkin ate dinner in their room. Larkin had French fries, chicken fingers, and a cup of chocolate pudding with whipped cream and a maraschino cherry on the top—she'd even eaten the stem of the cherry. She'd never tried any of these things before. CC's list of allowed foods stayed stuffed deep in Mary's suitcase.

Larkin watched the SpongeBob Christmas special during dinner. Her eyes were glued to the TV.

CC didn't celebrate Christmas anymore because she thought it was a capitalist plot. Or something like that. Mary's eyes glazed over when CC started talking about it. Since Larkin was born, she'd only allowed Mary to come visit after Christmas and she limited Mary to three presents for Larkin. She counted them! It just about broke Mary's heart.

This year, Mary had begged CC to let her show Larkin what Christmas was all about. She wanted to whisk Larkin away to Brooklyn, teach her to cut red and green construction paper into strips and make chain garlands and string them all over her condo, glue Popsicle sticks into snowflake ornaments and pour glitter all over them—and her kitchen table. She'd bundle Larkin up and take her skating at Rockefeller Center.

But CC said no celebrations. Allowing a few would be "confusing."

CC also didn't "believe in" cartoons.

"Cartoons are not a religion," Mary had argued.

Good thing CC was out to sea now where her cell phone didn't get reception. Otherwise, she'd be calling every fifteen minutes—*What are you doing now?* She was one of those overbearing kind of parents. Mary could swear CC was hovering over them in the igloo when Larkin was dancing around and singing along to the cartoon, "SpongeBob SquarePANTS!" Jumping up and down on the bed when she sang the word "pants."

Mary could almost hear CC saying, "Oh, Mother." In despair.

But Mary thought, *So much for your singing therapist. All the kid needed was a cartoon.*

She didn't know how CC had become so uptight after being such a rule breaker her whole life. It was ironic. Mary knew it was because CC was struggling to do everything perfectly. She read tons of books on child-rearing, subscribed to *Best Parents* magazine. But, ugh, going to CC's apartment was like putting on a straitjacket. Mary had to watch everything she did, every word she said, and she still screwed up!

CC meant well. It worried Mary because she saw CC trying to be supermom just like Mary had tried to be. From the moment CC found out she was pregnant, she had turned her whole life around one hundred eighty degrees, but she'd made way too hard a turn, Mary thought. Mary kept hoping that CC would relax some. But Mary understood the fear that your whole world would cave in if you stopped being hypervigilant. She'd had that fear herself. And she had to give CC credit for what CC had accomplished. She thought of that day in the therapist's office at

CC's college in upstate New York after CC found out she was pregnant.

The therapist said CC's self-esteem needed work before she had a child. Mary had chuckled at that and said, "Well, whose doesn't?"

But the therapist had been undeterred. She'd advised CC to put the baby—"If you insist on having it," she'd said—up for adoption.

Mary knew the woman was just doing her job. After all, CC had spent her whole first semester of her freshman year high or sleeping through all her classes and screwing around with half the lacrosse team, evidently. The woman thought CC was a loser.

CC had met Mary's eyes in that cold office where the window showed a landscape of snow and more snow and shook her head ever so slightly. Mary's heart lifted. CC wouldn't give the baby up. She'd do what she had to do. Mary could see it in the stubborn set of her jaw. Once CC made up her mind, that was that. Mary had been so proud of her that day, even though she had her own doubts about CC's competence as a mother. They'd linked arms and stomped out.

Larkin's father, Elliot, who was just nineteen years old at the time CC got pregnant, didn't want anything to do with Larkin, and Elliot's parents had, as CC put it, "bought his way out of fatherhood," giving CC a lump sum payment to "disappear forever." CC had taken the money. Of course she had. She had little choice. She was only eighteen herself at the time. She'd put the money to good use. She'd gotten her associate's degree online, put her "weedy days" behind her, and she was managing to raise Larkin herself. Well, she was smart. Brilliant, really. All her teachers said so. But it broke Mary's heart that CC was so obsessive. She understood that there were a million rules these days with children and that you could get all tangled up in the dos and don'ts.

"Trust yourself," she wanted to tell CC. "Trust the playful, creative child you used to be. Let *that* self out. Let *that* self be your guide with running your life and raising Larkin. *Feel* your life forward." But CC had turned into much more of a *think*-your-life-forward, *steer*-your-life-forward person.

Right before CC went on the cruise, she told Mary she wanted to send Larkin to a special preschool in the spring where they did calculus or something instead of squishing Play-Doh. CC was worried about Larkin's speech. She wanted Larkin to "get ahead"—wherever that was. CC had shown Mary the brochure because she wanted her to help pay for it.

"Listen," Mary told CC, "there's nothing wrong with Larkin's brain that she won't outgrow." The kid was sharp. She noticed everything.

When they got back to the room tonight, Larkin had asked Mary, "Why are Kipper's eyes so sad?"

Mary said, "I think because his son died."

"Did you cheer him up, Gramma?" Larkin had seen them laughing over their poolside drinks.

"I don't know," Mary said, helping to get Larkin into her weird nightgown. *Some soft cotton jammies*, Mary thought, *would be good right about now*.

"Mommy says when you cry, all your sad comes out."

"Is that what your mommy says?"

"And if you blow your nose really hard into a Kleenex, it helps."

"That's sometimes true."

"Joey Mantifucco from next door says that it's not sad coming out. It's just snot."

"What does Joey Mantifucco know?"

Larkin paused, looked at the TV. "I don't like James-Walter," she said out of the blue.

"Why not?"

"James-Walter makes me say my words reeeeealllly sloooowly."

"Oh?" Mary said.

Larkin watched the TV for a considering moment, then looked back at Mary. Her blue eyes were pale and speckled with brown.

Mary said carefully, "You can say words any way you want to say words, Larkin. Saying words in your own voice is one of the most important things in the world."

"You know what, Gramma?" Larkin said.

"What is it, my love?"

Larkin stuck her arms straight out from her sides. "Patrick is a starfish. I can be a starfish too if I want to."

"You're right," Mary said.

Larkin jumped up and down on the bed. In a few minutes, she collapsed, watching the TV. Mary gazed at her body all curled up in a ball. She loved the kid so much, but Larkin was going to disappear from her life again after this week. Could she bear that pain all over again? On top of losing Ron and her job and everything else in her life? She watched SpongeBob prance around the TV screen in a daze.

Mary got up and tucked a blanket over Larkin and kissed her on the forehead. She brushed Larkin's hair from her face, removed her glasses, touched her soft cheek.

There was no protection from love in the world, she thought. When it came over you, it rushed in like the ocean and filled you up. There was no stopping it. What even was the point of trying?

She said to herself, *You'll never have this time again. So live it up, girl. And do it your way.*

She felt a surge of pride. Today she'd taken Larkin fishing in her underwear, fed her chocolate, and the kid had survived. She'd had a good time.

She thought of Kipper and Ollie. *Yes, build the garden if you can! Go for it!*

She walked outside onto the porch and brought her phone and her glass of wine. She stared down at the blank screen. What was Ron doing now? Were he and Alexandra and Joanna sitting around his living room? Were they decorating the tree, baking cookies, drinking eggnog? She gritted her teeth. She'd blocked him on her phone and email, but she wondered if he'd tried to get in touch with her. How could he have canceled out of Christmas? How could he have let her go after all they had together?

Distract yourself. Focus on the present.

She picked up her phone. *Don't call Ron.* She called Joelle.

Joelle said, "How's it going?"

"Well, besides wrecking a boat and sending a guy to the urgent care, just spiffy." She told Joelle the story.

"Hmm," Joelle said. "So, you met a man . . ."

"It's not like that. He's definitely not a sorbet man. More like a brown-rice-and-veggie-casserole-with-an-arugula-salad man."

"With a glass of wine, that could work."

"We're going kayaking tomorrow."

"Really."

"But it's all about Larkin and Tripod."

"Is he nice? Is he cute?"

"Stop. He's not anything. He's sad."

"You have something in common, then."

"Oh, Joelle. No, he's *really* sad for good reason. I'm just stupid-sad."

"You're not stupid."

"I have been totally stupid about Ron."

"You've been loyal and stubborn."

"I have to get him out of my mind."

"Yes, get stubborn about that."

"I'll try."

"All right. Glad you're having fun."

"I'm not sure I would call today 'fun.'" Although she was smiling thinking of it, and she had a feeling Ron would be jealous if he knew. He was when she so much as glanced at another man. *Good*, she thought.

She hung up. The breeze swished around her. The moon shone through the palm fronds. The air smelled green. She had a bit of a tingly sunburn. She wondered if her whole life from now on was going to be, *Don't think about Ron.*

Well, it used to be real. Didn't it? They'd had a life together. He'd loved her. He'd understood her.

"I know your loneliness, because I have it too," he'd told her.

But could loneliness plus loneliness add together and become intimacy? It seemed to make sense that it would work that way. But that was the mathematical myth of their relationship. One plus one just equaled two separatenesses.

"I was never any good at math," she said aloud.

A woman walking by her igloo looked up. It was Ollie.

"Are you all right, dear?" Ollie asked.

"Just talking to myself," she said. She hoped Ollie couldn't see her face flushing. "Thank you again for the drinks," she said. "That was very kind. I owe you one. And Kipper owes you two. He drank your drink as well as his own."

"Kipper? Is that what you call Daniel?"

"Yes, well, Larkin started calling him that and it just caught on."

"He's lovely."

Mary said, "Yes. I think he is."

Funny how they had laughed together this afternoon—she and Kipper, after Ollie left—over such sad stuff too.

Kipper kept telling her, "This is terrible. Why are you laughing at me?"

And that just made it funnier. His wedding sounded dreadful. And then she told him about her wedding to Charles, and how Charles's family were "ultimate Christians," how they didn't "allow alcohol," how they didn't approve of public mouth-to-mouth kissing, so Charles had to aim below her mouth for the wedding kiss, and how he'd landed oddly somewhere in the vicinity of her chin and how she'd had to swallow her spurt of laughter and how it had come out as a loud burp and then she'd had the hiccups for the rest of the afternoon, how they'd had the reception in the church basement in a fluorescent-lit hall that smelled like pork because all of the church ladies had done the food potluck style and everything was a variation on a ham-and-noodle casserole except for the "cake," which was really a Jell-O mold in which Mary's and Charles's names had been spelled out in pineapple chunks, how Mary's college friends had spent the whole reception tailgating in the church parking lot doing shots of Fireball, and Kipper kept saying, "No. Impossible. Couldn't be."

Ron hadn't laughed when she'd told him the story of her wedding day. "Huh" was all she could get out of him. But Kipper kept sputtering and snorting. Then he'd rein himself in. As if he didn't feel like he *should* laugh, as if he didn't have the right to laugh anymore.

If my kid died, I don't think I'd feel like I had that right either.

Ollie stood in the shadows. She looked smaller than she had earlier, her white shirt billowing around her thin frame in the tropical breeze. She looked very alone on the dark path.

"Would you care to have that drink with me now?" Mary asked.

"I believe I would," Ollie said, climbing the two steps.

Mary went inside to get her a glass. When she came out, Ollie said, "I see you rearranged the chairs and the table on the porch."

"I'm sorry. It just made more sense this way."

"Don't apologize. It actually looks much nicer. And yes, I can see how it makes more sense." Ollie smiled and took a sip. "Very crisp. Thank you."

The old rattan chairs groaned as they sat down.

"Are you a decorator of some sort?" Ollie asked.

"Yes," Mary said.

"Ah, so that explains it."

"What?"

"How intuitive you were about the butterfly garden. How you wanted to make it a livable, usable space." Ollie's voice was wistful.

"That was fun to think about."

"And how you just made this porch so much more welcoming."

Mary smiled. She told Ollie about her writing job. Then she told her how, before that job, she'd worked at Oskar's—a chain of furniture stores. Though Oskar had hired her to do sales, he soon found that she could decorate his showrooms, and that the showrooms she decorated sold—the whole kit and caboodle. "I'll take everything just as it is!" the customers were likely to say of the "rooms" she put together.

"I miss that so much," she told Ollie. "Creating order out of chaos."

"Yes, I can see how that would be very satisfying," Ollie said.

"And I miss Oskar," Mary said, "with his big belly and waddling walk and his unlit cigar hanging out of the side of his mouth, barking orders at me, which I usually ignored. 'Why dontcha put that reclinah over heah, buckaroo.' He always called me 'buckaroo.'" Mary's voice hitched. She really loved that guy. When he died, she was one of the only people who went to his funeral. She remembered that gray October day. The sidewalks and gutters were filled with fallen leaves as though all the trees in New York had given up on summer at once.

"I met Ron," Mary said, "my boyfriend—well, my ex-boyfriend now—while he was buying an office chair in Oskar's showroom." Ron had come back three times, each time talking to Mary for an hour. Over an office chair? How many times could he roll himself around in different chairs testing the wheels? He seemed like he wanted to ask Mary out, but he didn't.

Now Mary told Ollie, "I should have known right then that he was a slow mover." Why was she telling all this to a stranger? *Because I need to talk or else I'll cry.*

"When Oskar died," Mary said, "and his daughter decided to sell the business, we had the liquidation sale, and Ron showed up. He asked me if I'd like to come work for him. He'd just quit his job selling insurance to start a home décor magazine.

"It's weird how you end up where you end up," she told Ollie.

"Yes indeed," Ollie said.

"What is it like to own a motel like this?" Mary asked.

"Oh, it's a joy," Ollie said, her eyes lighting up. "And then, it's, well, difficult. There's so much to be done."

"It looks like fun. I mean, it's such a quirky place, so much personality."

Just then the steel band started up again. They must've come back from a break. "Here comes Santa Claus, right down Santa Claus Lane," a man with a Caribbean accent sang.

Ollie said, "I'm lucky to have had my hotel dream for so long. I'm lucky that people have seen it for what it is, have loved it." Her voice broke. She shook her head. "I'm sorry I didn't get a chance to show Larkin the iguana or my birds today."

"Oh, I'm sorry too. But we were so busy. And there's tomorrow."

"Yes," Ollie said, looking off into the dark.

Mary looked through the trees at the lights twinkling through the branches, the warm glow of the windows in the igloo rooms.

A woman yelled, "Hon?" and a man answered, "Right here, my love." Mary smelled citrus and chlorine. The night felt very close, like a warm blanket drawn in. The band stopped playing except for one stray note on a steel drum. Someone laughed.

"Why did you come to this hotel?" Ollie asked. She leaned far forward as if she really wanted to hear the answer.

"It seemed to, well, have a soul," Mary said shyly.

"Yes. It does," Ollie said, smiling.

Mary said, "And I guess I needed an escape away from my life and myself."

"Actually, an ideal vacation is one that brings us closer to our real selves rather than further away, don't you agree?"

Real self? Zelda was forever talking about being real, being congruent—the outside self being the same as the inside self. She'd started Mary freewriting in a journal.

"Open yourself up. Let's see what's inside," Zelda had said.

Mary had read some of her writing to Zelda. Mary thought suddenly of Zelda's office. The soft hiss of the air purifier in the corner, the sound of Mary's own voice reading aloud. A few times, Zelda had taped Mary reading and then played it back for her. "So you can hear who you are. I think it's a stronger way to affirm your voice than just hearing yourself speak," she'd insisted when Mary had resisted.

She'd asked Mary to close her eyes and just listen. Mary had cringed at first at hearing her voice. Was that really her? It didn't even sound like her! But then she'd gotten used to it, and she actually looked forward now to that time that she'd hear her own thoughts. Strange, floaty odd words and fragments, thoughts and emotions, all weaving together.

"It's kind of like listening to a dream," Mary told Zelda.

"Yes. In both, you're making connections, making sense of disparate things. You're writing your own story," Zelda said.

Ollie seemed to hear her thoughts because she said, "You probably know a lot more about that real self inside you than you think you know."

Mary thought of her sketch pad with the lines running here and there like rivers, sorting themselves out and ending in dead-end lakes, or running out into rivulets or merging into bigger, stronger rivers. Ron had told her when they first started out that she had a unique writing voice. She thought he really valued that about her. But then, as time went on, he'd started putting constraints on her writing. He was under pressure, he said, to get the magazines perfect, to "professionalize their content." Mary did what he wanted, but she felt a sadness when she looked at her articles once they'd been published. Her words looked so wan on the page. Where did her creativity, her humor, her uniqueness go?

She thought of Luigi, the foreman when she flipped houses with Charles, and how he'd trusted her "vision." How he told her she could "transform" things. She thought of Oskar. How he used to say to her, "You see things the way nobody else sees them, buckaroo. You see how things fit. You see things simply and commonsensically, and that's a gift."

She had a gift. She smiled to herself. *It's Christmas*, she thought. *It must be time to open all my gifts.*

She asked Ollie, "How did you get to this place—I mean, come to own this hotel?"

Ollie explained how her husband had won it. "He was, I'm afraid, a bit of a gambler," she said.

"Really?"

"This island was undeveloped then. All the nature scared me.

Until it didn't scare me anymore. It began to work its magic on me. The gulf every day being so endless and blue. The sky so wide. And how you can see the storms roll in from far away, even see the line of rain approaching on the water. I love knowing what the tide is doing at all times. I love watching the sunset. I love walking on the beach and seeing something different every day. This place has taken care of me. I can't imagine living without it.

"Where do you live, dear?" Ollie asked.

"New York. Brooklyn. I never see the sunset or know when it's high tide. I wish I did."

"What keeps you there?"

"The usual, I guess. Job. House. Relationship . . ." Mary trailed off. *Nothing*, she thought.

"Ah. So you belong there?"

"Belong?"

Ollie waited.

It had been bothering her since she met Ollie what she reminded Mary of, and now Mary remembered.

When Mary was five years old and her parents died, she went to live with her uncle, her only relative, in a big old stone house with turrets and stone floors that echoed. Her uncle was wealthy and had lost his wife young to pneumonia. He'd closed himself off to all emotion after that. He worked all the time and rarely saw Mary. But she was provided for. She had a nanny named Mrs. Wilhelm, a stern stick of a woman whose job was to keep Mary in line.

There had been an old woman who lived on the neighboring farm who had two miniature ponies. The woman was a recluse and didn't have any children, and whenever she saw Mary, she'd come out of her front door like a cuckoo out of a clock door and yell, "Go where you belong!" in a voice that was crusty with disuse. Mary's nanny told her the woman had lost her husband in the war and that had turned her sour on people.

Ollie reminded her of that woman. She looked like her. But it was as if Ollie was a mirror image of that woman—everything reversed. All her hardness, softened.

Mary loved those miniature horses. She never knew their names, but she called them Blinken and Nod and fed them bits of carrot and handfuls of clover she picked from the field. Blinken had misshapen legs and wobbled a bit as he walked. Nod always stood by and watched over Blinken when Blinken grazed.

"Go where you belong," the woman would say, pointing at Mary, and Mary would step away from the fence backward, reluctant, yearning to stay and feel the ponies' soft noses nuzzling against her hand and touch their rough, tangled manes that hung over their eyes.

She had always wanted to yell back, "But I belong here . . ." She felt at home in that field with those animals, with the smell of crushed grass in the air and the green stains on her hands. More at home than she'd ever felt. But Mary never said anything, just backed away. Then the woman died, and Mary begged her uncle to take the horses. She would take care of them. She promised. She swore on her heart. But he wouldn't. And so the horses were taken away one day by some man in a van.

When she thought of it now, she still felt like she was falling off a cliff in her heart. She'd cried for months over those horses until her uncle sent her away to boarding school, hoping that would snap her out of it.

Go where you belong. Where was that? The phrase still echoed in her now.

"You're mine," Ron often told her, kissing her hard. It had always thrilled her to hear those words. But they weren't true.

"It's hard to know where you belong," Mary said now.

"Is it?" Ollie said. "I think you just do what you love, do it with the people you love, do it in the place that you love."

Mary thought, *I have none of that anymore.* It gave her an empty feeling. She said, "I wish it were that simple. I envy your life."

"Are you looking for a new life?" Ollie smiled at her.

"I'm just . . ."

It was odd, being in this place, how her perspective had shifted. Like she was in a Tilt-A-Whirl ride and everything she used to love and want now seemed upside down, and she wanted . . . what? To walk on the beach? To watch the sunset?

She said to Ollie, "I guess I am." *You'd better start figuring it out*, she told herself. *Because you're unemployed and your house is sold. And you're alone. Remember?* "I have a lot of things up in the air right now," she said.

Ollie finished her wine and put down her glass. "Ah, the air. Well, listen to the night. I believe it talks to us and tells us what we need to know. Listen for the black skimmers. They call to each other as they feed. It's quite high-pitched and beautiful."

"Are those birds?"

"Yes, they skim right along the surface of the water with their beaks."

"I would like to see that."

"Sleep well, dear," she told Mary. "Give your sweet granddaughter a cuddle for me," she said, and she disappeared into the night.

Mary's phone pinged. It was a text from Joelle. Found some nice properties for you to look at when you get home.

Mary didn't respond. She thought about the acrid smell of the city, the horns blowing, and the traffic. She sat thinking for a while about the butterfly garden, how exciting it had been to imagine building something like that.

Her heart felt jumpy and full of that kind of energy that seemed like fists were banging on the inside door of her heart. *Let me out.* She thought suddenly, *I want to write something. Something alive like that garden.*

So she picked up the empty glasses and went inside and found her journal. She sat down on the bed next to Larkin ever so gently and propped herself up with some pillows. There was something so lovely about a sleeping child. Mary couldn't resist being right there close to her warm body, hearing her breathing, her little moaning sleep noises.

Mary grabbed the Low-Key Inn pen off the nightstand and doodled a little flower on the page. Something was pushing up inside of her like a green shoot.

She started writing. It was like a letter, but to whom? Dear Zelda? She wrote fast, words spilling out of her.

It feels like a lifetime has happened to me today. I had a boating accident—well, actually, a series of accidents. And who am I at the end of this day? Dislocated. That's the word. I'm like a stranger to myself, like I'm a sea creature who got catapulted out of her shell somehow. I think those sea creatures make new shells for themselves somehow or find new ones. Or something . . . I should read up on it. It might be helpful to me. Right now, I feel like a naked pink little vulnerable creature crawling around the vast ocean, looking for a new place. I'm homeless. But it's so strange. I've spent one day here, and I feel less homeless than I've felt in years. In a spare little hotel room with none of my stuff. How is that possible?

I used to make these pillow houses when I was a little girl, with blankets stretched over the top like a tent. That was when I felt best and most secure, when I was in a soft, small place with the sun sifting through the weave of the pink blankets. I feel like that here. Like a child in a pillow house filled not with things but with ideas and imagination.

I met this little old woman. She runs this hotel. It's a beaten-down, odd place, but I like it. The old woman, Ollie, told me she loves to live where she knows what the tide is doing. Coming in, going out, high or low. I can see now why that's important. Low tide is when you walk, you look for shells, find what the ocean reveals when it opens itself up and you can see its bones. And high tide is when you sit and read and feel full. I would like to see a storm coming in here across the gulf.

Maybe I could live by the sea where the horizon is such a clear line, and the sky is so vast and arches over me. In a cottage on stilts with bright-blue shutters and a pink door, like being inside Larkin's rainbow, and maybe a hammock on the porch with the sea coming right up to my door. The cottage could just have screens, not even glass. That's so impractical, though, isn't it? I can hear Ron's voice saying that. But I love it on gray days when the moisture hangs like an intricate web on screens. I would like to show Larkin how it does that.

As I was sitting on my porch this evening right after Ollie left, I could hear the waves in the distance. They were little, but they made a soft lapping noise, which was like a lullaby. *I think I heard the black skimmers.* I heard their voices echo. And I think I heard the skim of their beaks along the water as if they were writing a letter on its surface like I am writing now: Dear Life, it's beautiful here.

OLLIE

Ollie was having coffee out by the pool, and her hands were shaking. She didn't know if it was from caffeine or anxiety. She'd printed out the QuickBooks statements from the past three years. She hated to look at them. Numbers told such a different story than words—just profit, loss, the bottom line. Failure. Nothing about the stories that could be told about this hotel and all the people who had passed through it over the years. Nothing about the little successes.

She thought about Amos Paul. He'd had such high hopes of being a Major League Baseball player when Ollie met him twenty years ago. She'd let him rent a room at a very low rate for two years. Honestly, she almost gave him the room. She could tell he needed it. She'd gone to a bunch of his Minor League games, sat in the right-field stands, watched him strike out time and again.

Oh, but those moments when he connected! The ball launched into outer space. Ollie heard the scouts saying they'd never seen anything like it. But he couldn't wait for the ball. He was always exuberantly swinging, out in front of nearly everything pitched his way. Big grin on his face no matter what.

There wasn't a chance he'd ever make it to the big leagues.

But he told Ollie that living at the hotel made him a different person. "I was so bent on hitting everything out of the park. But then I learned to be a real hitter, at least metaphorically," he'd told Ollie, winking. "I learned the value of a bunt, of moving a man around the bases, of letting someone else score." He said he was eternally grateful for the time he'd spent at the Low-Key Inn. "I found low-key-ness," he said. And he met his wife, Anna, who sang with a band that performed at the tiki bar. She had such a lovely deep voice—like a cello.

Now he lived out in rural Georgia and taught phys ed in the local elementary school. He spent his days coaching T-ball, trying to get those frenetic kids to not run around the bases backward, to not climb on the monkey bars when they were supposed to be playing center field. Oh, he had his stories! He and Anna were never able to have children of their own, so they'd become foster parents and ended up adopting twins. The whole family came back every year during the off-season to visit in that rickety old car that they had that was "kept together with spit and dreams," Amos loved to say. Every year, they sent a Christmas card with a nice handwritten note and a picture of them all dressed up. Ollie had just gotten it the other day. She had the photo taped on her fridge.

And Margaret Dunlop, the librarian. She'd been so shy, hiding behind her sunglasses around the pool. The Low-Key Inn was a kind of shelter for her. She came by herself for a week's stay for years. Always reading, always alone, Margaret had actually told Ollie one day at the hotel, "It's too peopley out there," waving her arm at the wide world outside the grounds. Then she'd met another hotel guest, Kim Sun. He was a mathematician from Taiwan who also came every year. Ollie had a feeling about them, knew somehow that they'd hit it off. Their vacations coincided one year—with a little scheduling help from Ollie. She watched them circle around each other for days, glancing at each other over their dark sunglasses. She finally just did her own fate intervention and asked them both to help her place a new birdhouse. She had Kim Sun up on a ladder and Margaret fluttering around him like a bird herself, saying, "Well, maybe a bit higher . . . Yes, that's it!" That had done it—the simple act of placing the house. Ollie had loved seeing them walk around the grounds, checking on the house together. They'd all celebrated with champagne when a bird couple moved in. The next year, Margaret and Kim were married, and then they had a child that they named after Ollie. Now they had three grandchildren they brought back with them every year.

Was it true what people said about the hotel being magic? People did change during their stays here. Ollie had seen it hundreds of times. But wasn't that true of every resort? People took the time on vacation to breathe, regroup, rethink their paths, reawaken themselves. A vacation anywhere could do that. But people insisted the Low-Key Inn was different.

Was it the scent of the flowers? The birds fluttering? Was it something that Ollie was growing in her garden? Some people thought the water that flowed out of the dolphin fountain made their dreams "funny." They called it "dreamy water." Ollie had heard all the theories. People had told her, "My arthritis is gone" after swimming in the pool. Or "I feel like a kid again" after a day on the beach. And people often found love here. That was undeniable. Love for life, or for each other, or for themselves. Ollie smiled to think of it.

But being magical wasn't necessarily a good reputation for a hotel to have. People said they wanted transformation and change in their lives, but really, did they? The outcome was too unpredictable. The locals shied away from the place, said it was "strange," even "haunted." Ollie had heard all the gossip about her being a witch too. That was just funny. A witch? Where was her broom, her book of spells, her black cat? Well, she did have those two burrowing owls in her yard. She smiled to think of that miniature pair. She could accept that *they* were magic, but not herself. She certainly wasn't working any magic saving this hotel, was she? Why didn't she concoct some potion for herself if she had so much power? Maybe she should get in the pool, sit under that dolphin fountain herself, see what happened . . .

Her phone rang. It was Frances.

"Any luck with Mr. Emerson?" Frances asked.

"No."

"Well, don't give up, Ollie. You can't give up. We'll think of something if he doesn't come through."

Ollie smiled. Frances was full of ideas. The other day, she told Ollie to turn the Low-Key Inn into an artists' retreat. Frances had the whole thing planned out. When she talked about it, Ollie could almost see the writers typing away in their igloo rooms, the game room converted into a studio with potters working at their wheels.

"Great idea," she'd told Frances. "But how?"

How? That was always the kicker.

Now Frances told Ollie, "We'll get together right after Christmas and strategize." Frances was off in Tampa for a week, spending the holiday with her niece.

"Strategize?" Ollie said, staring at the numbers on her profit-and-loss statements. Strategizing required money, and there just wasn't any. "Oh well," she told Frances.

"Don't give up, old girl," Frances said. They called each other "old girl" sometimes. It made them both smile and feel somehow not so old. But Ollie didn't smile this time.

After she hung up, Stephen brought her toast and juice on a

tray. He stood looking around her table for somewhere to put it. Her papers were everywhere in forlorn piles.

"Um," she said. "Wait, wait." She tried scooping them up, but a few papers slipped off her table and wafted away.

The man she'd seen in the pool yesterday was sitting at the next table. He bent to pick up the papers that scooted under his flip-flop. She threw up her hands. "Ugh," she said, meeting his eyes. "This is no way to start a day."

He stood up and approached her, holding out her papers. His face was as wrinkled as one of those Shar-Pei dogs. His grin was crooked. "Is it tax time already?"

"It might as well be."

"Hmm," he said. "Why don't you leave all this and come join me for breakfast? I could use the company. And you seem like you might need a break from that." He pointed to her piles.

She looked at him. He was still wearing that silly bucket hat. His blue-and-white-striped golf shirt was buttoned all the way up to his neck, and his plaid shorts were hiked up too high on his waist. Men! Some of them never figured out how to dress themselves. What they thought went with what was truly amazing. Still, he looked harmless enough with his white belt neatly buckled over his little belly. Schmoozing with the guests was her job, after all.

She said, "Maybe I *could* use a bit of denial."

"Denial is my best shtick," he said.

"Let me just . . ." She swept all her jumbled papers into her tote bag.

He took the bag from her and put it under his table. He gave it a kick. "There," he said.

Stephen put her food in front of her as they settled in.

"I'm Al," he said, reaching out his hand. "You're the owner, aren't you? The young girl pointed you out when I was checking in. You were out in the garden showing some children how to eat a fig."

"Ollie," she said, shaking his hand. It was knobby and warm.

She said, "We have a beautiful fruit garden here, and the kids love to help pick the figs and the sea grapes, the oranges and lemons and limes for the kitchen. Kids don't spend enough time in the garden these days. They say you don't need to explain miracles to children. You just have to show them a garden."

He stared at her. "Perhaps that's true," he said.

"It's one thing I can be sure of," she said, "when life gets to be a confusing mess." She glanced at her tote bag under the table. "I'd like to take my reality to the shredder."

"Is it that bad?" he asked.

She didn't want to go into it. But her worries were building inside of her like too much water pressing on a flimsy dam. She couldn't stop herself from saying, "Do you think we are an anachronism?"

"We?"

"Old codgers like us. Old ways of doing things. Old places like this hotel."

"I think there's still something to be said for us." He smiled.

"I should be strategizing right now, but it's all too much to think about before breakfast."

"Ooh, strategizing. I love strategizing." He leaned toward her.

"Really?" She peered at him as if he would be able to help her. A complete stranger. *Get a grip on yourself, Ollie.* "I'm sorry. You're on vacation; you don't need to deal with my problems."

"But I am a problem solver extraordinaire! Problems are my life!" He talked with his hands, grand gestures like he was leading a marching band. Ollie could almost hear "76 Trombones" blaring.

"What kind of a life is that?" She must have said it harsher than she thought, because he laughed.

"It gives me satisfaction resolving things. That click of a puzzle piece going into its place. Nothing like that sound."

"What do you do for a living?"

"Mostly consulting now. I have my hand in here and there."

Ollie felt herself almost blushing. She was looking at his hand, remembering how it felt when he touched her. *Oh, Ollie, what are you thinking?*

She picked up her toast and pointed it at him. "Eat your French toast before it gets cold."

He cut up his toast into even squares, then poured on the syrup. "Nothing like the real stuff," he said.

"Brown-colored corn syrup is what most places serve," she said.

"And the bread is excellent here."

"Mrs. Tilly bakes it for us and brings it in her van every morning. She does our desserts too. You could die for the carrot cake. She comes from Jamaica, and she's traveled all over the globe. She's amazing. And this is homemade grape jam," she told him, pointing to her own dish. "It's organic, made by this young hippie couple down the road. They raise bees, and we buy their honey too."

"What do you put in this tea?" he said, raising his cup. "It's tasty."

"Oh, is that our special tea? It's just a bit of this and that from the garden."

"It tastes like sunlight," he said, smiling. One of his cheeks had a dimple.

She smiled back at him. "Yes, I believe it does. They say in France the wine takes on the flavor of the nearby growing things—the lavender and the herbs. So why wouldn't the things in our garden take on the scent and taste of the sea, the salt air, the sun?"

She looked around her. It was a beautiful morning. Dragonflies were flitting about and the sun was sparkling gently on the pool. She could smell the gardenias blooming.

A bird swooped down close to her and landed near her feet and pecked around.

"That bird is so tame," Al said.

"They know me. I'm the crazy bird lady. This hotel is a haven for them. I have twenty feeders in my yard alone. I feel I have to take care of the birds. Did you know that there are three billion fewer birds than there used to be fifty years ago on this planet?"

"Billion?"

"I know. It's hard to believe. But the skies *are* much emptier."

They both looked up.

Al said, "I didn't notice."

"People don't."

"I hate news like that. Makes you feel so helpless."

"It does. But I read that in England the culture of feeding birds is so strong that many species are thriving there. So I'm doing my bit. The birds need me here."

"It's good to be needed."

Ollie watched the little bird. "Carolina wren," she said. It stopped and cocked its head, stared up at her, then looked at Al.

Al said, "He's watching us."

"Indeed he is. Curious little guy."

"Hmm," he said. "Can't say as I know one bird from another."

"It's a matter of looking at them. The details of them," she said quietly so she didn't startle the bird.

He stared hard at it. "It has a stripe that looks like a white bushy eyebrow. Like mine."

"Yes."

A woman at the next table got up, and the bird flew.

Ollie pulled her gaze away from where the bird found a perch in a palm tree. "Where are you from, Al?" she asked.

"Oh, I'm not really from anywhere. We never stayed put when I was a kid. My father got transferred a lot." His voice hitched. Ollie glimpsed then the little boy in him, the one nobody was friends with in first grade or second grade or third grade. *One of those lost kids,* she thought. Even now, under all those wrinkles and despite his confident shoulders.

Ollie thought of her own hometown in Ohio. It was a map dot of a place called Lilac. Her father had owned the hardware store in town. Her family's house backed up to farmland. Her childhood was a landscape of wildflowers and barbed wire, sheep dotting the scrabbly hills, the sounds of insects wheezing in chorus in summer, the cooing of mourning doves, the far-off smell of manure. It was a place she could point to and say, "The road started here." She wondered how it felt to start nowhere. *Floaty*, she thought. *No wonder he looks so alone.*

"Do you have family?" she asked.

"I lost my family a long time ago." He looked away.

"I'm sorry."

"My work is my life."

"I suppose mine is too."

They both ate quietly. Ollie rubbed her bad eye. It was so annoying. One of her eyes seemed to have a shade pulled half down over it sometimes lately. And it seemed worse today. Maybe it was because she slept hardly at all last night.

"Are you all right?" Al said.

"Just my eye. It's been bothering me."

He squinted at her. "Maybe you should get it checked out. Your sight is something you don't want to fool around with."

"You're right. I'm sure it's fine, though."

She bit her toast. It was dry and cold now and crumbled on her lips. She took a sip of her orange juice. She closed both eyes so she wouldn't see the shadow. *It's nothing.*

When she opened her eyes again, he was peering at her. "How would you like to be a tourist for a day with me?" he asked her.

"But I have work," she said, looking down at the bag at her feet.

"Maybe you should let all that go right now. Give it up to the universe. Isn't that what people say to do these days?"

"But—" she said.

"When was the last time you did something in this book?" He patted a magazine that was sitting on the table. It was the free guide to the island that the Low-Key Inn and every other local hotel and business distributed to tourists.

She shrugged.

"Never?"

"Probably not." Wilson never wanted to do anything. Never wanted her to do anything either.

"Oh, my dear. You have to open the door up to your life."

"The door?" Ollie thought of *Alice in Wonderland* where all the doors were locked, and even when Alice found a key to a door she wanted to open, she was too big and then she shrank and then she couldn't reach the key, and oh, that was a frustrating book. Like her life right now.

"I'm not sure there is a door in my life. One that I can go through, anyway," she said.

"Of course there is," he said. "There is always a door. Even if we can't see it. Yet."

He flipped through the magazine to an earmarked page and held it up to her. "See this?"

Ollie's heart fluttered. Did she really think that he was going to show her a picture of an actual door to her life opening? That was plain silly. It was a glossy photo of a miniature catamaran with a big engine. Two people were sitting on it, their smiles stretched wide by the wind, their hair whipped straight out behind them. A plume of spray fountained out of the back of the boat.

"I always wanted to rent a cat boat," he said.

"Really? It looks like you'd be very . . . exposed."

"Oh, they're supposedly great. If you like speed."

"Oh, well, speed."

"You're probably going to get wet though, so wear a bathing suit."

"Wait. Me?" She thought of her old blue-and-white polka-dotted bathing suit. She hadn't worn it in years. Did she even know where it was?

"You want to drive, or you want me to?"

"But—"

"You said you wanted denial." He got out his cell phone. "I'll call them right now and make a reservation."

Men got so intent upon things once they got going. It was like he was on the cat boat or whatever it was already, zipping along.

"It's gonna be fun." He smacked the table with his hand. "Yabba dabba doo!"

DANIEL

Daniel had gone to Sleep's boat, *The Maybe Girl*, earlier this morning to get the kayaks and pull them up onto the bay beach. He sat on the bow of his houseboat now, waiting for Mary and Larkin to show up. He glanced at the area of his boat that he'd painted. He'd only done a six-foot swath. He'd get back to work on it after Tripod left. It would give him something to do.

Or maybe he would just leave it the way it was.

Tripod's legs were twitching and moving as he slept on the deck next to him. Dreaming about something. The air smelled like drying fish. It was going to be one of those days, harsh around the edges, the sun so bright that sparks seemed to fly.

He'd had another bad night, and when he'd finally fallen asleep toward dawn, he had this crazy dream. Addie was here. But instead of coming in his door, she broke through the deck of his houseboat—chopped a hole with an ax—and dropped down to his bedroom floor wearing nothing but a Santa hat.

"I've come for the dog," she said, and reached out to Tripod.

Daniel said, "I'm sorry, but I have no hands, so I can't give him to you."

And he didn't! He had only stubs where his hands should be, and something was growing on them. Was it Spanish moss?

Why couldn't this dream be one of the ones that dissolved without a trace when he woke up? But no, it lingered, and he kept remembering more details. Addie wore thick brown lipstick in the dream. As far as he knew, she'd never worn lipstick in her whole life. And she had kissed him too. A long, smushy kiss.

He'd told her, "You taste like rust."

Tomorrow Addie would be here. How was he going to get through that?

First he had to deal with today. It was weird to think about spending the day with a woman. This morning he'd almost called to cancel. He'd gotten out his phone and stared at it. Then he thought of the little girl's face, those big clunky glasses of hers perched on the thin bridge of her nose, and he put his phone down.

Now he stood up as Mary pulled into the lot. What would she do to him today? Even when she wasn't destroying something, her energy was so up-and-down; it was like one of those bad EKG readings—all over the place—peaks and dips and stutters and spikes. Not what a heart was supposed to be like.

He paused. *Ta-dum*, *ta-dum*. He felt the muffled steadiness of his own heart—The Big No on the job again.

He watched her get out of the car. Her bag tipped and bottles of sunscreen rolled around her feet. When she bent to pick them up, she whacked her elbow on the car door, flinched, and dropped the whole bag. He smiled. She was such a klutz.

He went to help her.

"New look?" he asked her as Larkin hopped out of the car in a pair of flowered shorts, a pink tee with a unicorn on it, and some flip-flops.

"We both went shopping this morning in the hotel gift shop. That's why we're late. I threw out her JonBenét Ramsey beauty pageant outfit and, of course, the vomit shoes."

"Oh, those."

Larkin bent to hug Tripod, and Tripod looked at Daniel as Larkin half lifted and squeezed him. Daniel thought if a dog could roll his eyes, Tripod would be doing just that.

"Easy there," Daniel said to Larkin.

"He likes it," Larkin told Daniel.

"Oh," Daniel said. Maybe she was right. Tripod reached up his nose and licked Larkin's face.

Mary was pulling a cooler out of the car. Daniel bent to help her and started carrying the cooler, leading them toward the kayaks.

Mary said, "CC called me this morning, and you know what she said?"

He thought, *CC is the daughter. The one who went on the cruise. Why should I care?*

"They had to turn the ship around. Everyone got that cruise ship virus except for her and James-Walter."

"Turn around?"

Mary said, "So, you know what they're doing now? They rented a car and are driving down here. Right now."

"Here?" *They're coming on our kayak trip too?*

"Not here," she said, stomping along. Larkin scampered ahead with Tripod, hopping on one leg along with the dog. Larkin kept falling over and laughing. Daniel couldn't stop looking at them.

"They'll be here this afternoon. They're staying the night with us in our hotel room, CC informed me. Then they're whisking Larkin away to Disney. Disney! After all CC's talk about the harmful effects of cartoons. It's all because of that man she's with. James-Walter. He wants to go to Epcot and ride some ride."

He couldn't read her energy. She was talking so fast. He felt himself being hurtled into the "Thing Two Tornado," as he'd come to think of it.

"Is that good?" he asked.

She stopped short. "It's Christmas. They're taking my granddaughter away from me on Christmas Day."

"Ah," he said.

She said, "Disney is so overrated. I do not for one second understand those adults who wear Mickey Mouse shirts."

He didn't either. He and Addie had taken Timmy to Disney once when Timmy was six. Timmy had spent the day big-eyed and silent because the person dressed up as Winnie the Pooh had refused to talk to him. Daniel knew that the people in the costumes were strictly forbidden to speak, so he kept trying to distract Timmy, but Timmy didn't get it.

"What's wrong with you, Winnie? Don't you like me?" Timmy kept asking.

Winnie had shrugged, an odd smile planted on his fuzzy face.

The next day, instead of going back to Disney, Timmy said he wanted to go to a water park. He never watched his Winnie the Pooh videos again, and they had been his favorite.

"CC is going to hate it. And what will she do with Larkin? But there's no talking to her when it comes to that man. She'll do anything for him." Mary flapped her arms. A towel fell out of her bag and Daniel put the cooler down for a second, scooped up the towel, and tossed it over one shoulder. He thought of when he and Addie used to take Timmy to the beach, how much stuff there was to carry. He'd never minded that. He almost liked being laden down. *This is our stuff*, he used to think. *Ours*.

Mary said, "CC and men. She gets obsessed. I mean, why can't they just stay with me for the rest of the vacation the way we planned it in the first place?"

He shrugged. Here he was in the midst of a Christmas soap opera. His head was buzzing. He felt the ache of his stitches where she'd gotten to him yesterday. Now he put the cooler in the front of one kayak and bungeed it in.

"I'll take this boat with Tripod, and you two can take the other one."

Larkin said, "But I want to go with Try-Hard."

Mary looked at him.

"All right," he said. "Better let me take the dog and the kid, and you"—he pointed at Mary—"can take the cooler."

It was probably best that he decided to do it that way. Turned out she was a terrible kayaker. Her stroke, not that anyone would ever call it a stroke, was a cartwheeling kind of thing. She smacked the paddle hard into the water, then yanked it back. Her kayak swayed from side to side. The paddle kept jumping out of her hands. He'd never met anyone as uncoordinated as her.

He tried to show her, after they started off, how to dip the paddle, then pull through smoothly.

"Dip. Pull," he said.

She looked at him with slitted eyes.

"Just trying to help," he said as he glided ahead of her. *Let her cool down.*

Larkin sat with Tripod on her lap in the front of his kayak. He kept staring at her brown hair scrunched up into a messy ponytail and her pale neck with the tiny bumps of her spine and her new pink tee shirt with the tag sticking up out the back. SMALL, it read.

Timmy used to dress himself with his tee shirts inside out and backward when he went to that preschool in the Church of the Innocent's basement. Timmy had really hated that preschool. Why he and Addie insisted Timmy go, Daniel couldn't really remember. Addie would force Timmy to go back to his room and re-dress himself, but when Timmy came home from school, his shirt was all backward again. His teachers said he was dyslexic or dysfunctional or dys-something. They couldn't decide. They just knew Timmy needed therapy.

Daniel didn't think it was worth making a fuss over. Let the kid dress any way he pleased. It wasn't hurting anybody. But Addie had insisted Timmy go to the therapist. Why had he just gone along with so many things? Then Timmy had started dressing right. Except he came home from preschool every day and his tee shirt was soaked through from his neckline to his chest because that damn school made him so anxious that he sucked on his shirt. Day after day, Daniel saw those wet shirts and never did anything about it.

His paddle smacked the water hard. If he had just done one thing different back then, could it have changed the whole course of Timmy's life?

He pointed to a nest on top of a channel marker. "See the baby ospreys?" he said.

Larkin nodded back at him, her eyes wide.

Mary crashed into his kayak. She was looking up at the nest. "Oops," she said.

"That's probably the female," he told her. "The male could be off hunting. They come back to the same spot every year. They mate for life."

Mary looked away and started paddling. *What's up with that?* She wasn't wearing a ring, he'd noticed. Divorced, he guessed. Here she was, alone at Christmas. That said something. *What do you care?* he asked himself.

He hung behind her and watched her back. She was wearing a different bathing suit today. *Did she just buy that?* She had faint tan lines already on her shoulders. There was something so sexy about tan lines. He pulled ahead of her.

They aimed for a little island that Daniel knew. After they pulled the kayaks up on the sand, Daniel showed Larkin where to look for sand dollars, showed her how they Frisbee-floated toward the beach where the water was shallow and the ocean floor flat. She got busy hunting for them, collecting them like they were gold pieces. Mary did too. Larkin found a dead sea urchin, so he showed her how to hollow it out with a sharp shell to clean it. It was a nice purple one. A dolphin gently rose and dove, rose and dove right in front of them in the aqua water.

Mary said, “What is this place called?”

He told her it was called Broken Beach. “Many years ago, a storm cut it off from the mainland. The Seminoles considered it sacred ground. If your spirit or your heart was broken, you came here to make an offering of a shell. There’s a shell pile right up there.” He pointed back away from the shore. “People still come here from all over to put a shell on that pile.”

“Can we go see it?” Mary said.

He nodded. “I want to look for driftwood anyway.”

They left Larkin on the beach with Tripod. “I’ll be right there where you can see me,” Mary told her.

“They’re fine,” Daniel said. “They’re in their own world.”

They walked toward the shell mound. “Do you make something with the driftwood?” she asked.

“Carvings of people.”

They looked around as they walked. She found a nice piece—a graceful, twisty branch—and gave it to him. He could tell she loved the thing, just the way she held it in her hands.

“You can keep it for yourself if you want,” he said.

“No,” she insisted. “You make it into something else.”

When they got to the shell mound, she said, “Oh, it’s big.”

“Yeah,” he said. It was a good ten feet tall and double that in width—a squat, looming thing. He looked at the dark shadow it cast. He always thought of Stonehenge when he came here.

He took a shell out of his pocket. A scallop. It felt smooth in his hand. He walked over to the pile, put it down. *Here you go, Timmy*, he said to himself. *One for the team*. It was what he said. Every time he came here. And he came here a lot, made his offering, left. He didn't really understand how to pray. What was he supposed to say? This seemed better. Simpler.

Mary was looking at him. "What does it do?" she asked.

"What does it do?" he said. He looked at his shell on the pile. "I don't know."

"Can I?" she asked, holding up a little lightning whelk she'd been carrying.

He looked at her. *What is broken in her life?* He shrugged. She put her shell on the pile next to his, walked back. They stood looking at the pile.

He reached down and got a handful of sand. He told her, "They say the sand here is the softest sand in the world."

"From all the shells?"

"From all the sorrow," he said. He let the sand run through his fingers.

They walked back to the kayaks in silence. Daniel lugged the cooler up to the dune where there was a little clearing in the mangroves. Then he took out a piece of canvas that he had in his backpack. It had grommets in it and was strung with rope, so he tied it to a mangrove branch and then stretched it to another few branches so that it made a square tent roof over the clearing. Mary arranged the lunch the Low-Key Inn had made for them on a beach blanket: turkey sandwiches, PB&J for Larkin, a cluster of red grapes with slices of cheddar, chocolate chip cookies for dessert, a screw-top bottle of white wine, and a juice box for Larkin.

Mary had picked a flower when they were in the dunes, a little white one. She poured some of her bottled water into a conch shell she'd found and placed it in the middle of the blanket. It made a nice centerpiece, he thought.

"Wow," he said, sitting down.

Larkin ran up with Tripod. They sat down together and shared Larkin's sandwich. One bite for her, one piece for him. Tripod waited patiently for his pieces and nibbled them from Larkin's hand.

"What a good boy," Mary said.

Daniel was grateful to her for liking Tripod. Tripod seemed happier than usual. His tail wagged and his eyes were bright. It was good for the dog to be around a kid, he thought. Or maybe it was something about female energy.

"We're getting spoiled, us guys," Daniel said. He was hungry. Hungrier than usual. It seemed like they all were. They ate up every last bite.

He hadn't spent a day on the beach like this for years. He and Addie used to take Timmy and go to Wildwood every August for a week because Addie's family rented a house there. But that was always an awkward vacation. Addie's sister Debbie didn't like sand—something about the texture. She didn't go to the beach. She just stayed in the kitchen strapped into a starchy apron, and she cooked vats of odd food for them all. Grape soup was one dish that he remembered well. It was green.

Addie's other sister Darla was a ditzy thing who married and divorced, it seemed, every few years. He could never keep track of who was the current husband. One year, there was a Jonathan. The next year, there was a different Jonathan, but this one, for some reason, wanted to be called Andy. The sheer pace of the woman was dizzying.

And then there was Addie's mother. She sat on the couch all

day and did the rosary. She wouldn't let Timmy watch *Scooby-Doo* because she said it had magic in it, which was the work of the devil. Scooby Dooby Doo, for God's sake.

When lunch was over, he said to Larkin and Tripod, "You guys want to decorate a Christmas tree?"

Larkin hopped up.

"We have to find shells that have holes in them," he told her. Then he showed her how to hang them on the branches of a big dead mangrove tree that had tipped over and was leaning in the sand.

Larkin followed him for a bit, then took off and scampered around the beach, hunting for shells on her own while Tripod trooped after her. She kept a conversation going with Tripod. "Now we put this shell here . . . Now we hang the seaweed. That looks pretty, doesn't it? Let's go find a big shell . . ."

Daniel sat back down on the blanket.

"That'll keep her busy for a while," he said. He looked at the sky. A black cloud was moving toward them fast. "We may get some weather. Maybe we should get back before disaster strikes again." He looked at her pointedly.

"You really do think I'm Thing Two, don't you?"

"I just meant . . ."

"I know what you meant." She winced when she said it.

Why did I have to say that? he thought, frowning at himself. He wanted to take it back. He said, "It'll probably just be one of those pop-up storms."

She looked at the approaching cloud and said, "Next up, locusts. Then plague."

He half smiled. "You're not that bad. You're just . . . eventful."

"Ha," she said.

"You're fine," he told her.

Even though the sun was still shining and the cloud seemed far off, it began to rain. First a few huge drops, then faster and faster. He and Mary ducked under the canvas while Larkin ran around in circles with Tripod getting drenched. It was nice to see that kid looking happy. And Tripod was yipping and hopping around like a puppy. Every few minutes, Daniel touched the canvas roof, and the collected rain poured off in a waterfall.

Mary was silent, staring out somewhere. The warmth of her body pressed next to him. He closed his eyes. When he opened them a minute later, it was with a start. His body was listing hard to the right. He'd almost lost his balance, tipped into her.

She didn't seem to notice, though. She turned toward him. "Thank you," she said. "For this. For this whole day. It was generous of you."

"No problem," he said, glancing at her. She was so close. Her eyes were smiley and sad at the same time. *Uh-oh*, he thought. He cleared his throat. "No problem at all," he said again.

MARY

The sun was starting to slant in the sky, and Mary and Larkin were back at the hotel. Larkin skipped ahead of Mary toward the pool. They wound around through the igloos. Mary was following Larkin and not really watching where they were going. They must have made a wrong turn, because it was suddenly quieter. They'd turned away from the pool and the people. The flowers and bushes were denser here, and the trees were full of fluttering birds. Larkin was standing in the path ahead, staring at something.

Mary came up behind her, and both of them looked at an igloo. It was painted Creamsicle orange with mint trim around the windows and a wooden aqua door. Ollie was sitting on the covered porch with her sketch pad open on her lap. She was sipping a drink. The igloo was surrounded by gardens and bird feeders hanging from branches and a water fountain burbling in the middle of it all.

"Halloo," Ollie said, beckoning to them.

Mary followed as Larkin skipped toward Ollie. The shade of the porch looked tempting and cool. Mary's skin was tight after being out so long in the sun, and her arms ached from all that paddling.

"Look," Ollie said, showing them her sketch pad. "I was trying to get one of these swallows." She looked at the sky. "But they're too fast for me." She put down her pencil and rubbed her eyes. Her sketch pad page was filled with crossed-out images of wings and bird shapes.

"Is this your house?" Larkin asked Ollie.

"Yes," Ollie said, smiling. "And look, you're just in time to meet my friend. Here comes Frederick."

Mary and Larkin turned around.

A huge green lizard was waddling toward them.

"Yikes," Mary said.

"Oh, he won't hurt you, dear. He comes every day for the hibiscus flowers I feed him. I've been waiting for him to come down from his tree."

Larkin's eyes were huge. Mary took her hand as they followed Ollie down the porch steps.

"Come here, Frederick," Ollie said. She took a flower out of a big pocket in her shirt. She bent down, and Frederick hurried over.

"He walks funny," Larkin said.

"Yes, he's a bit bowlegged," Ollie said.

Frederick took the flower in his mouth and munched on it. What a startling green he was. "He doesn't even look real," Mary said.

"Do you want to feed him?" Ollie asked Larkin.

Larkin nodded.

"Now, he doesn't have teeth, but his mouth is sharp, so you want to hold the flower by its stem." Ollie gave Larkin a flower and showed her where to put her hand.

"You're so brave," Mary said. She was a bit taken aback by the lizard. It had to be four feet long. It was longer than Larkin was tall. But there Larkin was, bending down and holding out the flower. Frederick snatched it and then wheeled around and raced back toward his tree.

"He moves quick when he wants to," Mary said.

"He's sometimes shy around new people," Ollie said.

They watched him clamber up a palm tree. Mary put her hand on Larkin's head.

"Why are there so many birds here?" Larkin asked, looking at Ollie.

"The birds live here with me. They are my friends."

"I would like to have a bird friend."

"Here, then," Ollie said. "Come with me." She walked to her porch and came back carrying a can. "Put your hands together," she said to Larkin, and she filled her hands with sunflower seeds. "Now stretch them out as far as you can reach. Can you stand very still?"

Larkin nodded.

Now that Mary was looking around, she thought she'd never seen so many birds in such a small area. They were lined up on the branches and swaying on the stalks of flowers, all different colors and shapes and sizes. They were singing and cheeping.

Larkin put out her hands. A bird swooped near her, and she flinched.

"It almost flew into me," she said.

"They won't. They are very smart and very good fliers," Ollie told her.

"Will they bite me?"

"You'll feel their beaks, but it won't hurt."

Larkin tried again. She stood for a minute, two minutes. The birds seemed to be considering her. Mary was proud of her for standing there. A yellow bird landed gently on her arm.

"Oh," Larkin and Mary both whispered.

Mary glanced at Ollie, and Ollie was smiling.

The bird hopped once along Larkin's arm, then to her wrist. It looked at Larkin's face and cocked its head. Then it took a quick peck at a seed. Larkin's eyes were wide and bright. It pecked again. A brown bird flew down and joined the bird in Larkin's hand. Larkin's mouth was open. Mary could hear her breathing short little breaths, "Oh, oh, oh."

"You try, dear," Ollie said to Mary and poured a bit of seed into her cupped palms.

Mary could smell flowers, hundreds of flowers, and greenness and redness and yellowness. She could see the smells and feel the colors. It was as if the senses were all blended here. The air was soft the way air is when it's near water. She held out her hands.

A bird swooped near her. She closed her eyes as the bird landed on her shoulder. A little flurry of breeze touched her cheek. She opened her eyes. A brown bird sat there looking at her. Her breath hitched.

The bird hopped onto her hand and began eating. She felt its hard beak like a probe against her. A probe like a doctor would use to poke her— *Are you alive in there?*

Mary smiled so wide her cheeks pulled. It was beautiful. It was more than that. *I love this*, she thought.

She stared at the bird. It cocked its head, which was reddish brown with tiny white specks, so fine, so soft.

"Why?" Mary asked Ollie. She didn't know exactly what she was asking her, but Ollie seemed to know.

"There is plenty of food for them in the feeders. But they like to come down. They need a bit of touch," Ollie said.

Larkin was laughing. She had birds fluttering around her. So did Mary. Mary laughed too.

"Their hearts are beating so hard," she told Ollie. She kept her voice soft. It didn't seem to bother the birds.

A lawn mower started up in the distance, and the birds all flew up into the trees.

"Look, Gramma," Larkin said. There was a feather at Larkin's feet.

"That's a gift for you," Ollie told her.

"It's beautiful," Larkin said, picking it up. And it was. A rainbow of grays ending in a fluff of pure white.

"They want you to fly like them, my dear," Ollie told Larkin.

~~~

Ollie walked with them toward the pool. Larkin ran ahead. She didn't want to leave the birds, but Mary promised they would come back. "If that's okay?" Mary asked Ollie.

"Of course. The birds will always be happy to see you. And so will Frederick."

"Thank you again for setting up that picnic lunch for us today. It was great," Mary said as they walked.

"You had a nice day?"

"I didn't wreck any boats."

"Success, then."

"Larkin had fun with Tripod. I can't believe that dog is leaving. Larkin is going to be lost without him. Kipper said he'd bring Tripod over early in the morning to say goodbye."

"She is attached, isn't she?"

"And Kipper is too. There's something wrong in the way he's just letting Tripod go. He should fight for that dog, but he doesn't seem like he has any oomph left in him." A riled-up-ness was churning inside of her. *Fight for what you love*, she'd wanted to tell
~~~

him. But look at her own life! Larkin was skipping down the path in front of her. She needed to fight to be in that child's life. She needed to find a way to heal things up with CC.

"Ah, oomph is a greatly underrated quality, I think," Ollie said.

"Yes, they should invent oomph classes."

Ollie laughed. "I'd go."

"Me too."

Ollie rubbed her eye, then stumbled a bit.

"You okay?" Mary said.

"Oh, I'll be fine, dear." She kept walking. "I probably just overdid it today." She told Mary that she'd spent the day on a boat too. "But this one was like a rocket ship. Al and I lifted right off the water a couple times. I thought we were going to fly away. I was absolutely drenched by the time it was over. 'Isn't this great?' Al kept yelling at me. 'No!' I told him a hundred times."

Mary laughed.

"And then it poured on us," she said, throwing up her hands.

"Oh, us too," Mary said. Saying the word "us" gave her an odd feeling. She and Kipper and Larkin were an "us." How funny. A few days ago, they'd been strangers.

Ollie said, "Al's traveled all over the globe. He's been to places I've never even heard of, done everything a person could possibly do—rode elephants and giraffes across deserts."

"He rode a giraffe in the desert?"

"It was something like that, anyway. When that man starts talking, he goes on and on—town after town, story after story."

"And you believe him?" Mary asked, then immediately wanted to take it back. She'd been thinking of Ron and all his lies or half-truths or justifications. Whatever they were. Funny, she hadn't thought of him most of the day. She'd been way too busy. And every time the thought of him had popped into her head, she shoved it away. *Don't. Just don't.*

"It's all quite amazing, but I think I do," Ollie said quietly.

"I'm sorry," Mary said. "It's my issue. I have trouble with trust these days."

Suddenly, the path opened up, and they were at the pool. Ollie said she had some things to do to get ready for the Christmas Eve party.

"Are you coming?" Ollie asked.

Mary nodded. She was looking forward to it. She'd seen the signs posted in the lobby announcing it. Maybe it would be one of those hokey luau events where some guy wears a grass skirt and eats fire and all the guests drink out of pineapples and do the Macarena, but nonetheless, it would be fun. And Larkin would love it.

Mary sat down at a table and Larkin jumped into the pool. Mary was tired, but it was a good tired. She was quiet, watching Larkin toss Tutu, then swim to get him. The clouds were lit with pink streaks from the setting sun. A woman with a flowered bathing cap did steady laps in the pool. *Keep on going*, Mary said to herself.

Larkin looked up. "Mommy!" she said.

Mary hadn't told Larkin that her mother was coming. She told herself she wanted to surprise Larkin, but the truth was she didn't want Larkin to see the sadness she felt over CC coming to whisk Larkin away.

Mary watched CC clicking across the patio in a white sundress and gold heels. James-Walter was lumbering behind, looking overheated in black jeans and a black button-down shirt. Larkin scrambled up the pool steps and threw her body against her mother's legs.

Mary wanted to cry looking at that clutching hug of Larkin's. To be held like that!

But then James-Walter said, "Don't get your mother wet, Larkin."

Mary had to look away so she didn't have to watch Larkin pull back.

Then CC was walking toward her and Larkin sprinting ahead. Mary blinked back her tears. She wouldn't cry. But she felt all gushy seeing them together.

CC gave her a one-armed hug. "Mother," CC said.

Mary didn't know where she got that "Mother" thing. When Larkin was born, Mary became "Mother" to CC instead of "Mom." She didn't know why. It was like a shove against her chest, though, every time she heard it.

James-Walter shook her hand, his fingers damp.

Mary wrapped Larkin in a towel, and they all sat down and ordered drinks.

"How was your trip down here?" Mary asked.

"Florida is such a cliché," James-Walter said.

"We stopped off to see the manatees at the power plant on Paradise River. They are so sweet," CC said.

Mary said, "I love manatees."

"They look like blobs," James-Walter said. "They act like blobs too."

"Beautiful blobs," Mary said.

"They let you touch them there, but you can only use one hand," he said.

"Why?" Mary said.

"Exactly," he said.

"He used two," CC said.

"I don't follow stupid rules," he said.

Mary had tried hard not to dislike him the only other time she'd met him. She'd hoped it would be better this time around.

The drinks arrived. Larkin had a lemonade. Mary and CC, wine. James-Walter had a martini with three olives.

"Three is exactly the right ratio of salt to bitterness," he'd told the waiter when he ordered. Mary cringed when James-Walter asked, "Does, perhaps, the hotel have blue cheese–stuffed olives?"

"No, sir," the waiter said.

"Figures," James-Walter said.

Now James-Walter waved his martini. "Some place," he said.

Larkin nodded. Mary looked around at the Low-Key Inn and its faded pink façade. The dolphin had a red Santa hat perched on its head.

"Great fountain," James-Walter said, following her gaze.

She bit her lip. "We adore it," she said, suddenly defensive.

"Mommy," Larkin said, hopping in her seat, "I have a new friend named Try-Hard, and I door him too."

James-Walter looked at Larkin and said, "Can you say 'aahdoor'?" He stretched the word out slowly. "Say 'aah' first," James-Walter told Larkin.

Larkin's head drooped forward. "Ah," Larkin whispered.

"Then, 'door,'" James-Walter said.

"Then door," Larkin said, still looking down.

James-Walter frowned.

Mary said quickly, "He's a dog."

"That's good, honey," CC said. CC looked tired. Her eyes were red like she hadn't been sleeping well.

"Are you okay?" Mary asked her.

"I'm glad to be off the ship of disease."

Mary wanted to say, *Why did you have to go in the first place? You should have come with us*. But she didn't.

"I have a surprise for you, Larky-Loo. We're going to Disney tomorrow!" CC said. Her voice was high-pitched and strained. "You, me, and James-Walter. They have rides to go on. Isn't that exciting?"

Larkin looked at her blankly.

"Don't you want to go on the rides?" CC said.

Larkin's eyes went to Mary, who gave Larkin a weak smile.

"James-Walter bought us tickets. Wasn't that nice of him? Can you say, 'Thank you, James-Walter?'"

Larkin looked at Mary. "But I want to see Try-Hard."

~

Mary was alone in the room. CC and James-Walter and Larkin had gone for a walk on the beach to catch the sunset. Mary thought she might take a nap, but the moment she got on the bed and put her head on the pillow, she got this image of Ron standing in his tux in her living room. When they'd first started dating, he'd decided to surprise her with a private prom because she'd told him her uncle had never allowed her to go to her high school prom. He'd gotten all dressed up and brought her a lily corsage and a silver heart balloon and then boogied her around her living room all night. They drank too much champagne and laughed and laughed. When a slow song came on at the end of the evening, he held her and rocked her gently in his arms and sang quietly in a cracking-with-emotion voice, "Have I told you lately that I love you? Have I told you there's no one else above you?"

Mary felt a huge wave of sadness wash over her. She sat right up. *Don't close your eyes. Don't relax your guard*, she thought. She'd been protected by anger and indignation up until now, but those kinds of walls only lasted so long. Especially with her. When pushed to the limit, she could get a good head of steam up, but she couldn't sustain it. She knew she couldn't.

She took out her journal and started writing another letter to Zelda.

I have to focus on the present moment, right? The feel of the pen moving in my hand. The fresh smell of a newly turned page. Out the window, the green swaying trees. The darkening sky. Focus on now. Not the past, not the future. Focus on my senses—what I can see and hear and touch and smell and taste. And feel grateful for every single moment that I notice. That's how I'm going to get through this.

I'll think of being with Larkin. Thank God for her. She distracts me from myself.

I'll go outside in nature. It forces me to see how vast and alive the world is, and how small my own feelings are.

I'll look at Kipper. How do people bear loss like he does? How do they go on? Forget one day at a time. He has to do one moment at a time. I have to do that. Build a present like that—one tiny block at a time. Like a Lego. One moment clicking into the next. Start anywhere. Red, green, blue. What am I building? I don't know. A foundation?

Right now, I feel like an explorer setting forth in a liquid world where I don't know if I'm ever going to find anything solid again. But maybe that's what we're all supposed to be doing with our lives. Just tossing off our lines and sailing into nowhere, being guided by what? Stars? Storms? Intuition? Want? I guess that's the big one. Want. That big yearning ache inside. What do I want?

Not Ron. Don't think about Ron. Don't text Ron. Don't call Ron.

Think about Larkin. CC. Ollie. Kipper. My motley crew of the present tense. Not James-Walter, though. Ugh.

Maybe I'll start a new storyboard about my new home. What could it look like? I'll gather up scraps and ideas from everything around me. Colors. Textures. Shells. Flowers. I'm excited to start it. I wonder what it will turn out to be. I have no idea yet. I'll just let it become what it wants to be.

I see a collage in my mind, a blurry one. A strange composite of new things.

I'd like Larkin to add to it. She has such a mind! And I'd like her to feel at home wherever I end up. I wonder what CC could add to it? And Ollie, little old Ollie and her funny rainbow hotel?

And what about Kipper? With all his gardening and sea knowledge. I have to incorporate some of that on my storyboard. Let him add a seashell onto the pile. It was weird today. I almost felt like I was flirting with him. But how could I be?

Last night, I sleepwalked again. It scares me so much when I wake up and I'm not in bed. Zelda, what if I wander away from my life?

I woke up in the bathroom. It was dark but the mirror was glowing the way mirrors do in the dark. I looked at it, and my face was like a ghost of myself. Am I a ghost? I wondered. I turned on the light, and there I was. Alive. It was like hearing my own voice, that moment of seeing myself. Startling and strange. Oh, it's just you, I thought. And I didn't feel scared anymore.

Remember the last time I met with you, when you did that guided meditation with me, and I was standing in a field, and I told you that I was alone? And you said, "Tell me about being alone," and I started crying. And I told you I was always alone in my childhood. And in my marriage to Charles. Even with Ron, I was alone.

Then you told me to imagine another person coming into the field. I saw someone coming like a shadow through the tall grass and the wildflowers. At first, I was scared, but then the person got close and I saw it was another woman. I told you. And you asked me to ask her what she wanted. I did. And she just smiled at me. I told her I was fine, that I didn't need her help or anything. But she didn't leave. She just stayed in that field with me. And I kind of felt weird about it but not in a bad way. Not like, "Get out of my field." Just, "Okay, I guess there's enough field for both of us."

And then you brought me out of the meditation and asked me how I felt, and I wasn't sure. I really liked the field, though, and all the wildflowers. It was peaceful there.

Tonight I'm thinking that the woman in the field, that was me, wasn't it?

OLLIE

Ollie was getting dressed. It was time to take out the sequined shift again, the dress that made everyone say, "Why, you're glowing!" She'd smile at them and nod. She'd be among many people, but still, she'd feel alone. Everyone else was celebrating something, being on vacation or with family. She'd watch from the sidelines as people danced. Sure, she'd help string the lights at the party, orchestrate the music, encourage people to boogie together, but it wasn't her party. Her life was filled with acquaintances, with people coming and going. She thought of Al. Today was a day to remember. She hadn't belly laughed in forever, and with him, she couldn't stop laughing. But he was just a tourist too.

No one stayed.

She loved her job so much that the loneliness was okay. It really was. It was a floating kind of loneliness. It had its own high. She was like a bird observing it all from above. She laughed. Yes, she was like a bird.

Ollie dressed more carefully than she had in years. This might be the last Christmas party at the hotel. "Well, let's go out with a bang!" she said to her empty room. "Let's Thelma and Louise it! Accelerate as we're going off the cliff."

She put on her star-shaped earrings. She loved how they shone.

For goodness' sake, she even got out her silky underwear, the pink ones that said LOVE, LOVE, LOVE on them in all different languages. She'd ordered them years ago from some catalog when she and Wilson were in that period where they went to a couples counselor, trying to save their marriage. Now she felt illicit even holding them. Like it was subterfuge. She was an old woman. What was she doing?

She'd never worn the underwear. She and Wilson had stopped going to the counselor after two times. Ollie had the cash for the woman in the jar on their dresser. But Wilson found it, and he gambled it away. That was a big argument. She told him that he stole not only the money, but their chance at happiness. He'd looked at her so sadly then. As if he'd let himself down as well as her.

Why had she kept this underwear in her drawer, deep at the bottom, buried all these years? What was she doing? She slid the panties on. They felt like ice, were smooth like a baby's skin. She stood stock-still in her dim closet. One evergreen candle was burning on her dresser in her bedroom a few feet away, so she smelled forest all around her. They fit. Her body was still slim, almost girlish.

She replayed in her mind this afternoon with Al. She'd never met a man like him before. That energy, that smile—contagious. But he was much more too. His blue eyes seemed to reflect the whole sky. Lost—that's how she felt when she looked in them. And found somehow too. It was confusing. Her heart beat hard right up into her throat when she was with him. Even now, just remembering, it was like little shimmery fish were swimming through her veins.

He'd gotten a phone call after they finished their boat ride. He walked away from her, stomped down the dock, waved his hands in the air like he was trying to sweep the clouds right out of the sky. She tried not to listen.

"I have to go," he told her when he walked back.

"I had a nice time."

"Nice? I take you on a humdinger of a ride and all I get is a 'nice'?"

"Very nice." She smiled. She wished she didn't have that shadow over her eye, that odd shadow that had started last week. It was darker than usual today, wasn't it? She blinked. So stupid, really. Of course she couldn't blink it away. It was getting so bad she'd have to go to the doctor. This was such a perfect day. She'd forgotten all about the hotel. Why did the shadow have to be there?

More than anything else in the world, she wanted to tell him right then, "I'm afraid." She wanted to lean her head forward, rest it on his shoulders. Just for a moment, just a little rest.

But that would ruin everything.

"I wanted to take you to this outdoor bar called Diggers," he said, "buy you a drink, listen to some blues. I hear there's a great band there today."

"Mmm." She tried to keep the sadness out of her voice.

"But . . ." The word came out heavy.

"It's fine. I have to get back anyway," she said. She smiled brightly at him.

He drove fast, humming something to himself. It was like he was constantly hearing music, that man. His mind, she could tell, was miles away already. Even though he was right there next to her, it was as if he'd left her behind by the roadside. She got an image of herself sitting on the hot pavement, sand gritting her skin, the hot whoosh of wind as cars passed her by. Ridiculous to feel so abandoned by him. The poor man was doing nothing but humming.

She watched the green blurry world out her window.

When he pulled into the parking lot and stopped at the pathway to her door, he said, "I won't be able to make the dinner. There's somewhere I have to go." He looked straight ahead. Then he turned to her. "I might be able to come later. Don't count on me, though."

"It's all right."

He shook his head. "I'm sure it will be a wonderful dinner."

"Thanks," she said, and patted his shoulder. His tee shirt felt soft. She wanted to let her hand rest there, but then she thought, *No.*

He turned his head toward her hand, and for a moment she thought he was going to lay his cheek on the back of it. He hesitated. Then he nodded and said, "Thank *you.* I needed a day off."

"Me too."

The silence hung in the car. It was a rental car and smelled like other people, like car cleaner, like dust. It had been many places. She could just tell. He got out of the car. She heard the *thunk* of the door and silence settling into the car. She watched him walk around the front of the car as if in slow motion. *I don't want this day to end*, she thought. It had been years since she thought such a thing.

He opened her door for her.

"Madam," he said, and swooped his hand to send her on her way down the winding mossy path scurrying with geckos and back to her room, which was really just a hotel room. It had a number on the door: 12. That struck her today.

Now she was all business setting up for the party. She'd always loved arranging things, making the humdrum patio by the pool into a stage. The setting was such a huge part of the event. These old wooden picnic tables made people feel like they were part of a huge motley family. The home-style meal forced them to turn to the person next to them and say, "Would you like some?" A bond would already be formed as the bowl was passed, as fingertips met and glances were exchanged. A lot could happen over a bowl of mashed potatoes. Ollie had seen it many times.

The power was all in the details. The sign on the path welcoming the guests to the dinner read WE ARE SO HAPPY THAT YOU ARE HERE! Who couldn't be pleased by that little kindness?

Ollie tended to like the kitsch of Christmas, but for this occasion, there were only white candles flickering in frosted glass globes on the tables. Tiny fairy lights strung between the palms twinkled as if the stars had come down from far away to eavesdrop on the event. She insisted on simplicity. She swore that the bare-bones-ness of it all worked a kind of winnowing magic on people, cut away what she called "the stuff and feathers" of people and encouraged them to be more honest with each other. Although Wilson had always called this party "Ollie's Age of Aquarius Love-In."

In the center of each long table Ollie set up a rustic wood sign. She'd painted these signs years ago, and she pulled them out of storage every year. Now she picked them from the box randomly, allowing her fingers to choose for her, then placed them on whichever table they seemed to look best. One said OPENHEARTED, another FEARLESS. There were HOPE, LET GO, THANKFUL, and JUST BE, with a little image of a bumblebee looping around in the corner.

It seemed so simple. But Ollie had learned over the years that these little words had power. They called out to people, and people chose where they wanted to sit based mostly on these signs. It was uncanny how people who didn't know what the heck was up with themselves or their lives could sort themselves out and sit where they somehow *needed* to sit.

The table with the BREATHE sign always filled up first. What that said about people's lives these days! She shook her head.

The clouds were amassing high above Ollie, piling up on top

of each other. The breezes stirred. The twinkle lights whooshed back and forth between the trees like swings in a park that ghosts were riding. The signs on the tables kept flipping over. How could Ollie prop them up? With rocks? No. There really was nothing she could do.

At a certain time in any party, there was a point of no return. It had begun. It was going to go where it was going to go.

The LOVE sign fell flat. It slapped the table.

Ollie's heartbeat raced.

On the beach, the water was churning up in the dark. She could hear waves building and crashing. The air smelled heavy and salty and mixed with so many mysterious things—fish and seaweed and lizards and flowers—like a beachy potion brewing on a steamy night.

DANIEL

Tripod kept looking at Daniel funny. That dog always knew when something was up.

"Don't give me those moony eyes," Daniel said as he swept the floor of the houseboat. He'd already swept it twice. Why was he doing it again?

Tripod looked away, then back at him.

"You know, don't you, that I can't do anything about this? I mean, I would if I could, but it's out of my hands. Time will go by quick, and you'll be back here before you know it."

Why was he lying to Tripod? He'd never take the dog back. He couldn't go through this coming and going again. It was too much. Already his chest felt empty and the dog hadn't even left yet. He'd been running the same scene through his head for days now—Addie walking away from him holding Tripod's leash, Tripod's tail wagging at first, then slowing, Tripod looking back at Daniel once, twice, three times over his shoulder with his big eyes, hopefully, sadly, then accepting, then turning his head forward. Giving up on him.

He shook his head. *Stop. Just stop.*

All relationships, when it came down to it, were just hello-goodbye. Why should he ever put himself through that mess all over again? Addie could keep Tripod. They would be fine together. He would forget about Tripod after a while, and Tripod would forget about him.

"Let's get real here. You're a dog," he told Tripod.

Tripod cocked his head.

Daniel swept a small line of wood shavings into a neat pile. He'd put all his carvings in the back bedroom already. He couldn't bear to see Addie touching them, smiling at him the way she did. She'd always been patronizing about his attachment to nature as if it were a weakness. She was a city girl. When they got married and moved into the suburbs, both of them had thought that it would be a realistic compromise. Isn't that what marriage was all about?

But the suburbs weren't for either of them.

Addie never got the hang of being in a small town. She'd say, "I don't like it that they know all our business at the pharmacy" and "I swear those checkout girls at Murphy's market look at me funny when I'm buying groceries—like they're keeping track of the amount of ice cream I eat or saying, behind my back, 'Why, she's not eating her share of vegetables.'" Addie would always drive far out of her way to go to a generic CVS or a BJ's just so she didn't have to endure the small-town eyes.

Daniel could never get over the groomedness of the suburbs. Even though his business was, in large part, keeping those yards looking so neat and clean-cut. He really loved the haphazard ways of nature. He hated those overly manicured look-at-me yards, the bushes pruned into balls or the flowers lined up like fierce little soldiers or, worse, the rosemary bushes transformed into painfully twisted topiaries. He felt sheared down himself as he mowed lawns.

For all the years of their marriage, he was haunted by dreams of trees that fell. Splintering, crashing, thudding. The sad smell of sap. Addie thought he was insane, and maybe she was right. Now he sat down on his deck chair and listened to the waves lapping at his boat. Being on the water among the tangled mangroves soothed him. He'd felt an easing within himself when he moved here. No one could touch these trees.

The wind was picking up. It was going to storm tonight. What if Addie's flight got canceled? His heart gave a little rise. But what would that do? Give him one more day with Tripod. It was best to just get it over with. Get Christmas done.

Mary had texted him earlier. Come to the Low-Key Inn party tonight. ☺ But she had her whole family there. He didn't want to be in the middle of someone else's family.

It would be too much to look at Mary all night too. It was tough enough today. *Get a grip*, he told himself. Two days ago, she was nobody in his life. Now the thought of her was like one of those moths that kept beating around a tiny light deep inside of him—stubborn, insistent. *Don't let her in! What are you going to do with a woman who's just passing through, who will never pass this way again? Nothing. That's what. I'm no kind of light to beat around anyway.*

It was stupid. Stupid. But the air between them as they paddled the kayaks home today was alive. He couldn't stop glancing back to check on her. She kept halting halfway in her uneven strokes to look at him, her boat wobbling. She was even klutzier on the way home, if that was possible. He kept shaking his head, laughing.

"What?" she'd yelled to him, smiling.

"Nothing. Nothing," he'd said.

He shouldn't have told her anything. But this morning, under the canvas with the rain coming down all around them, he'd relaxed his guard. If a man lets a woman see a crack of vulnerability, a sneak peek, they're all over it with a crowbar, prying the crack open. Although Thing Two wasn't that way. She just listened. But listening could crack a person open too.

Now there was a bond between them that wasn't there before he'd opened his big mouth. It couldn't be undone. All it could be was ignored. He shouldn't have said a word.

But, "See that?" He'd pointed.

"What? That beach?"

"It looks like nothing. Well, it's beautiful, but it's like a lot of other beaches."

The palm trees were swaying, sweeping warm rain down all around them. He felt the ground under their blanket give a little.

"I paddled up there one day and Tripod hopped out of the boat. By the time I pulled the kayak up and looked over at Tripod, he'd sunk up to his chest."

"Sunk?"

"I didn't have time to think. I just ran over to him, and then I was in. Up to my knees, my thighs, my chest. I was holding Tripod up in the air. He was very still. I could feel his heart beating. I wanted to throw him, but I didn't think I could get him far enough. And I thought it would be best if we were together."

He could hear her breath catch. She stared at him.

"I stayed as still as I could. Although I wanted more than anything to struggle against it, thrash out at it somehow. I don't know why we didn't keep sinking. We kind of stopped. Although I knew it was more of a pause than anything."

Just thinking about it made him shake. Sometimes he woke up in the middle of the night in a sweat, dreaming that he was breathing in wet sand.

"What happened?" she said. Her voice was thin.

"The tide. It started coming in. The sand got wetter and the water started washing up around us. I thought we'd drown then. I thought that would be better somehow. Cleaner. Less suffocating."

He shrugged. "But the water lifted us. It was slow, but it kept buoying us up until we could kind of slither our way out. Bodies are hollow, really, when it comes down to it. We float.

"I put a buoy out there, right off the beach, a red one with a danger sign on it. I don't want anyone else to go there. Even though I'm not sure it's still there. Maybe it was just one of those sinkholes that appear out of nowhere. The solid ground just opens up and sucks you in, but then, when you go back the next day, the sinkhole isn't there anymore. It filled in or got solid or something."

He heard his own voice rising. He was trying to convince himself that it was gone. It had returned to wherever it came from.

She didn't say anything, just sat there next to him.

They watched the rain. The sky got slowly whiter, then broke into ragged clumps of cloud with glimpses of blue sky. Soon it was just a drizzle and then the sun would come out and they would pack up and paddle home, and things would go back to normal. Except they didn't.

"There are probably a lot of places like that out here," he'd told her, looking at the horizon. He shouldn't have said that, but it was true.

She'd nodded.

The silence between them was like a dare, he thought. A dare he'd thrown down to see if she'd step into it like a trap. It was unfair, he knew, but there it was. She let the silence between them sit, though, not trying to fill it in or dismiss it, like Addie would have. Soon he was aware of how it wasn't really silence at all, but filled with tiny birdcalls, the soft swish of wavelets on sand, Larkin's and Tripod's padding footsteps.

Mary picked up a mangrove pod from the sand and twirled it in her fingers. Her fingers were interesting, he thought, long with no rings, no polish, her nails a little ragged around the edges as if she chewed on them absently when she was thinking. He imagined her doing that and smiled to himself.

She held the pod up like a little umbrella. “Ollie explained what these were to Larkin the other day. How one seedpod drops down from a branch and just drifts around in the water, gets carried by currents, and then wherever it catches, it puts down roots.”

“Yeah,” he said. “The islands build up around the seed.”

“All these islands,” she said with wonder. “Ten thousand of them, right?”

“At least.”

She’d gotten up then and walked to the water’s edge and threw the seedpod into the water. Her throw was awkward, and the seed didn’t go far. It whirred down a few feet away, but a tiny wave came and swept it sideways. She stood there watching it for a long time, and then Larkin and Tripod ran up to her.

“Look,” she told Larkin, “I just started a whole new island.”

“Can we live on it?” Larkin said.

Daniel expected her to say, “No. How silly. Of course not.” But she didn’t. He realized he was holding his breath as she watched the seedpod float away.

“Maybe someday, when the island grows up,” she said, touching Larkin’s head. Her voice was wistful. Then they turned and walked back toward him.

Daniel thought about that seedpod drifting around now. It could have gone anywhere. He looked at Tripod. “Let’s take a ride.”

Tripod hopped up to his feet. He loved to go for rides in the truck. Daniel lifted Tripod onto the passenger seat, and Tripod put his paws on the door handle, leaned his body against the seat back for balance, and stuck his head out the window. He peered ahead. What did he see that kept him so rapt? Daniel couldn't see anything but the road, a Home Depot, a red light, a man in droopy shorts ambling down a sidewalk, a woman swinging a purse.

It was sunset. The sky looked violent, like its blue shell was breaking open to show a fire underneath. He found himself on the road to the Low-Key Inn. He slowed when he got to the entrance. He looked at the arch of hibiscus trees, thought he heard music in the distance. He wanted to turn, but he drove past. There was somewhere else he needed to go. Someone he needed to talk to.

The VFW was a small white one-story asbestos-shingle house that someone had once donated. It sat in an overgrown grassy field where there were several sand mounds, the kind that gopher tortoises and burrowing owls make, and there were stakes and ropes protecting those areas. He pulled into the dirt parking lot where a line of cars was parked. The other time he came, Jorge, the bartender, told him that he was welcome anytime, but now he hesitated. The truck idled. He was surprised, really, that the place was open, that anyone was here on Christmas Eve.

When he came before, it was for a PTSD meeting his doctor had told him about. He'd felt out of place. All those people had actually lived through stuff, bombs and people shooting at them. Daniel had lived through nothing, except his son.

But they said they understood. They'd accepted his presence there like he was one of them. But he didn't feel that way.

Jorge had talked to him afterward, told him, "This is a safe place." He told him that there were "others." Parents. Spouses. Grown children. Not to feel alone. But that was just it—Daniel did feel alone. As if his life had turned into a dark, echoey hall, and he was the only one wandering around in it.

He hadn't come back here. It had been four months now. He'd driven by it every once in a while, but he never pulled in.

Before Daniel left, Jorge said, "Don't just disappear on me, now." They both knew what he meant.

Daniel had promised Jorge then, "I won't do that to you, man."

Daniel didn't break promises anymore. Not for years now. Not since he'd told his father he'd come back to see him in the nursing home and he hadn't. He'd been going every night for a month when his father was at the end of the bone cancer. He'd pull his father's diaper up, feed him tiny spoonfuls of applesauce, put ice chips on his tongue. They'd listen to baseball games together. His father had always been a radio buff, a Yankees fan. So they'd listen every night, his father's head lolling on the pillow the whole time, but Daniel refused to miss a day. His father had barely known or acknowledged him, just stared at him with black eyes. "Hi, Dad," he'd said. Then, "I'll be here to see you tomorrow, Dad." Barely anything in between.

They hadn't had much of a relationship Daniel's whole life. His father and mother had been fused together, their kids more accessories than essentials. Daniel never really even minded. He was fed and clothed and provided for. He spent his childhood outside, happily creating worlds of his own imagination. His parents didn't interfere. He was thankful to them for that.

But he found that he loved his father in those final days, those quiet days when they were together. He looked forward to them. Then, one night, Daniel didn't go. He'd been filled with anger for his father. It had come out of nowhere and he found himself bound in by it as if his skin had turned to metal. *I'm a man in a can*, he'd thought. He couldn't seem to move at all, never mind get himself to the nursing home. He sat on the couch and stared at the wall. He left his father alone, and his father died that night. The nurse told Daniel, "He asked for you. He wondered where his baseball pal was."

His baseball pal.

His father had never once in his life even thrown a ball with him.

Tonight, dust swirled around his truck. His hands clutched the steering wheel. Jesus. He was scared. Of what? Nothing was in that building except a bunch of wounded people. Why was that so terrifying?

"Just go," he muttered to himself. Tripod turned to stare at him, and they both started for the door.

Some sort of meeting was going on. He stopped in the doorway as he saw the chairs in a circle and all eyes turning to him. "Oh, sorry," he said.

Jorge stood up. "Daniel, come in. Pull up a chair."

"I don't . . ."

"Come on in, hon," a heavyset, gentle-faced woman said.

He pulled over a straight-back chair next to her, sat down hard. She nodded at him, and he caught the scent of Bounce dryer sheets. Everyone was looking at him. Their faces were kind but curious.

"I was just driving around," he said.

"We're talking about the breakfast tomorrow. We all volunteer doing the pancake breakfast at the church," Jorge said. Daniel remembered that Jorge had told him he was a retired principal. Everything about him was curved—his nose bulbous, his lips plump, his eyes round, the lines in his face all arcs and parentheses. He wasn't fat, exactly, but he was a solid bowling ball of a man. Even his hands, when he set them on his lap, seemed like they'd roll right off. There was something steamrolling about his words too. The room seemed swept up by him. Daniel bet this guy really knew how to run a school.

Daniel looked at Jorge.

Jorge said, "We're going to meet here. There's a lot of setup to do. We're going to serve almost five hundred people. How are you at flipping pancakes?"

MARY

Mary was trying to ignore James-Walter, but he was standing in the middle of their igloo room. He said his back hurt from driving, so he didn't want to sit, and he was complaining about how long it was taking CC to get ready—how long it *always* took CC to get ready. He wheezed when he breathed, and it seemed like he was using up all the air in the room. She wished he would stop talking. And breathing like that.

Mary poured herself a glass of wine and forced herself to say nothing.

When CC finally came out of the bathroom, Larkin said, "Oh, Mommy, you look so shiny!"

CC was in a tight gold dress with matching earrings and shoes. Even her eye shadow was gold. Mary thought she looked like she was trying too hard. But Mary often felt that about CC lately. She thought CC was most beautiful undone-up and natural. But CC was always put together these days. Always in an outfit.

James-Walter said, "Babe." He nodded at her.

CC smiled. A thin, wavery red line. She said, "Mother, we're going for drinks now. Are you sure you're okay with watching Larkin?."

"Of course," Mary said. She tried not to sound eager to see

James-Walter leave. It was too bad he had to come. Who knows how it would have been with just CC and Larkin? *My two girls*, she thought, and her eyes got a little teary.

CC said to Larkin, "Let's get you dressed before we go."

"She can dress herself. You go have fun," Mary said.

"Mother, I've got this. I want her to wear the black party dress," CC said.

"But I want to wear the uniform shirt," Larkin said. She was standing on the bed in her underwear.

"Unicorn?" James-Walter said. "Can you say 'you nah corn'?"

"Yes," Larkin said. "Yes, yes, yes." She jumped up and down on the bed.

"It's Christmas Eve," CC said, and yanked the black dress out of the closet.

Larkin looked at Mary. Mary looked into her empty wineglass. She'd gulped it down.

Larkin said, "I want . . . I want . . ." She started sobbing quietly. She was shaking, holding Tutu by the hair.

"Where's your nesting doll, anyway?" CC said.

Larkin shook her head hard and clutched Tutu to her chest.

CC bent down and tossed shoes around on the floor of Larkin's closet. "Where are her good shoes?"

"I don't know," Mary said. That was true. They could be in a landfill by now for all Mary knew.

Mary told CC, "Remember how stubborn you were about dressing yourself when you were Larkin's age? You always wore two different socks and two different sneakers. Nothing ever matched."

CC said, "You never stopped me."

"No," Mary said.

James-Walter said, "She still gets away with everything. She's a brat."

CC looked toward him.

He shrugged and said, "You know you are."

"I want . . ." Larkin hiccupped.

"You'll do what I tell you," CC said. Mary saw James-Walter kind of nod. Mary told herself, *Don't say a word.* She wanted to, though. Oh, how she wanted to tell CC, "Let the kid be. And stop looking at that James-Walter fellow. Who cares what he thinks?"

CC handed Larkin the black lace dress. Tears ran down Larkin's face, but she took the dress and yanked it over her head. It hung crooked, and CC reached to fix it, but Larkin pulled away. She stood staring at her mother, her arms hugging herself.

"Let's go," James-Walter said to CC. "I need a drink."

The moment they left, Larkin wilted into a heap on the bed. Mary peeked outside and watched them walk away. She felt how tight her shoulders were, hunched up around her ears, and she forced herself to ease them down. Branches slapped against the window. A storm was brewing out in the gulf. It was so cozy in here. It would be nice to just curl up next to Larkin and read, skip the whole evening, listen to nothing but Larkin's soft breathing. Now, that would be a strange but wonderful way to spend Christmas Eve.

She couldn't bear to think of being here without Larkin. How could she stand watching them all leave tomorrow? Maybe she should just fly home herself.

She thought of her living room that she'd been packing to move in with Ron—her stripped-bare walls, the corners piled with packed cardboard boxes, the gray city outside her windows. She thought of the dent in her couch, the spot she always sat in waiting for Ron to call, for Ron to come over, for Ron to get his act together and commit. *Time I lost.*

Mary said to Larkin, "Let's read a book." She started piling pillow after pillow on the bed until it was a big mound.

Larkin watched her. "What are you doing, Gramma?" she finally said.

"I'm fluffing us up," Mary said, plumping the pillows. "Here." Mary grabbed a book off the nightstand and hopped on the bed. Larkin leaned back next to her. She fell back between the pillows. Her legs kicked out. Her little voice came out of the pile. "I'm fluffocating!"

Mary kind of laughed, then stopped short. She pulled Larkin's arm and Larkin emerged out of the pillow mound. "You're right," she told Larkin.

She and Larkin threw all the pillows off the bed one by one until there was a big pile. Then Larkin jumped off the bed into the pile laughing.

"This is all we need," Larkin said, handing a pillow to Mary. "Just one for me and one for you." She scrambled back onto the bed.

Mary laughed. "You should write a book, Larkin," she said, "about simplifying life."

"Okay," Larkin said.

They rearranged themselves on the bed, and Mary opened the book. Its spine crinkled. It smelled new. The bedside lamp threw a yellow pool of light on the page. Mary smoothed the book open with her palm.

"The book is happy that we're reading it," Larkin said.

"I think you're right," Mary said.

Larkin lay her cheek against Mary's shoulder.

After a few pages, Mary heard Larkin's breathing get slow and even. Larkin's head drooped. Mary closed the book gently. She looked around the room—the dated yellow dresser, the aqua mirror hanging above it, the worn-thin chenille spread, the primitive but happy oil painting of a hut on pilings on a beach. She looked at Larkin's sleeping face on the pillow. She smiled. Two pillows *was* enough to get them to this happiness.

I don't want to leave this place yet, she thought. *This funny, sweet place. Something is happening to me here, living this hotel-small life. Could I live this way when I get home? Get rid of most of my accumulated stuff? I don't need it. Why did I ever need it? Maybe I'll leave it all in boxes, give it to Goodwill.*

She breathed in slowly, synchronizing her breathing to Larkin's. *I'm not ready to leave tomorrow. I don't even want to leave five days from now. Well, that is how everyone feels on vacation, right? Maybe I can come back here someday. Make it a tradition and come back every year with Larkin and CC. Maybe, each time, I'll book a fishing trip with Kipper. It could be like that movie* Same Time, Next Year. *Except that was a romance, wasn't it? Oh, how silly. I shouldn't have drunk that glass of wine so fast.*

She'd have to think of something to do with herself tomorrow if she wasn't leaving. She thought of the storyboard she wanted to make to get ideas for what she wanted in a new home. A new start. *Maybe I can borrow some of Ollie's paints for a day just to play around with colors.*

She got herself up and started dressing for the party. She'd wear the red dress she bought this evening in the gift shop. She'd looked at it before when she bought the new bathing suit for herself and the new outfits for Larkin. She'd fingered the gauzy material and the fine gold threads that ran along the neckline, then walked away from it. The way she usually did with colorful clothes. These days, almost everything she wore was black or gray. Joelle called it her "Draculina look."

Well, that was because Ron always told Mary, "I like you to be understated. I like classic."

So she'd complied. But when had understated become invisible? How she dressed these days had a lot to do with Ron's jealousy. She never wanted to stir it up. So she'd dressed to not stand out. But Ron wasn't here now, was he?

When she'd stopped in the gift shop tonight, the dress seemed to be waiting for her. She didn't even try it on. "I'll take it," she told the woman at the desk, who winked at her.

"Attagirl," the woman had said as she folded the dress into tissue paper.

Now she slid it over her head and looked in the mirror, curious to see if it would fall the way she envisioned it. The dress draped around her in loose folds. It moved so beautifully that even when she was standing still, it seemed to dance around her. The threads of gold made her eyes sparkle.

She looked at herself. She looked different. *This is not you*, she thought. *You're not flowy. You're straight-lined. No. That was what Ron wanted you to be.*

"What do you want?" she whispered to the mirror.

She stared back at herself. Her face was getting tan. Her nose was pink. Her hair—was it lighter? Maybe it was. She felt lighter all around. Who was she, though? She was "Gramma." She smiled. That was fun. She was "Mother"—well, that was difficult. She'd been Charles's wife. That was a long time ago. She'd been Ron's what? His everything. His nothing now. She kind of shivered. She was alone. It was scary. But it was kind of exciting. She could be anything, do anything, go anywhere. She could move to Iowa and be a waitress. For goodness' sake. She imagined herself in a pink apron, MARY stitched in black on the front, living in a rented room, serving truckers eggs and bacon, calling them "hon." No, that wasn't her. She'd probably end up decorating the restaurant, moving all the chairs and tables. Yes, that was her.

She liked the idea of going somewhere that no one knew her, though. Seeing where she would land if she threw her life up into the air. Seeing who she was if she were really left up to her own devices.

It somehow felt powerful.

She thought suddenly of Oskar. Once, he'd told her, "You have a persuasive way about you. I don't know how, but you could make a door believe it's a window." He'd smiled at her, and she'd been stunned. Her?

She thought of all the letters Ron had received over the years about her work. Fan letters to her. "That woman makes it all make sense." Or "She's an inspiration." Or "She changed my whole perspective." He'd been proud of her. She sold magazines, and he knew it. It made Ron a little mad, though, too, Mary thought.

She'd seen the way Kipper looked at her today. Did he even like her? It was hard to say. But she liked who she was with him. Honest. Out in the open.

She thought of his hands on a fishing rod, the sure way he cast a line. A little zip of energy went right through her. She wondered if he'd stop by the party. She'd invited him. Maybe it would be best if he didn't come, though. She needed to be with her family, focus on them tonight. It was their only night together.

Oh, Larkin. Mary looked at her curled-up sleeping form. Larkin moaned softly and murmured. Mary caught her breath. That fierce little face. Those fragile bones. Mary had bought her a puzzle of a dog for Christmas, a book about seashells and one about a dolphin, and a pink snorkel-and-mask set. Four presents, not three! She had them all wrapped up under the bed. She'd put them out in the morning so Larkin could find them. She couldn't wait to see Larkin's face when she opened them.

Larkin seemed confused about Christmas, excited but also full of practical questions about how Santa's sleigh flew and how he got to Florida without snow, and how he was going to get into the hotel room without a chimney. Already a realist. Mary told her that Santa would find a way. He always did. She told Larkin that nobody could really explain magic. "You just have to trust it, honey."

Ha. There was that trust thing again. She should trust herself more.

Larkin stirred on the bed and turned over. Mary poured herself another glass of wine. "What the hell," she whispered. Ron always told her she got "crazy emotional" when she drank wine. Three glasses and she'd start telling everyone what she felt. Well, maybe it was time for crazy emotional. It was the season. It was Christmas.

Mary put her hand on Larkin's back and shook her gently. "Time to go to the party."

Larkin hopped right up. Then she went into the bathroom. She was in there a long while. When she came out, she'd put her unicorn shirt on over her fancy dress and she was holding something in her hand.

"What's that?" Mary said.

Larkin bit her lip and said nothing. Mary looked hard. It was Larkin's ponytail. She'd chopped off all her hair.

"I want to look like SpongeBob," she said.

Mary took a breath. "But SpongeBob is a sponge."

"I know that, Gramma."

Mary walked over to her and looked at the back of her head.

Larkin had cut it in a ragged line. *Ouch*, Mary thought. The ponytail holder was still in her hair. Mary pulled it off, fluffed up Larkin's hair, held her shoulders, and turned her around. She looked so cute with a crooked bob.

"Oh boy," Mary said. "Well, how about I tie your hair back again and you wear my baseball cap tonight, because I don't think your mommy is going to be happy."

"She doesn't like cartoons."

"I know."

Mary put her yellow BEACH HAIR, DON'T CARE cap on Larkin's head and stood back to look at her. The hat was way too big and looked like a mushroom cap on Larkin's thin stalk of a neck. But at least it hid her hair.

~

The steel band was playing "Deck the Halls." Mary could see lights twinkling through the trees. People were milling around the outdoor dining area, drinking and talking. All the servers and bartenders were wearing caps with gold reindeer antlers sticking out of them. Ollie was at the hostess stand, and she gave all the children, and any adult who wanted one, a Rudolph nose on an elastic band. Mary helped Larkin put hers on. Ollie reached out and squeezed the nose, and it squeaked. Larkin's face lit up.

"Gramma, you wear one too," Larkin said.

So Mary put one on. She and Larkin looked at each other and laughed.

"Let's get one for your mommy," Mary said, taking an extra.

Ollie said, "It looks like we're going to get some weather, so unfortunately, the boat parade is canceled until New Year's, but the children's parade is still on!"

"What is that?" Larkin said.

"Would you like to be in the parade with us?" Ollie asked Larkin. "All the children make it snow so that Santa can come," Ollie told her.

"Snow?" Larkin asked.

Ollie nodded.

"May I go, Gramma?" Larkin asked.

Mary nodded. She was so happy that Larkin seemed to be coming out of her shell, opening up. Ollie had a lot to do with it. So did Kipper and Tripod. And maybe her grandma too. So there.

Ollie said, "We're lining up now. Come with me." She stuck out her hand and Larkin took it and they walked away together.

CC and James-Walter walked over to Mary.

"Where's she going?" CC asked.

"She's in the parade. Here, I got you a nose." She held it out to CC, who, to her surprise, put it right on. James-Walter frowned. "I didn't think you'd want one," Mary told him. He shook his head.

The steel band stopped. The lead singer said, "It's parade time!"

People gathered together. The band struck up "Rudolph the Red-Nosed Reindeer." Ollie appeared wearing a red nose and playing a kazoo. All the little kids in red noses followed behind her. The littlest ones came first. They each had a plastic sand bucket full of flower petals, and they threw the petals up in the air as they walked. As they marched, the path around them became white. Soon all the children were covered in flowers. And the guests too. The air fluttered, and the fragrance of flowers was everywhere, mixed with sea smells. *Dreamy,* Mary thought.

Mary's chest was full watching Larkin march with her knees pumping high. She was tossing flower petals and singing. The whole crowd was singing. Larkin's face was lit up. How simple and hokey it was. But how joyous. Mary turned to look at CC.

Tears were running around CC's red nose. Mary smiled at her and reached back and touched her arm. James-Walter looked away.

Then came Santa in a golf cart decorated with lights and shiny balls. The band played "Here Comes Santa Claus."

"Ho, ho, ho, merry Christmas," Santa said. Mary thought it looked like Stephen in a beard. He had a Rudolph nose too.

The parade dissolved as the kids scampered to their parents. The band started playing "Moon River" and people took to the dance floor.

"You were great," Mary told Larkin. Larkin stood next to her and shyly slipped her hand into Mary's. Mary held it ever so gently.

They watched CC and James-Walter dance. Mary hummed and swayed to the song. She'd never really listened to the lyrics before. *Two drifters, off to see the world . . . such a lot of world to see.*

CC had taken off her nose. Her dress was so stiff it looked like armor. James-Walter was all in black, his belly pushing hard against the buttons of his shirt. She looked like an exotic dragonfly and he like a beetle. But moving together, they were surprisingly graceful. They were staring in each other's eyes as if in a trance. *Hmm*, Mary thought, *so that's what it's all about.*

James-Walter could move for a big man. He was whirling CC around like she weighed nothing, swooping her this way and that. People were moving aside for them they were so good. Mary remembered what CC told her one time on the phone, when she'd just met James-Walter, in one of her rare opening-up moments: "He's like a magician. You know when they can just open their hand and, out of nowhere, pull a whole rainbow of scarves out of thin air? Well, he makes me feel like that. I feel like I'm appearing out of the nothing and the nowhere I've been my whole life."

You haven't been nothing, Mary wanted to tell her. But she didn't say anything. She was happy that CC was telling her anything at all.

Now as she watched them dance together, she felt a catch in her heart. He *did* have moves, and he looked at CC like she was the only thing in the world. And CC was shining, literally shining in that sparkly dress. *Oh, dream maker. You heartbreaker.* But she could also see how James-Walter was spinning CC. Tossing her outward and then catching her when he'd almost let her go too far.

Mary understood what it felt like. Ron made her feel that way too. Like she'd been invisible her whole life, and then, with him, she was seen. But magicians . . . couldn't they also put you in a box? Cut you in half? Make you disappear?

"Let's go find a table," she said to Larkin.

Larkin wanted to sit at the table with the JUST BE sign. So Mary sat down next to Larkin on the bench. She looked around at all the hotel guests. People seemed to know each other, greeting each other and laughing as if they'd been coming to this party, this hotel, for years. There were some big extended families. One group at a table all wore red tee shirts that said THE MADDALONIS' ANNUAL CHRISTMAS PARTY and green elf hats. One family had leis around their necks, but the leis were half jingle bells and half flowers. Mary loved to see big families together. There was something so warmly chaotic and slapdash happy about them. She knew they could be as dysfunctional as the next family. But when she looked at their faces, she didn't see that brittle individuality of her own family. People looked softer. Maybe their bones were not hard things, but more like pipe cleaners. *Yes,* she thought, looking around, *these look like fuzzy and pliable people.* Maybe it was all the wine she'd drunk. Or just the wistfulness of Christmas that was getting to her. She wished she'd thought to buy some pipe cleaners for Larkin. They could have played with them together, making families of people that linked together with colorful arms.

After the song ended, CC and James-Walter came back to the table. "I'm pooped," CC said, climbing over the bench to sit down.

CC looked at Larkin and narrowed her eyes. "What's with the hat and the shirt?"

Mary hurried to say, "Could you please pass the rolls?"

The steel band started playing again. "The look of love is in your eyes," a man in the band sang a little off-key.

James-Walter said, "Interesting rendition."

Mary pressed her lips tightly together. *It's CC's life. Let her figure it out for herself.*

The man sitting next to CC turned to her. He was a young man with a swoop of blond hair over his forehead and gold wire-framed glasses. Mary thought she'd seen him in the pool the other day swimming. Such a young man by himself stood out in a crowd. He looked rumply and nerdy and a bit lost. He smiled at CC and asked her where she came from. Mary heard him say his name was Paul and he was here applying for a job.

"What kind of work do you do?" Mary asked him to avoid speaking to James-Walter.

"I'm an engineer. I used to work for a plastics firm in Germany."

"Ah."

"It was my family's company. I was, how do you say, railroaded into it." He tucked the cloth napkin into the neck of his tee shirt as a kind of bib.

Mary smiled at him. What a sweet young man. Kind of John Denver–ish.

He said, "The place where I interviewed here converts plastics into reusable materials. They called me back for a second interview. I'm waiting to hear from them."

"That's great."

"I'd like to be part of the solution rather than part of the problem," he said, patting his bib.

"It's good to do something positive for the world."

"What do you do?" he asked Mary.

"I write. Well, I used to write about houses. Big houses mostly, fancy houses." Ron was always telling her that the goal was more to impress, to make readers long and dream and want. While she was always trying to make homes accessible and real. It was a constant battle between them.

She flapped her hands. "Lots of décor stuff." The word "stuff" hung in the air, a dense cloud of a word. Mary wanted to whoosh it away. It wasn't about stuff! She'd always had trouble describing what she did, why she did it, how excited she got with every assignment. Maybe *this* assignment, she'd see the home of her dreams! Maybe *this* assignment, she'd see people who really *got* it. Who found peace in their home. Who managed to really bring the outside world in. To bring life in. To achieve simplicity. But so many people missed the mark. It didn't matter how much money they had or even taste or style. It was so disheartening to watch how people screwed up their spaces. Mostly, they buried themselves in their belongings. Belongings—such a beautiful word, and yet, wasn't it all just stuff? She thought of Larkin with the pillows—*one for me and one for you*. Just enough.

CC looked at her. "I forgot, Mother. You have to look for a new job, huh?" Of course, Mary had told CC about breaking up with Ron. CC had been delighted. She'd always disliked Ron, called him "Ron the Con."

Mary nodded. "And a new place to live."

"Did you decide yet what you want to do?" CC asked her.

"Not yet," Mary said. She thought about her Mary-the-waitress idea. *Not even close.* "I probably need some time away from writing about homes." *Too much Ron-ness in that,* she didn't say. "I don't know what I want," she said. She got an image of herself dragging furniture around Oskar's showrooms. Pulling a couch here? No. There? Yes. "And I don't know where I want to live. Maybe I'll just put everything in storage for a while and rent something until I figure it out."

James-Walter said, "Do you know how many Americans have storage units? Multiple storage units? On top of their three-thousand-square-foot filled-up homes?"

"No," CC said. "But a lot, I bet. Too many."

"Millions," James-Walter said. "It's a storage-unit culture."

Paul said, "I just sold everything I own. All I have are the clothes in my suitcase."

Mary felt a jolt of excitement. "Wow. How does that feel?"

She suddenly pictured herself living in a small room. Where? On a beach? A window open to the sea, sort of a Zen mood, everything sand colored, a handmade pottery vase with one white flower stuck in it, a soft throw on the bed, a comfy chair, a worn wooden worktable. What more would she need? Mary the beachcomber.

Paul said, "It feels scary but free."

James-Walter took a roll from the bread basket. It steamed and smelled yeasty. Mary's mouth watered.

"Pass the oleo," he said to Paul.

"I'm sure it's not oleo," Paul said as he passed him the butter dish.

"Whatever." He spread a thin dab that barely moistened his bread.

When he was done, Mary took the dish and buttered some bread for Larkin. She used too much butter to compensate, and it dripped off the roll.

"Yum," Larkin said.

Mary saw Ollie approaching the table. She had a basket and was handing out placemats and crayons to all the children at the tables. She gave one to Larkin and patted her head, left to go on her way. The placemat had a maze on it in the shape of a heart.

"You start here," Mary told Larkin, "and you try to end up here." She pointed to a star at the end.

Larkin plunged right in. She started going down every path, humming her way along, her tongue sticking out of her mouth. Every once in a while, she'd change the color of her crayons.

"You have to look ahead and see where to go," CC told her, leaning across the table.

"But I like to do it this way," Larkin said, barely looking up.

"But you have to find the right way."

"Let her do it the way she wants," Mary said. She looked at Paul, and he was leaning over to watch Larkin draw. James-Walter was frowning, looking at his fingernails.

"But she's going every which way," CC said. "She's just making up her own paths and crossing over the lines."

"She's making a rainbow heart," Mary said. "It's pretty."

"Jesus, Mother, don't you believe in directions at all?" CC's knife clattered onto her plate.

Mary tried to smile but her lips felt tight. "It's just that I don't believe you get any points for going in a straight line."

"What are you saying?" CC said.

“Nothing.”

“Why don’t you just come right out and tell me you think my life now is one giant straight-line mistake?”

“I don’t think that at all. I just wish you did, I don’t know, more loop-de-loops. Followed your dreams even if they led you nowhere.”

“As if your life has been so loop-de-loop adventurous,” CC said.

Mary looked down. Larkin’s hand was swirling around the page. Sometimes she’d hit the end of a trail and she’d double back, find another road. Sometimes she’d just ignore the lines completely and plow right through.

“As if you’ve been such a dreamer,” CC said.

Mary felt sudden tears welling in her eyes.

Larkin put her crayon down and folded up the paper tighter and tighter into a little square. They all watched her.

Paul asked Larkin, “Have you ever had a sunshine pie?”

Larkin shook her head.

“I used to have tea parties with my granny, and I’d make her sunshine pies,” Paul said.

“What are those?” Larkin asked.

Paul moved his hands like he was shaping dough into a ball and rolling it out. Everyone was watching him. His eyes were intent, and his face was scrunched up in concentration. “You make the crust like this,” he said.

“There’s no sunshine left today. But you can still make a pie just thinking about letting the sun in. Then you stir it up.” He swirled his hands. “Abracadabra.” He tipped his hands and made a pouring motion. “There. Then you let it be, and it bakes in an instant!” He looked up, smiling.

Larkin got busy right away making one of her own. Mary watched her. Every little motion made Mary smile.

Larkin reached her hands out toward Mary. "Do you want some of my sunshine pie?"

Mary pretended to take the pie. She put it down on her bread plate. She picked up her knife and fork.

"Gramma!"

Mary looked up. "What?" she said.

"You don't eat a sunshine pie like that." Larkin pushed her own hands to her open mouth. "You eat it big like this." She swallowed and laughed. "Yum."

"Oh," Mary said. Mary put her knife and fork down. She felt a blush creeping up her neck. Was she really going to eat a sunshine pie with utensils?

She took a deep breath. *I want*, she thought. *I want what? I want to eat sunshine pie like Larkin*, she answered herself. Well, that was something. In a world where she seemed to know nothing about where her life was going, at least she knew that.

"So, what are you planning to do at Disney?" she asked James-Walter just to break the silence.

CC and James-Walter looked at each other. Then James-Walter said, "We'd like to do Drinking around the World, where you have an adult beverage in each country in the World Showcase. And CC booked a spa morning for herself. I'm going to fly the *Millennium Falcon* in the Star Wars exhibit."

"He loves Star Wars," CC said.

Mary looked at Larkin, who was galloping Blanket around her dish. "What will Larkin be doing?"

"Oh, we hired a childcare specialist for one day, and the other day, she's going to Camp Dolphin," James-Walter said.

"Childcare specialist?" Mary said slowly, like the two words were fragile and needed to be handled very carefully.

Paul asked CC, "Is the camp one of those things where you swim with the dolphins? That sounds so cool."

Larkin looked at her mother.

"It's a day-care center," CC said. "They make their own organic Play-Doh."

"Play-Doh?" Mary said. She couldn't seem to form a sentence that wasn't a question.

Paul said, "I always loved Play-Doh."

"Me too," CC said. Her voice was soft and happy. "How about when you squeeze it through that plastic press thing that makes shapes?"

"Oh yeah, I used to make star shapes in a big, long worm and then slice them up," Paul said.

"Worm stars," CC said, smiling at him.

They looked at each other for a long moment. The steel band stopped suddenly.

"Could you pass me the bread?" James-Walter asked CC.

"Again?" CC said.

"So what?"

"I thought we were cutting our carbs."

It got very still.

"I have never been, but I hear that Disney is a much-loved place," Paul said to CC.

"*You* will love it, anyway," Mary said to James-Walter.

"It's not like that, Mother," CC said. "We're just not into the Dumbo the Elephant story."

"What's wrong with Dumbo the Elephant?" Mary said.

"It's about bullying and the cruelty of the circus," James-Walter said.

"It's also about the mouse teaching Dumbo to use his ears to fly," Mary said.

James-Walter shook his head at Mary.

"It's about magic," she insisted.

"It's about exploitation," he said.

Larkin's head was turning back and forth between them.

"Actually, the circus doesn't even exist anymore," Paul piped up.

"What about It's a Small World? Is that exploitation too?" Mary said.

"That's so dated," James-Walter said.

"Dated?" Mary's hands balled up the napkin in her lap.

"And stupid," James-Walter said.

Mary blurted, "It's so easy to be negative."

"No, it's an intelligent response," he said.

"So you're saying that I'm stupid," Mary said.

CC said, "He's saying *it's* stupid, Mother."

Mary looked at James-Walter. He stared back at her. He dabbed his lips with the napkin. Two tiny, little dainty dabs.

"Why don't you just leave Larkin here for Christmas?" she pleaded. She could hear her voice almost breaking. "And I'll sing her stupid life-affirming songs," she added. The words came out of her sarcastic, but she didn't mean it that way.

"What songs?" Larkin said.

Mary looked down at her plate, her untouched roll. Nobody said anything. The silence was jagged.

Then Paul started singing, "There is just one moon . . ." He had a clear tenor. He paused.

CC piped up, "And one golden sun." Her voice was high and lovely.

Mary used to sing her that song when CC was a baby, but she didn't think CC remembered it.

"And, I don't know, something else . . ." Paul sang, laughing.

"It's a small world after all," they sang together.

The breeze suddenly shifted and the notes hung in the changing air.

"How cute," James-Walter said.

The waiter walked up to the table. It was a waiter Mary hadn't seen before. A young girl. "Hi, my name is Daisy. I'll be your server tonight. Would anyone like a drink, or are you all set?"

Paul fumbled in his shirt pocket and came out with a little monkey finger puppet, which he slipped on. The puppet said to the waitress, "I'll have a Shirley Temple."

Paul was really good. His lips didn't move at all. The puppet was felt and had a red-and-white-striped shirt on and arms that stood straight out.

"What's that?" Larkin said, staring at the puppet.

"Oh, it's so cool. It's pink and it has a maraschino cherry in it," the puppet said.

"I love marvelino cherries."

"Me too," the puppet said. "Marvelissimo!"

"What's your name?" Larkin asked the puppet.

"Pooky," the puppet said.

"I love you, Pooky," Larkin told Paul's finger. Paul's finger bowed and he reached out across the table and hugged one of Larkin's fingers with his thumb and middle finger. Her face crimped up with glee.

"When have you ever had a maraschino cherry?" CC asked Larkin, her voice tight again.

Larkin looked up at Mary.

Mary shrugged. "I'll have a Shirley Temple too," she told the waitress.

"I can share with Pooky," Larkin said.

James-Walter said, "For God's sake."

CC said, "It's pure artificial crap with red dye in it."

"Yummy," the puppet said to CC, but CC was staring at Mary.

"You didn't listen to me at all, did you, Mother? You just went and fed Larkin whatever you felt like feeding her, didn't you?"

Mary sighed. "I'm her grandmother," she said, as if that explained everything.

"You're passive-aggressive."

"And you're a control freak," Mary said so fast she couldn't stop herself.

Paul's eyebrow went up and his eyes kind of crossed.

"Uh-oh," Pooky said, bowing his head.

Just then, Larkin dropped Blanket. She crawled under the table to pick him up off the ground, and when she reappeared, her hat was gone.

CC's hand went to her mouth.

"Oh shit," Mary said.

DANIEL

They were taking it for granted that Daniel was here to volunteer to help out at the pancake breakfast. How had he gotten himself into this? He sat stiff in his chair and let the talk of the preparations swirl around him. An old man in the corner with a white bucket hat on looked familiar to him somehow.

It smelled like old men in here, like beer, like Brut cologne, like mothballs. The knots in the knotty pine paneling looked black as bullet holes. From the other room, there was the sound of a pool ball knocking against another, the heavy sound of a ball falling into a pocket, rolling inside the table down a chute, then clunking into the other balls.

He heard someone say, "Good shot, man."

When he'd almost leaned into Mary this afternoon, he'd pulled himself back so sharply he'd gotten a ping in his neck, one of those stinging nerve sensations that arced through his whole body. *Don't rest your head anywhere. Keep your distance,* he told himself. *You should have stayed the course tonight, not turned in here. But where was that? Just a black road.*

He could be driving around now, going nowhere. But it had scared him tonight. The blackness was more black, and the wind made the world seem to tip and sway like the ocean. He felt almost seasick.

Daniel shivered. The AC vent was blowing on him, but it wasn't that. He shouldn't have come. But he had to. Tripod was sitting on his foot. Daniel felt the warmth of Tripod's thigh, the wriggle of his butt.

The talk transitioned away from the pancake breakfast. People talked about what they were doing for the rest of Christmas Day. Someone had bought a set of Tupperware for her daughter. The family needed it, she said. They always had too many leftovers. It was a useful gift, she insisted. A guy said that he just gave his kids money. There was a discussion about Amazon gift cards. Some liked them, some didn't. Artificial trees or real trees? Decorate your golf cart or not? Then the voices died out.

"I feel like I could do more, that I *should* do more," the man with the bucket hat said.

Nobody said a word for a long minute. Then someone said, "You could go crazy thinking like that."

Some people nodded.

"We gave five hundred dollars to the food bank this year," Jorge said. "We built a ramp for the old woman down the road when she couldn't manage steps anymore. We helped Jamal when he had to move. We did his garage sale. And we switch off driving Conrad to dialysis twice a week."

The man said, "I feel this sadness sometimes now. Maybe I have to go to grief counseling or something. But it's not just for my own personal losses. It's bigger than that. It's for the climate, the bees, the people in Haiti . . ."

"Ugh," someone said. "I can't even think about it. I can't read the newspaper anymore or watch CNN. It's all too much."

"I can barely get through my to-do list every day without worrying about all that," another person said. "I'm always tired."

"Maybe it's my age," the man in the bucket hat said. "I'm so aware of time slipping away. What have I really done in the way of good?"

"Mother Teresa said, 'If you want to change the world, go home and love your family,'" someone said.

"Family," the man with the bucket hat said.

The woman who bought the Tupperware gift started talking about being allergic to something in fruitcake. She couldn't figure out what it was because there were so many ingredients. Another woman reached out and patted her hand.

Jorge brought out a platter of cookies and said his granddaughter made them. They were misshapen gingerbread men that she'd put silver bead eyes in, red or green sugared heads, raisin ears sticking out of their arms or their bellies. Jorge said they were alien gingerbread men. Everyone took one and passed the plate along. Daniel held his in his lap. He couldn't bring himself to bite even a foot off it.

The man with the bucket hat was rustling around in his corner chair. He brought out a guitar and tuned a few strings. "You mind if I play a little something?"

Jorge nodded at him. The man propped the guitar in his lap. Played a few stray notes. Tuned one string. Everyone waited. He looked up. "I'm not very good," he said. A few of them smiled.

"Sigh-a-lent night, Ho-a-lee night," he sang a little off-key, grit in his voice.

A woman with a high, vibrating churchy voice chimed in, "All is calm."

Daniel clamped his mouth shut. He felt shame flush through him. Would he be expected to sing along? He stared at his feet.

There was Tripod. But he couldn't look at Tripod. *Addie will come tomorrow to take Tripod. I can't watch that. I can't.*

"All is bright," a few shaky voices sang.

He looked at the wall. A paper garland with tinsel fringe glittered in the pale light. JOY, JOY, JOY it said.

He kept saying the word to himself. *Joy is just a dish detergent. Joy is bubbles,* he rambled to himself so he didn't hear the voices singing that sad song. It was a sad song, wasn't it?

He thought of Timmy. Timmy used to take his hand when they crossed a street, as if Timmy were protecting Daniel. He was such a careful child. And they were so careful with him. Careful got you nowhere in this world. This crazy world. What got you anywhere?

"Sleep in heavenly peace," someone's voice broke.

Daniel looked at the door. *Sleep*, he thought, *would be a welcome thing.* He felt like he was ready to sleep forever. *Tonight. Tonight.* The word settled into him. He liked the sound of that word.

Who will take Tripod out in the morning, though? I'll text Mary. Maybe she'll come over and take Tripod out for his morning walk. I'll leave a note for her—what to feed him for his breakfast.

Then Addie will take him away, and I won't have to watch. I can't say goodbye to him. I can't.

When the song was over, people clapped. Daniel moved his hands together, steepled them, then stood up. He was leaving. He wouldn't stay for another song. But it seemed everyone was leaving. People were milling around the doorway hugging each other and shaking hands, saying "Merry Christmas" and "See you in pancake world." He hung back.

Jorge was standing next to Daniel and turned to look at the bucket hat guy, who was packing up his guitar across the room. He told Daniel, "That guy lost everything once. His wife and daughter in a fire. In this house."

"This place?" he said.

"He used to own it. Years and years ago. He was a builder. Built a lot of stuff around here, and then his wife and daughter died, and he moved away. Got rid of everything. Donated this house to the VFW with some money to repair it. He pays the taxes on it every year. I've never met him before now."

How did he survive? Daniel wanted to ask, but he didn't. Although he really wanted to know. Some people seemed to have more elastic in their hearts or something. More bounce-back. *How do you get that?* He looked over at the guy.

Jorge said, "He's never been back."

"Why did he come now?"

"Maybe it was time." Jorge turned and looked hard at Daniel. "Can we count on seeing you tomorrow morning?"

Daniel looked down. "I just came to say thank you."

"For what, man?"

Daniel shook his head. *For trying*, he thought, but he wasn't going to say that. He'd given Jorge his word that he'd come back here. And now he'd done it. He'd come back. Now he knew Jorge was trying to pin him down, get Daniel to commit to something else tomorrow. Then Jorge would get Daniel to commit to something the next day. Then the next. That's how people strung you along. Got you to live.

The man with the hat was walking toward them. A woman hugged Jorge as she was leaving, asked him a question about the pancake breakfast. The man paused by Daniel and bent to pet Tripod. Tripod's tail wagged.

"That looks like a happy dog," the man said.

"He's lost a lot." Daniel didn't know why he blurted that out.

"The world can really get to you with subtraction," the guy said. "I'm Al." He reached out and shook Daniel's hand.

"Daniel," he said, almost flinching at the touch of Al's hand. Some people ran so warm. He didn't want to feel that right now.

The man said, "You have to keep adding or the minuses catch up to you."

Daniel looked at him.

"You keep throwing grains of sand in the bucket. It seems like nothing some days—just one grain of sand. One moment. But it's not nothing. By the end of the day, it weighs something. I'm starting to learn that at my late age."

Daniel said nothing.

"Now I guess I have to learn to give back the same way. One tiny gift to the world at a time."

Daniel shook his head. He thought of the shell he'd left on the pile at Broken Beach. One little shell.

"Grief is a big thing," Al said.

"Yes, sir, it is."

"Hard to put your arms around."

Daniel swallowed. When was the last time he'd put his arms around anyone? He didn't even hug Tripod. He said the dog didn't like to be hugged, but Larkin had been doing it and Tripod didn't seem to mind. Didn't mind at all. *It's your own issue*, he told himself. *You don't want to open your arms up to anything.*

Al was in shadow but Daniel could see the outline of him. Al said, "But it's also hard to hold yourself in so tight."

Daniel felt how stiff his body was.

"It's a tough spot," Al said. "If you yield, you could crumble away into yourself. If you don't yield, you could turn into a statue."

I'm the statue, Daniel thought. He saw himself sinking into dark water, landing on the bottom, tipping over. Fish would swim around him. He'd become a part of the ocean floor. There were worse things.

"I've been the statue," Al said. It was as if the guy were reading Daniel's mind. "For a lot of years. But even statues can get lonely. Turns out statues are people too. You know what I mean?"

Daniel peered at Al in the dim lighting. Who was this guy?

"Don't give up on yourself, son," Al said.

The word "son" seared through Daniel.

"I gotta go," Daniel mumbled and turned and walked out the door. Tripod hopped behind him.

The wind was whipping the palm trees along the road. The blowing sand stung Daniel's face. A car's headlights swept the dark aside. Then the car pulled out of the lot, and the dark poured back like syrup. Another car started up. A few drops of rain fell around him. They sounded heavy as stones. The air smelled suddenly like wet pavement and exhaust and trees.

He knew he shouldn't have just taken off. It was rude, and the guy was just trying to help. But he had to get out of there. He felt Tripod leaning his warm body against Daniel's leg. Daniel jerked his leg away fast, and Tripod stood on his own.

MARY

CC stood up, yanked Larkin by the arm, and announced, "We're out of here."

She stomped away. Larkin kept looking back at Mary. She said "Gramma" once, but Mary put her head down. James-Walter grabbed another roll out of the basket and followed CC. Mary watched them disappear down the path. There was stunned silence for a few moments. Then a thin rain began to fall. Lightning crackled through the sky. Mary didn't move.

Ollie got on the band's mic and said, "Everyone grab something. We'll move the party inside."

Paul was staring at her. He said, "Are you going to join the party?"

Mary shook her head.

"It's raining," he said.

"I know."

She stood up slowly.

"She is passionate, yes? Your daughter?" he said.

Mary nodded. CC was leaving. She knew it. CC had that closed-up look on her face that meant she had decided. And once CC decided, it was like she locked herself into a room where nobody could get in and no words could penetrate. "The stubborn room" Mary used to call it. Mary believed that CC herself didn't know how to get out of that room.

"I can't let them go," Mary said, starting to walk.

Paul got up and fell into step with her. "No party for you either?" she asked.

He shrugged.

The path was narrow. Mary kept getting slapped by cool, damp leaves on her bare arms. Lights shone up from the ground and made the palm trees glow. She heard geckos scurrying on the ground around her.

She couldn't get the sound of Larkin's voice calling to her out of her head. Should she have gotten up, argued, insisted? How? No, she couldn't have. She had no right as a grandmother to demand anything.

Had she really called CC a control freak? She winced. No wonder they were leaving her.

Paul was quiet walking next to her, seemingly deep in his own thoughts. "The holidays. They are much stress," he said.

"Do you miss being home for the holidays?"

"Home never felt so much like home to me."

Mary thought of herself as a child, alone in that big empty house she grew up in with her uncle, and how she'd stare out the window at the wide-open fields. She'd dreamed of becoming a forest ranger then, being able to ride a horse all day, cutting paths through the forest. Living high up in a tree house, swaying with the breeze. She'd loved the idea of nothingness around her.

Her nanny hadn't liked her going outside to play, though, wanted her close by to keep an eye on her, so Mary could only sneak out occasionally. Mostly she'd been stuck inside. She learned the internal ways of houses then, of corridors, doors, and closets. She'd gallop her imaginary horse down the hallways. *I wonder if that's why I write about homes*, she thought suddenly.

"I don't think I've ever lived in a real home," she said.

She felt his eyes on her. She felt herself blushing.

He didn't say a word, but she could hear him breathing. "Your daughter is . . . ?" he said.

"What about her?"

"She is married to that guy?"

"No. NO! Ugh," Mary said.

They both laughed.

"Is she gone?" he asked. They were standing in front of Mary's igloo room. It was dark except for the porch light. Mary knew they were gone.

They walked up to her porch. The rain began to increase.

"Where did you learn that ventriloquism thing? You're very good."

"My parents had my two sisters early in their lives and then had me when they were in their forties. It was like being an only child. They were busy with their careers. I was left up to my own devices. Pooky was my first friend. When he talked, it was like he was the voice of a different part of me. Actually, Pooky is a much better person than I am . . ."

"It's probably all my fault CC is so bad at choosing men," Mary said. "CC's father was a skinnier version of James-Walter, when I think about it. I remember how Charles used to pick at his food in restaurants. Like somebody might have slid a worm into his beet salad."

"I have not always been so wise myself about relationships," he said.

Mary just nodded. What could she say? *Oh, me too?* What an understatement. Best not to say anything.

"Will you be all right?" he asked her.

"I'll be fine." Although she wasn't so sure of that.

"Well, merry Christmas," she and Paul both said to each other simultaneously, then stopped. There wasn't much merry about it. He smiled at her and walked away down the path.

The igloo felt hollowed out. They must have torn out of here. She looked in CC's room just to be sure. What did she think, that CC was hiding in the closet? She slid out the drawers one by one. One white, fuzzy thread was curled into the corner of the bottom drawer like a dead caterpillar. Mary closed the drawer. A hanger was on the floor. She picked it up and hung it in line with the others. She walked into her room. Larkin's things were gone, but her presents were still there unopened. Mary stopped short. Blanket's legs were sticking out from under Larkin's bed. Oh no—Larkin would be lost without him. She picked him up and clutched him to her chest, felt her heart beating.

There was no note. The aloneness pressed in on her. She walked around the room, her sandals echoing on the tile. She ran her hand along Larkin's bed where the chenille blanket was still rumpled from her nap.

Was she going to cry? No, for God's sake, no. She couldn't give in to it. She had to keep on going, keep moving.

She thought suddenly of Ron. What was he doing right now? What if she flew home and knocked on his door?

No, she almost said out loud. She shivered. *I'm afraid*, she thought. *I can't go back out of fear.*

She picked up her phone and called Joelle.

Joelle was at a party. Mary could hear a Christmas carol and people's voices. She'd forgotten for a moment that it was Christmas.

"Um," Mary said. She tried to hold back a sob.

"Uh-oh. What's up?" Joelle said.

"I shouldn't have bothered you."

"It's all right. It's just my crazy family having dinner. My uncle Guido is doing his animal impersonations. He does a good walrus, but I could use a break from this. Give me a minute. Let me find a quiet spot."

Mary heard footsteps, a door shutting. "I'm sitting on top of a pile of winter coats," Joelle said. "I'm on my second glass of my cousin Franco's mead. This stuff is deadly. It has like eight different alcohols in it and some chocolate and cloves and I think chili peppers and then they ferment the stuff. It tastes a little like kerosene, but it's helping me get through the day with my family."

Mary knew that Joelle loved her family. Her parents were Italian and very loud. Every comment was a rib, a jab, a joke on you. The first time Mary had met them, she had a frozen smile on her face the whole time and her cheeks hurt for a day afterward. She hadn't been able to figure out what to make of them.

"Give it right back to them," Joelle had told her.

And now she did. Last year at Joelle's mother's birthday party, she'd gotten into a pillow fight with Joelle's little nieces and nephews and ended up hitting Joelle's father in the jaw with her left arm. They never let her get over that one. The whole family called her "Mo" now, after Muhammad Ali. She always rolled her eyes at that, but secretly she loved it. The next time she went to Joelle's family's house, she'd given Joelle's father a wrapped box—a pair of boxing gloves.

That was the only nickname she'd ever had. Well, "Thing Two." She smiled to herself. She even liked that.

Mary was always getting dragged along to Joelle's family outings because Mary was closed out of being with her own family, and, lately, Ron always had "something going on with Joanna."

Now she looked around her empty hotel room. Closed out.

Joelle said, "I was just going to call you anyway. Ron is looking for you."

"What?" Mary gulped.

"He called me three times today, asking where you were. He said he had to see you and talk to you. I didn't want to tell you. I figured it was best that you were away from it all."

"You didn't tell him I was away, did you?"

"He knows you're away. He went by your condo. He interrogated your neighbors." *Uh-oh*, Mary thought. Mrs. Engleson knew she was on vacation and was bringing in her mail.

"Oh no," Mary said, but she felt a little satisfaction, too, knowing he was worrying. Suffering. Good. Let him suffer.

"I said I didn't know where you were. But he didn't believe me."

Mary was quiet. Did she tell Mrs. Engleson where she was going? Maybe to Florida, but not specifically, she didn't think. She hoped not.

"Don't get suckered back in," Joelle said.

"I know."

Mary looked at the nightstand with the pad and pen. Larkin had scribbled a picture of Tripod on it. Three stick legs, a curly tail, a body like a rectangle, a big grin on his pointy face.

"CC was here. Now she's gone, and so is Larkin." She told Joelle the story. The rain was coming down harder now, pounding on the roof. "It's pouring here," Mary said.

"It's snowing here."

"Of course it is. I'm missing a white Christmas."

"You're just feeling sorry for yourself."

"What am I going to do?"

"You're going to wake up tomorrow and start again."

"From scratch?"

"Scratch is a wonderful place to start."

After Mary hung up, she stared at the rain slashing the window. She thought of when CC was born. Mary and Charles were renting a dingy apartment in Yonkers, and Charles was going to school at night, working all day. The drafts blew through the front door. She had to wheel the little portable washing machine over to the kitchen sink and connect the hose to the faucet to wash their clothes, and she had to wheel the dryer over to the window, rubber-band one of Charles's socks to the end of the exhaust tube, and poke it out the window so it would vent outside. Everything about the place was dreadful. The brown couch was covered in a musty faux suede; the bed's coverlet, a thin quilted thing, was orange with a sprinkling of spotted mushrooms.

Every afternoon, Mary would fill the sink up with sudsy water and put CC in it. CC would sit for hours blowing bubbles and squeezing squirt toys. "Little Fishy," Mary called CC back then. The kitchen was always puddled when Charles came home from work, rubber squeeze toys strewn on the counter. Mary and CC were curled together on the couch napping, no dinner at all cooking. It always pissed him off. But that time had been golden for Mary. It didn't matter how bad the apartment was, how annoying Charles was. It was a good start, a loving start, wasn't it? The love was pure.

That's what had held her together through all those years with Charles—the love she had for CC. It was an engine that drove her through the days. And after Charles died, as she was struggling to meet the bills because Charles had sunk too much into flipping houses, it was her fierce and protective love for CC that made the long hours working at Oskar's okay.

Mary had never thought much of her own needs back then. Zelda said that Mary hadn't really had a chance ever to take care of her heart, that she didn't really know how. Oh, she had her moony nights when she watched *You've Got Mail* or *Under the Tuscan Sun* over and over and felt herself wallowing in want. She read romantic fiction and dreamed of someday being the heroine of her own love story. But it felt impossible. Where was the time for love? Where was the energy for love? And the world seemed like it was made up entirely of strangers back then anyway. Maybe *she* was the one who had Bubble Wrap around her heart. Around both her and CC. Protection from the risk of feeling anything.

Then Ron came along. He was like a tornado that swept her up to the Land of Emotion. Mary thought of when they first started going out. Ron had read to her in bed some nights. She'd close her eyes and rest her head on his chest and listen to his voice rumbling. She'd never been read to in her life. Or maybe she had when she was very young before her parents died, but she couldn't remember it. Those were some of her happiest moments with Ron. He'd read her Raymond Carver short stories. Those were his favorite. The clean, spare prose was like a lullaby. Mary had never felt so loved. She thought Ron had loved those times too, but then he stopped reading to her. He was too busy at night working late or too tired to read after he came to bed. That's what he claimed anyway. She offered to read to him, but he said no. Mary just thought he'd gotten scared of the intimacy. He'd been afraid more than he'd been moved. Well, that was the story of their lives together. There was nothing Mary could do to change that now.

Mary looked around her empty igloo room. She really did have to start from scratch with her heart. At least she'd had that time with Larkin. She'd read to Larkin. When Larkin cuddled up in Mary's lap to be read to, her little breaths going in and out, her finger rubbing the page, trying to follow along with the words, her voice repeating some of them in a whisper, Mary wanted to lay her cheek down on top of Larkin's head as she'd done with CC so long ago and weep with joy.

But they were both gone now.

Her phone pinged. It was a text from Kipper. I can't come to the hotel tomorrow morning. Something's come up. It's an emergency. Is there any way that you can feed Tripod and let him out tomorrow morning? He'd typed in the address of his marina.

She looked hard at her phone. *Emergency?*

DANIEL

Daniel and Tripod were driving around in the rain. They'd been driving for half an hour. Nobody else was on the road. Of course they weren't. They were all busy with their families and their mistletoe, playing that Charlie Brown tinkly piano music and stuffing the turkey. He'd always hated stuffing the turkey, sewing the pale skin flap shut.

Maybe he'd turn vegetarian. Sure, he would. In his next life.

Tripod was sitting on the seat looking at him. He could feel the dog's eyes. The windshield wipers swiped back and forth. The rain pattered on the truck's roof. It would have been cozy at another time. A palm frond blew into the road. He tried to swerve around it, but the front tire hit the branch, and the truck jounced.

"I gotta get new shocks for this thing," he told Tripod. "No, I guess I really don't."

He loved this truck. Kept it real neat—no receipts floating around on the floor, no dust on the chrome. He washed down the outside with the hose once a week. It smelled like butterscotch because he kept a little bag of butterscotch squares in the center console. Even though they got gooey in the heat sometimes, he still liked to have them there. Just to pop one into his mouth and feel it melt.

Tripod shook himself, and the tags on his collar jingled—the tags that had Daniel's name on them and his phone number.

"You know I just vacuumed this truck," he told Tripod. "So don't go shedding on me now. Even though you're not much of a shedder, you're always leaving little bits of yourself around.

"And don't go looking at me all squint-eyed like you know everything in this whole wide world. Because you don't."

Daniel stared straight ahead at the road. The headlights lit up only a few feet ahead. But that was good. Best not to look too far into the darkness.

"I want to tell you . . ." He paused. He regrouped himself.

"You know you'll be fine. Don't you, boy?"

Daniel hadn't ever called him "boy" before. He didn't know why he said it now. The word felt wrong and squirmy-like in his mouth. Like a lie did. Like he was telling Tripod that they were a duo, just you and me, old buddy, old pal, two guys in it together until the end of time. And they weren't.

Daniel pulled over to the side of the road and did a U-turn, started heading to the boat.

"I'm sorry. Okay?"

~~~

Daniel was sitting on his houseboat under the canopy. He was waiting to hear back from Mary. When he'd typed her that text, he said to himself, *It's true, isn't it? This is an emergency, and there's no one else to ask*. Still, he felt bad to ask.

Maybe she was at the party and didn't bring her phone. But it was raining. Maybe she was busy with her family in the hotel room celebrating. Or maybe her silence meant no, she wouldn't help him. Well, he couldn't leave without knowing one way or the other.
~~~

He thought of taking the fishing boat out tonight, puttering along in the rain, going out deep, getting to the right spot.

He wasn't looking at Tripod. But he was aware of Tripod lying at his feet, breathing softly. Tripod grunted and half turned over so his white belly showed. Daniel was going to reach out his bare foot and rub Tripod's belly the way Tripod liked it, but he stopped himself.

He should write a note or something to Addie. People felt better if you wrote a note. Just to let her know it wasn't her fault, that it had really nothing to do with her. Well, maybe something. But not really. Everything connected though, didn't it?

He looked down. His book was sprawled open to the page he'd been reading. But somehow it seemed wrong to read right now. If Daniel picked that book up now and started in on it, he'd maybe want to find out what happened next. He was right in the middle of a mystery. A Robert Parker with the alcoholic ex-ballplayer cop who worked in a town called Paradise. He loved Robert Parker. He could really write a clear sentence. God, he wished that guy hadn't died. The irony of that thought struck him. It was almost funny in an awful kind of way. Maybe he'd meet up with Robert Parker in the afterlife, if there was such a place, and they'd float around in the clouds together or something. He hoped there weren't clouds. And harps. Jesus. Who wanted harps playing background music all the time? He hoped there was a dark bar kind of like the Marker 8.5 with an old pool table that was a little crooked so you had to adjust your shots to the lean of the table. He hoped there was cold beer.

He grabbed his phone, scrolled around idly for something to distract himself. He didn't understand how people could spend hours on their phones. What were they doing? He felt so bored by it. People curling their eyelashes with a new gizmo. People losing belly fat. An article claiming, "Don't eat bananas, whatever you do!" The ice caps were melting. The elephants were getting poached for their ivory tusks. *Jesus, this place. What the hell are we doing to this world?* he thought. *I'm glad to be getting out.*

But he didn't feel glad. He felt an uneasiness like a storm had opened up in his belly and the clouds were roiling. Should he leave a list of what Tripod liked to eat? The treats he preferred. Those funny chicken tendon things he liked to chew on. And his floppy-eared rabbit that squeaked that he liked to sleep with. Maybe he should pack a little bag for Tripod, put a list inside. *No.* He shook his head. *No. You can't control anything, you fool.* Especially now.

Addie would figure it all out. Addie was a smart woman. Addie could be kind. She had kindness within her. She was capable of kindness. Who was he kidding? She didn't have real warmth at all. Not the through-and-through kind. Not the radiate-from-within kind. She had the kind that sits on top of your skin, like one of those ice-cream cones that they dip in warm chocolate and it freezes into a thin shell. She was the chocolate-shell kind. And no sprinkles. Oh, there was not a chance of a sprinkle on top of Addie. He kind of smiled. He'd found that out in his life. A little too late.

And who would take over his houseboat?

There was nobody. Sleep already had a houseboat of his own. Addie? No. Definitely no. Maybe Mary would. But that was stupid. Why would Mary want to live in his houseboat? She had a whole life somewhere else. Still, she would at least appreciate his wood carvings. What would the person do with them who had to clean out his houseboat? He couldn't imagine Addie doing it. She'd just call some sort of removal service. He imagined a whole group of people in matching green tee shirts—JOEY'S BOAT CLEANUP SERVICE or something on the back with an image of a mop and a broom dancing together on a boat deck. He didn't like the idea of strangers swarming all over his boat. Maybe they'd laugh at all his carvings. He could just see them holding one up and then another. Guffawing.

Maybe he'd just throw them overboard now while he waited for Mary to text him back, save them the trouble of clearing out his stuff. It wasn't just being considerate. He felt suddenly worried about the tree people. He couldn't think of them going to a landfill stuffed inside a black plastic contractor bag. How suffocating that would be. And what an indignity. To have been a wild branch on a beach and then to end up like that. It was just plain wrong.

He got up and went into his kitchen, a heaviness in his chest. He opened the drawer. There it was, the face looking out of a knot. It did look like Timmy. He couldn't leave it in the drawer for the cleaning people. This one, especially, he couldn't leave behind.

He'd set it free.

He walked up to the deck, holding it in his palm.

Daniel had played baseball in college. Center field. Well, he'd been fast, and his arm was good. Not good enough to get drafted, but good. He'd loved the pace of the game, the grace of a ball soaring and how he seemed to know in his belly where it was going before it got there. How he'd feel like he was flying as he reached out and caught it. He should have joined some sort of adult league. Well, it was too late for that now.

He'd given Timmy his old mitt. Timmy had loved that thing. Even brought it with him to Afghanistan. What did Timmy think he'd be doing there? Actually, Timmy *had* played baseball with some of the local children. He and a couple of other guys had taught the kids. They didn't have real bats, but they'd used a stick and a rubber ball. He could imagine Timmy showing them how to catch a ball in that mitt, how your hand had to yield to it.

Daniel had taught him, "You have to allow the ball to land soft."

It was raining steadier, and he thought, *It will get wet in this rain*. But that was okay, wasn't it? It was natural. He couldn't think about it. Couldn't think about one more thing for one more minute. He heaved back and threw the carving as far as he could.

"Land soft," he said. His voice was thick.

He heard a small splash. He peered into the black night, imagined it bobbing all alone out there on the dark sea. He tried to see it but couldn't. Panic rose up in him. Jesus, it was just a piece of wood. It was going back to where it came from. Let it go. But his eyes searched the dark. Maybe it sank, or maybe it just floated away on the current. He swallowed hard. The rain was coming down all around him, dripping down his face, into his eyes, down his cheeks. No, those were tears. He hadn't cried yet. Not once about Timmy. After all this time. And now this.

OLLIE

Ollie witnessed the scene with CC and Mary. She saw CC's exit. She saw Mary's body slump as Larkin was pulled away.

Ollie had met CC and James-Walter when they were at the bar before the party. She bought them drinks. She knew she was in no position to be doling out freebies, but she couldn't help herself. James-Water was giving Mr. Green, the bartender, a hard time because Mr. Green didn't know how to make some drink concoction. A Face Slammer. Or some such thing. CC was standing by, blushing as James-Walter instructed Mr. Green about what ingredients to add in what order, when to stir, when to muddle. CC's lips were a thin line. Her eyes were far away. CC was wearing big hoop earrings and a dress that looked like it was made of metal. My goodness, she was trying so hard to look . . . hard! And yet she looked like a little girl too. So bright and Larkin-like. Mary had told her she was a nutritional coach of some sort. "'Nutritional' in big capital letters," Mary had told her ruefully. CC had been gracious accepting the drinks. When CC smiled, Ollie could see that CC was one of those people who worked, no, toiled away at being happy. She seemed like one of those marathon runners who ran for days at a time, hundreds of miles, even running while they slept—how was that possible?—in search of a high.

It was a shame that CC and Mary were battling. And on Christmas Eve!

Ollie had seen Mary change so much in the past few days—her face soften, her shoulders loosen. And Larkin too. She'd seen Mary and Larkin bond. Ollie had watched it happen before—a person arriving for a weeklong vacation and leaving as someone else. Entire family dynamics shifting. *The hotel,* she thought, smiling. It gave people a nudge to shift gears, to relax into themselves, to grow. It granted them permission. It told them, "Yes."

It was too bad about the storm, but the activities barely missed a beat, actually, when the party got transferred to the dining room. Thank goodness the air-conditioning had been fixed in time. Ollie stood and watched as people ate and talked and laughed. Another celebration at the Low-Key Inn. Ollie felt proud. She'd opened her home to a bunch of strangers and they'd all become friends.

She was tired, though. She kept rubbing her bad eye. It had been a long day. She decided to leave early. The party would go on without her.

On a hunch, she packed up a few plates of leftovers.

She hurried through the rain and knocked on Mary's door. "I saw your light on," she said as Mary opened the door. She closed her umbrella, leaned it against the wall, and handed Mary a plastic bag. "I brought food. I thought maybe you and . . ." Ollie looked behind Mary at the empty room.

"Larkin's gone. They're all gone," Mary said.

"You look a bit . . . Are you all right?"

Mary said, "Come in. Come in."

"Thank you, dear. It's a wild evening."

"How's the party?"

"Oh, a little rain can't stop Christmas. I brought you something else too," Ollie said. She reached into her shoulder bag and handed

Mary a rolled-up piece of paper tied with brown twine, a feather tucked into the knot. Ollie had been carrying it around all day, waiting to get a chance to give it to her. Now would be a good time.

Mary slid the feather out.

"That's from a least tern," Ollie said.

"Lovely," Mary said. But Ollie heard sadness in her voice.

Mary unrolled the picture. It was a watercolor that Ollie had painted of three people and a dog. Ollie liked how it had come out. It was a quick gestural study but the shapes were recognizable—there were the bent shoulders of Kipper, the eager but hesitant shape of Mary, the happy little form of Tripod, and the flashing motion that was Larkin. They were on a beach.

"Why, that's us!" Mary said.

"I like to do portraits for the guests. It's a hobby of mine." It was hard for Ollie to explain why she carried that sketchbook everywhere these days, why her hand had to constantly be moving, how her art helped her to see. Especially now with her eye acting up. She'd do these quick character studies and then write words under each picture to title it or explain it to herself.

"It's in the shelter of each other that people live." Mary read the caption Ollie had written in her loopy scrawl.

"I believe it's an old Irish proverb," Ollie said. "I remembered those words as I was drawing your picture. They just came to me."

Mary said, "I get that too. Out of nowhere, words come to fill up my pages when I write."

"Do you do journal writing?"

"Yes." Mary paused. "I started writing these letters recently, though. Letters that seem more like journaling than letters."

"How interesting."

"I wanted to ask you if you had any extra paint and watercolor paper I could maybe borrow tomorrow? I have a project in mind, and I'm eager to get at it."

"Of course," Ollie said, fumbling around in her bag. She handed Mary a compact set of watercolors, each color in a round tin, and a small pad with a brush. "I always carry these with me. You can have them. I have bunches of them. I can't resist buying art supplies."

"Oh, I couldn't."

"Yes, dear, you can. And you must. Merry Christmas. Do your project and your letters. Maybe combine them and see what happens!"

"Oh, Ollie." Mary gave her a little hug. "You're an angel."

Mary looked again at the picture and ran her hand gently over the art. "This is exactly what it was like on the beach today. But how did you know?"

"Sometimes my hand knows more than I do. At first, when I started, it was just you and Larkin on a beach, but then Kipper and Tripod appeared like they wanted to be in the picture too."

"Thank you." She held it to her chest. "I'll treasure it." Her eyes got teary.

Mary's phone pinged. "Oh," Mary said, picking up her phone and looking at it. "It's Kipper again. He wants me to walk his dog tomorrow morning, something about an emergency. He said that he needs to know one way or the other." She frowned.

"He said it's an emergency, did he?" Ollie said.

"It's strange."

"I hope he's okay," Ollie said.

"Me too."

Ollie let the pause lengthen between them. She looked at Mary. "Well, dear, have a good night. And merry Christmas."

"But I don't need all this food. You should take it back."

Ollie smiled and she was gone, out the door, into a whoosh of rain. On the porch, she took her old umbrella from where she'd leaned it, popped it open, and walked away. The trees and bushes whispered with falling raindrops and pinged on her umbrella. She pulled her thin sweater around her shoulders.

When she got to her porch, moths were beating around her yellow light. She'd forgotten to leave a light on inside. She fumbled for her key. She heard hurried footsteps behind her on the path. She turned. It was Al and he was soaked. Rain poured off his white hat.

Her heart did a little jitterbug. "Come in out of the storm. What are you doing in all this?" she said.

"I love storms." He stood in the rain.

"Me too."

"And I forgot to eat. I thought there might be something left in the kitchen."

"I'm sure there's a lot of food left. The party is still going."

He hesitated.

"But I think I might have something in my fridge," she said.

Al ducked onto her porch. She opened her front door, and they both stood in her living room. He was dripping wet, but he looked around and smiled. "This is a step back in time," he said.

"Nice to be overlooked by change sometimes," Ollie said. "Let me get you a towel." Then she looked again at him. His shirt and shorts were drenched. "Get out of those clothes," she said. "I'll throw them in the dryer. Here, take this." She grabbed a robe hanging behind the bathroom door.

A few minutes later, he came out of her bathroom with a sodden mass in his hands. He was wearing her pink fluffy robe. His arms stuck out of the too-short sleeves. She smiled at him.

"What?" he said. "I can't pull this look off?"

She rustled around in the fridge and made a plate of salami-and–cream cheese roll-ups with some dill pickles on the side. While she arranged everything on a platter, he strolled around her kitchen. She was aware of him looking at her collections. While other people collected china or figurines, she collected shells, bits of sea glass in glass jars. And feathers. Hundreds of feathers. They all stood in old bottles and vases and chipped pottery mugs on her shelves.

"What's with the feathers?"

"I've collected them my whole life. I think there's a little magic in each one. Think of how with just that bit of softness, they fly."

She looked at him. He was reaching out and touching one gently. He smiled at her. "Amazing."

"Would you like a glass of wine?" she asked.

"I believe I would."

"What color goes with salami and cream cheese and pickles?"

"Anything," he said.

She opened a bottle of red and poured them two glasses.

"Let's go outside and watch the storm," he said.

As they walked through her living room, he pointed to the paintings on the walls and said, "Who is the artist?"

"Me," she admitted.

"These are so delicate," he said, peering at them. "So alive."

She bowed her head, hiding her smile. She led them outside, and her wooden screen door slapped behind them. She loved that sound. They sat on Ollie's porch swing and watched the rain. Ollie was aware of the warmth of his body next to her. His arm was only a few inches away, and sometimes his elbow brushed her as he reached for the food or his drink. She pretended not to notice.

They didn't talk at first, just listened to the rain.

"The rain makes a wishing sound," Ollie said.

"What do you wish for, Ollie?"

She looked at him. He looked at her. He was so close. She shook her head. It must be her eye acting up again. He looked almost transparent. He seemed like millions of atoms floating in a shape of a man. She couldn't tell him what she wished for. She couldn't turn this moment into money talk.

"Anything wrong?" he asked.

"No, no," she said.

He leaned back. "It's nice, this just sitting here. I don't get to do this a lot."

"It is nice."

"You know, Ollie, you've got it all right here."

"Oh?"

"The birds around you. Your feathers. Your art. This place. I would like to have your life."

"But your life sounds so exciting. All that travel. You're a businessman of the world."

"I think I've done some things wrong."

"Well, we've all done that."

"I mean, lately I can't stop thinking about what I could have done differently."

"Vacations can sometimes do that for you."

"You know, I started my company all by myself. I thought I knew it all. I was young." He smiled. "And I've run it all along by myself."

"That must be hard."

"I was running away."

She looked at him.

He nodded at her. "I'm old now. And it's time to come back, circle around to deal with things. Before it's too late."

"Things?"

"My wife and daughter died on Christmas Eve."

"Oh, Al."

"It was many years ago."

"Still."

"I went back there tonight, to where it happened."

"That must have been hard."

"I thought it would be. But it was so different now. Other people's stories have grown over that place." He stopped. The sounds of the rainy night were all around them. "Time has grown over me too. I'm an old moss-covered rock."

"With a heart."

"I'm trying to scrape around and uncover that."

She smiled at him in the dark.

"You are a good woman, Ollie. Gentle." She could feel his eyes searching her face. "You've created a place of love and kindness. You've done a good job."

She sighed. "No, I haven't."

"You've opened your heart up. You're everywhere."

"It's not all it seems."

"No?"

"Maybe it's not enough to have heart in life."

She wanted to tell him everything right then, unburden herself. "I've run away myself . . . This place is testament to that."

"What do you mean?"

"My marriage to Wilson, well, it wasn't the best marriage in the world. He was a stubborn old coot. So set in his ways like one of those electric cars you set on a track that connects to a groove and you watch it go around and around the same circle."

Yes, Ollie thought. *I was stuck in his rut.*

She surprised herself by saying, "He was a depressed man, I

believe, his whole life." Was he? Yes, now she saw it. "He would never have admitted it. Wouldn't have gone to a doctor or taken any medication. No. He just gambled and gambled like he was trying to fill some deep hole inside of him. Fill it with what? Money? I never understood it. I thought we had enough. But he didn't.

"He fell off the roof a year ago fixing a shingle because he couldn't ask for help. Now, I think, I'm the same. Afraid of change. And I can't ask for help either."

"Things may work themselves out. Sometimes they do."

"Not this time."

The sky was very dark and the rain fell all around them.

"What about all that talk about this being a magical place?" he said.

She said, "I could use some of that magic right about now."

"Maybe with magic, you need to meet it halfway," he said. He gestured with his hand in the space between them.

"Halfway?" she asked.

She turned her wrist over on the armrest. His arm brushed against hers. And there they were, suddenly, sitting on the porch swing holding hands.

MARY

Mary texted Kipper back. Are you okay? But he didn't respond. Why didn't he respond?

She sat down on her bed. She reread his text. He had an emergency that was going to last all night? That really didn't make any sense. He was asking for her help. He didn't have anyone else except his dog. His dog who was leaving. She got a bad feeling in her stomach.

She looked out the window. It was pouring. She paced around the empty room. She couldn't stay here and do nothing. *Stop thinking. Just go*, she told herself. She pulled on a sweatshirt over her dress and grabbed the plastic bag of food and her pocketbook and went out the door.

The whole world was liquid. The trees looked like they were steaming. She kicked off her shoes and left them on her porch and ran barefoot down the path. It was slippery, and gusts of wind sighed through the palms, sending cascades of water down around her, dousing her face and back.

She got in her car. "Whew," she said, and her word hung in the empty car. She was shaking. Not from the cold. It was a warm rain. From what? All the electricity in the air? She felt little hairs standing up on her bare arms. The rain beat on the hood. It was going to be hard to see.

Just go.

She punched Kipper's address into the car's GPS and started along the winding road out of the hotel complex. She could see warm yellow lights in the hotel dining room. She felt a moment of longing to be with others celebrating, then shoved it aside. She had something to do, somewhere to go.

She hunched over the wheel. The windshield wipers slapped violently back and forth, back and forth. Her headlights barely cleared a path. There were no other cars on the road. There was no one to follow. She couldn't really see ahead, but she kept on going. She wound down empty streets. The blankness made her scared, and she pushed harder on the gas pedal. *Hurry.* She turned right, then right again. *Where is it?*

Ahead was a white sign. The marina? *Yes.* She turned onto a narrow dirt road pocked with deep puddles. She bumped through them, waves of mud and rocks splatting against her windshield. The road opened into an empty lot with the black of the water beyond. She couldn't see where the land ended and the water began. *Don't drive into the water, Mary, whatever you do*, she told herself. She stopped the car. *I'm in the middle of nowhere*, she thought. The water sluiced down all around her. It wasn't letting up. She'd have to run for it. Run where? *Run toward the blackness.* She'd have to trust that she could find the water, the dock. Maybe she could smell it or sense it somehow.

She got out of the car. She looked around. *There. That direction*, she decided. She didn't quite know how. But there, it looked like water, and maybe the dock? The dim glow of piling lights? She moved toward it, her body bent and huddled forward, trying to see. *Yes. There.* Just ahead of her, dark forms of boats were rising and falling like the water itself was breathing underneath them. He'd said his was the third boat in. Was that a light on one of the boats? She followed the path of the piling lights on the dock. The boards felt slippery under her feet. She was filled with urgency, but she forced herself to walk slow. *Don't go down and hit your head and fall in. No one is here to save you. Where is he? Did he go somewhere? He had an emergency*, she kept thinking. She got to the third boat. There was a swaying strand of lights casting jittery shadows on an empty boat. The boat sloshed in its slip.

"Hello?" she yelled.

She saw some difference in the light, a kind of dark within the dark.

"Hello?" she said to it.

She must look like a lunatic, she thought. The rain was running down her face.

"I brought us dinner," she yelled, holding up the bag. The shadow got up and moved toward her.

When her eyes adjusted, she could see it was Kipper. He had no shirt on and he was drenched. His hair was matted to his head and his eyes were wild.

"What the heck?" she said.

"I went for a swim," he said.

~

She was in his tiny bathroom, which was more like a wooden closet than anything else. She rubbed her hair with a towel. She was wearing his sweatshirt and a pair of his sweatpants. She had to roll them up on her waist, and even then, they kept sagging down. She draped her dress and sweatshirt over one of the towel racks. She looked in the round mirror. She looked like a crazy woman. Her hair stood out at odd angles and her makeup was smeary. She ran her hands under the water and stuck her face into her hands and rubbed it. It felt so good to clean her face. The towel felt soft and smelled nice. Like Kipper's soap.

She looked around. It was neat as a pin, nothing strewn about or out of place. Extra white towels were neatly folded into a cubby. Shaving cream smell mixed with the smell of the cedar paneling. She breathed. Her lungs felt achy. Had she been holding her breath?

When she went out, Kipper was in the kitchen sitting at the table, which was little more than a card table screwed to the floor. A small light glowed over his head. He was looking down at a piece of wood he was holding in both hands. Tripod sat on his feet under the table.

The carving seemed to be of a face. He kept staring at it. His tears fell onto the piece of wood. They kept welling in his eyes and flowing down, and he didn't reach up to wipe them away or anything. He didn't make any noise. He was perfectly still. It was scary how still he was.

She walked quickly over to a blanket that was hung on the arm of the couch and wrapped it around his shoulders. She tucked it around him. He smelled like salt and sea. There was a place near his temples where his hair was receding in a gentle scoop. She wanted to run her finger along the edge of his hairline. But she couldn't. She didn't. She stood behind him. She didn't know what to do next. She could tell he was still crying. She felt his sadness. It was so big it filled her chest.

She sat down at the table across from him. It was as if they were going to play rummy. But they weren't. She felt tears running down her own face. She wanted to reach across the table, but she didn't. She thought, *Two people crying is better than one*. They had their separate sadnesses, but they were in it together too. Like two people swimming in the same river.

The rain pounded on the deck above. There was a blue-white flash of lightning, then a huge explosion of thunder.

"That was close," Mary said.

He nodded.

"We're not going to sink, are we?" she said. She was thinking of his tears filling the whole boat, *Alice in Wonderland*–ish.

He shook his head and kind of smiled.

Mary heard a clock ticking somewhere, but time seemed to be hovering. She heard the rain ease. The thunder lessened and got more distant. The lightning became far-off glows. The rain got peaceful, steadily tapping on the deck close above them. She heard Tripod breathing. He was sleeping. She didn't want to move. She felt glued to her seat.

She allowed herself to think of her own losses. Ron. CC. Larkin. Her home. Her job. What a Christmas! She wondered if CC and Larkin were okay driving in all this rain. She wondered what Ron was doing right now. Ron didn't cry. Or she'd never seen him cry. She bet that whatever he was up to, he wasn't crying about her right now. She must have said it out loud. Kipper looked up.

He raised one eyebrow.

She decided to tell Kipper about Ron. Maybe it would distract him? Maybe just the sound of her voice would help? Talking was its own kind of river too, wasn't it?

She told him about the snow globe. She told him why she came to Florida. She told him she thought she fit with Ron, which was why she stuck with him so long. "He made me feel like I belonged somewhere in the world. And I never felt like I belonged. I always felt like I was on the outside looking in. And he opened the door and invited me in, and I never wanted to leave. I just wanted to stay in that warm glow. But he kept pushing me away. Saying he wasn't ready to let me in to stay, saying things were not ready . . . Ready. Ready. I hate that word.

"People spend their lives getting ready. People waste their lives getting ready. I wonder what the average percentage is for how much of their lives people waste. You think, like, what—most people waste forty percent? Not counting sleeping. That's not really a waste. I mean the waking hours. I think I'm in a top percentile here. I think I'm about eighty percent."

He shrugged.

"You're right not to care. Why should you care? But I care." She stopped. She wiped her nose with the back of her hand, kind of slapped herself on the cheek. "I do not want to be twenty percent alive. How did I get to be that?"

He looked at her. She noticed the tears were slowing on his face. *Keep talking to him*, she thought. *Talk him through it. It.*

"You don't have to talk to me if you don't want to. About anything, really."

He nodded.

"But I have to warn you that if you don't, I might keep doing my big run-on-sentence thing, and I'll go on and on for perhaps hours about my own stupid issues because I just feel nervous as hell about you right now and I barely know you, plus my life has turned into a pile of garbage."

His mouth twitched.

She saw that he was shaking. "Why don't you get out of those wet clothes?"

He didn't move.

"Let's get you out of those wet clothes," she said. Enough of the questions. He wasn't going to answer her. *Just tell the guy what to do*, she told herself. *He could use some taking care of.*

She pulled on one of his arms. His bicep was sinewy, ropy, strong. *Hold on to the ropes inside yourself when you're drifting out to sea*, she thought to tell him, but said nothing. What did that really mean, anyway? But there *were* ropes inside of us. Stubborn, tough old things that kept us holding on.

Kipper hesitated. Then he stood up. He let the blanket fall to his chair. He walked into the bathroom. Tripod looked at Mary.

"He's going to be all right in there, isn't he?" she asked the dog.

She went and stood near the door. Nothing. *What the hell is he doing?* Then she heard a small noise, and the shower went on.

"Nothing bad can happen while he's taking a hot shower," she told Tripod. The dog's forehead was creased with worry. Mary opened some cabinets and drawers. She found two wicker placemats. She took out the meals she'd brought and warmed them up in the microwave and placed the containers on the table with the plastic silverware Ollie had thought to include.

"Voila!" she said to Tripod as she opened the lids. She pulled a piece of turkey out of her Styrofoam dish, let it cool in her palm, then offered it to him. He took it carefully. She watched while he chewed. He looked at her and cocked his head. "More?"

"All right," she said, and gave him another piece. The smell of turkey and stuffing and green beans filled the room.

She looked around in the cabinets and found an old candle half burned in a yellow jar, a matchbook stuffed in with the candle. She put it on the kitchen table and lit it.

Tripod was watching her every move. His head was on his paws, but his eyes followed her around.

"There," she said. Tripod blinked.

Kipper came out with a towel wrapped around his middle. Steam followed him out of the room. The hair on his chest was dark and tapered down to a line on his belly. Mary imagined running her finger along that line and then told herself, *Don't.* She shouldn't be looking at him that way, shouldn't be thinking anything. He was lean and rangy. His structure showed through, not like Ron, who was all rounded muscle. She shouldn't be comparing them.

He disappeared into a dark room and shut the door.

"He'll be okay," she told Tripod. But she didn't really know that. Just as long as she heard rustling around, though, he was fine. She'd check on him soon if he didn't come out.

She kneeled next to Tripod, scritched the fur on his back against the grain so it stood up. Then Tripod rolled over and she rubbed his belly. He made tiny moaning noises. "Good boy," she kept whispering over and over.

DANIEL

It was dawn. The air still smelled like heavy clouds. A gust of warm, clearing air whistled along the dock, though, and shook the seaweed-shrouded lines. A crack of pink appeared at the bottom of the gray sky.

Daniel had gotten up to go to the head, and his eyes scared him, they were so red. He closed them now as he stood on the deck and breathed in the air. Tripod sat on his foot. The dog hadn't left his side since last night. Followed him like glue. His body felt shaky, like he was coming down with something. But he didn't think he was getting sick. He felt Mary coming up behind him. A shift in the air, a degree warmer. He turned. She was in bare feet and his clothes.

"I heard you get up," she said. Her voice was graveled and rough. Her hair was sticking up at the top and drooped into one eye. He wanted to reach out and move the one strand, tuck it behind her ear. But then again, he kind of liked how mussed she looked. One leg of his sweatpants was pulled up to her knee and the other was slumped down on her ankle. Her feet were a little tan, and her toenails were painted a pale coral. There was something childlike about her toes.

"I'm not jumping overboard," he told her.

"I didn't think . . ."

"Storm is blowing out. You can see the line of it."

The sky was brighter already, the pink becoming a blaze of orange and shooting veins of light across the grayness. The end of the storm was just that—an end. A clear, straight wall of cloud disappearing.

"Nature doesn't usually do straight lines. Except with storm fronts and tails," he said. "Sometimes it looks like the sky is cut in half." His own voice didn't sound like himself. He sounded gruffer. *I've aged. And not well. If Timmy could see me now . . .*

He'd seen Timmy swimming next to him last night when he went after the carving. He'd been far out. He'd felt the depth of where he was, the weight of the water all around him. Then Timmy came out of the dark and said, "This way, Dad." And Daniel had stroked hard toward him. But Timmy stayed ahead, always ten feet ahead. Daniel wanted to catch up to him, but he couldn't.

"Wait for me," he tried to say, but there were waves in his mouth. "I just want . . ." What did he want? To grab Timmy, to roll him over and hold Timmy on his chest like he'd learned to do when he was a lifeguard at the Y that one summer, to float with one arm around Timmy's body and the other arm paddling back to the boat together. To save his life. Except Timmy seemed fine somehow. *I'm the one who needs saving.* He almost laughed.

All he wanted to do was to touch Timmy, feel the warmth of his skin under his hand. Just one more time.

But Timmy kept swimming ahead. His voice was so Timmy-sweet and textured, that ironic edge with kindness underneath it. Daniel could see a shape, and he knew it was the shape of Timmy. Even in the dark and the rain, he recognized the sprawly way he swam, reaching too far left and right and not straight ahead.

Daniel had tried many times to straighten out Timmy's stroke, but it was just the way he swam—more turtle than fish.

It seemed like Timmy led him straight to the carving. It was bobbing in the water and Daniel's hand hit it. It submerged and then popped back up. He grabbed it tight, looked around.

Timmy said, "It's okay." Timmy's voice was growing fainter.

"What do you mean?" Daniel had yelled. It wasn't okay. Nothing was okay. He was in the middle of the goddamn ocean. Did he mean the carving was okay? Timmy was okay? Daniel was okay? Daniel was not okay. He would never be okay.

"Really, Dad?" Timmy said. Daniel almost laughed. It was so absurd to hear Timmy's voice like that, saying what he always said to his father, "Really, Dad? Really?" the way he just reflected back Daniel's emotions and made fun of them, but in a loving way. Daniel could see himself when Timmy was around. He could see exactly who he was in Timmy's eyes. A bumbling scarecrow of a man with a too-big heart.

"Why are you talking in riddles? Just tell me. Tell me what to do. I don't know!" Daniel yelled. It was hard to yell and tread water at the same time. He was losing his breath.

"Stay within range of my voice," Timmy said, and then he was gone. Daniel felt his absence the way he always felt it these days, a kind of hole in his heart that his life was pouring out of.

"But how? Where did you go? Where are you?" He'd yelled until he was hoarse, swimming this way then that, making circles, treading water. His words got swallowed up by the night, which was close down on top of him. Lightning cut the sky once, and he could see for miles, it seemed, in the odd blue glare of it, and there was nothing. No one. He hadn't imagined it, though. He knew Timmy had been there.

Then he heard a bark. Then another bark. And the sound of Tripod was a thin line of light that pulled on him. So he swam toward it, with that carving in his hand. He kept swimming, one stroke after another. And Tripod was sitting there, waiting for him under the canopy.

Daniel stood with Mary now, and they both watched the line of dark move across the sky. He'd woken up on top of the covers with a blanket tucked around him. He remembered her tapping on his door after he'd showered, her tiptoeing in, lying down next to him. and he hadn't objected, just let it happen to him. He remembered her lying down next to him too.

"I'll stay here and keep talking, okay? Feel free to go to sleep. I mean, I would, if I were you," she'd told him.

He knew she was guarding over him. She couldn't have done a thing if he'd decided, really decided, to go back swimming. That's how he thought of it—swimming. Although it really wouldn't be swimming.

But she said, "Scooch over," and she laid herself down like a wall. He had to smile at that. A soft wall, a mush of a wall. It was nice of her. Who would spend their Christmas Eve like this? She'd talked and talked. He'd fallen asleep and woke up a couple of times and she was still talking. It was okay. She talked softly, and she was really talking to herself, and he knew she needed to do that. At first it was really angry. She could be tough on herself. Then it was as if, sometime in the night, she decided maybe she'd give herself a break. She asked him questions, but she didn't expect an answer, he knew, so he kept his eyes shut. She answered herself most times. "Am I really unlovable? My uncle told me that once, when I was a little girl. His voice was sad. 'Mary, you are just one of those unlovable people.' I looked in the mirror after that and thought and thought. Which feature makes me unlovable? I tried to pinpoint it.

My imperfect nose? Is my forehead too high? Or was it something internal that shone through? Those words stuck into me. I carried them around for years. My whole life. I still do. Believing it. Disbelieving it. Fighting against it. Accepting it. I tried it all. The only thing that ever made me feel lovable was the way the ponies ran to me all those years ago. Across that wide field. They whinnied when they saw me and ran toward me like their hearts would break and head-butted me over the rail, nibbled on my fingers like I was the sweetest grass in the world. Maybe one other time. When I had CC and she was a baby, she cuddled into my arms and reached into my hair and rubbed my earlobes and said over and over, 'Ears, ears, ears,' like it was my name, like she loved me so much she couldn't get over the softness of my ears, or that she was able to touch and hold a tiny part of me. And now Larkin . . ."

She stopped.

Daniel held himself very still with his eyes shut so she didn't stop. *Don't stop*, he thought. *Just keep talking, telling me things*. It was like she was reading him a bedtime story.

"You are very peaceful to be around," he'd said to her when they were lying together. He'd reached out then and touched her face. He slowly traced her features. Her cheekbones, her nose, her chin, her lips. Oh, he wanted to kiss her. He wanted to. So badly. But it seemed wrong. They were both so raw. And this seemed better. It was almost as good as being naked. He wanted to keep touching her, trying to figure her out—the planes, the rises, the dips, the falls, the freckles, the little scars and lines.

"I wish I had met you earlier in my life," he said. He hadn't meant to say it out loud. But he did, and it had made him feel even more naked. But it was fine. She just smiled at him, and she reached out and touched his face in return. She traced all his lines. He'd let her. They'd done it to each other.

Now he said, "I'm supposed to go to this pancake breakfast thing this morning—I mean, I'm supposed to go help and flip pancakes. It's for people who don't have anywhere to go. They're homeless vets or wounded." He really had no intention of going last night, but this morning, it seemed like something to do. And he knew he'd have to keep finding something to do next, and to do next . . . To get through.

He didn't want to be alone this morning waiting for Addie. *When Addie gets here, that will be that.* His stomach dropped. *Don't think about it.*

"I'm a person who has nowhere to go," Mary said.

"Me too," he admitted.

"I'll drive to the hotel so I can get some clothes first because I don't think I can go like this." She looked down at herself in his rumpled too-big clothes.

"You look beautiful," he told her.

~

Daniel picked Mary up at the hotel and they drove to the church hall together. The place didn't seem to be one denomination or the other. It was a modern white building with some wooden pews, and the hall attached to it was the size of a small gym and smelled, Daniel thought, a little like a gym, a little like holy water. The walls were painted yellow and there was a big bulletin board on the wall advertising Bible classes and a "Ram Truck 4 Sale" and when the next clothing drive was going to be happening. In cutout construction paper letters, the heading proclaimed WE GIVE BACK.

He and Mary were right on time, but the building was already bustling with people setting up tables and unfolding chairs.

Daniel saw Jorge across the room. Jorge smiled and waved them over. Daniel introduced Mary, and Jorge said, "Thanks so much for coming. All of you." He bent down and gave Tripod a pat.

"Tell us what to do," Mary said.

For the next half hour, they worked flipping tablecloths onto tables and putting out dishes of butter patties and carafes of syrup. Someone started cooking the bacon, and Daniel's mouth watered. He didn't think he'd ever been this hungry. But he put off his hunger.

A truck pulled up, and Daniel and Mary unloaded crates of organic blueberries that a local farm had donated. Mary's face was intent. When she got started on something, she really focused. Her mouth was scrunched up in one corner. She kept pushing at her flopping hair to get it out of her way.

Daniel hadn't been in a place like this in a long time, where people were all working together hard. It was a good, clean energy with a distinct beat to it. People walked with purpose. They kept saying, "You got that? Let me help you with that."

Tripod followed them around but stayed out of the way.

A woman handed Daniel and Mary long linen aprons.

"Can you mix up the batter?"

"With the best of them," Daniel said. He felt a lightness as he said it. He and Timmy had loved making pancakes, creating faces on them with chocolate chip mouths, raspberry noses, blueberry eyes. Timmy was gleeful standing on the kitchen chair, watching as the pancakes cooked and the expressions on the faces changed. Yes, he remembered, and it stabbed at him, but he smiled too. He could almost hear Timmy's voice so full of laughter, the words bubbling out of him. *Stay within range of my voice.*

Mary measured the pancake mix while Daniel poured tin cups of water into an industrial-sized beater, and then Daniel pressed the button and they watched the batter clump up, then get smoother and smoother. Little pockets of dry pancake mix stubbornly hung in there, and Daniel poked at them with a wooden spoon until they finally yielded. Then he passed the bowl to a guy who lined it up on the counter.

Daniel kept looking at Mary's face as she peered into the huge bowl of batter. She looked tired and sometimes a shadow flitted across her face, but mostly she was just concentrating on measuring and pouring and mixing just as he was. It was very quieting, even among all the bustle, to focus on getting the batter just right, then adding the berries, bursting mounds of them so ripe they were almost black folding into the pale batter.

After they'd finished another bowl, Mary popped a few blueberries in her mouth. "Open wide," she said to him, holding a blueberry in her hand.

He opened his mouth, although he knew she would miss. The blueberry went flying over his right shoulder.

"Oh," she said, and picked up another. This one hit him in the eye. "Wider," she told him.

"Wouldn't make a bit of difference," he told her.

"You're moving too much."

"I'm breathing," he said.

"Oh shoot," she said as one hit the back of the guy standing behind Daniel.

"I'm taking you out of the game," he told her. "You can't throw a strike."

"Give me another chance."

"Nope."

She threw a blueberry as he turned away. "That would have gone in if you didn't move," she said.

"In your dreams."

The words hung between them. Daniel thought of last night, how he felt the heat of her body inches away and how good it felt to not have to do anything or say anything, just to be next to her. He'd been thinking, *Is she real? Or is she just an idea of a person?* Weird stuff like that. Well, his mind definitely wasn't right after he'd seen Timmy. Or thought he'd seen Timmy. He'd needed to touch her just to make sure she was there. The relief that washed over him when he felt her soft skin made him draw in his breath.

He'd fallen asleep eventually. They both had kind of faded away. It was a comforting sleep. Not like sleep usually was. It was like he was in a very soft place, kind of like a hammock made of clouds suspended in the air. And even though he hadn't slept long, he felt rested in a deep way. When he woke up, he felt his own chest to see if he was alive. He really did. He'd never felt that out of it before. But his heart was still pounding.

Now they opened the doors to the hall, and people filed in, got in the food line. The air was full of sizzling sounds, the salty smell of melting butter, and a low hubbub of voices. Someone had turned on Christmas carols on the PA system—schmaltzy, crooning ones that always made him think of *White Christmas*, the movie, when Bing opened up the stage to see the snow falling and the sleigh going by with the shaggy horses and the bells, and he kissed Rosemary in her little dance outfit and her perfect coif of hair behind the huge tree. That moment was Christmas to him.

Mary had a smudge of batter on her cheek, and Daniel was going to tell her about it, or even reach and rub it off, but then he decided he wouldn't. Every time he looked at her, that smudge made him smile. His little secret.

They made batter for over an hour. Vats of it, it seemed. Then Jorge told them, "That's enough. Go get a plate. Sit down."

So they did, him and her at a table with a bunch of old guys.

The one next to him was named Franklin and was in his nineties, neatly dressed in a suit, with his hair Brylcreemed so that the lines of the comb showed. The one next to her, Willy, was in his seventies and in a wheelchair and hadn't shaved in a week and smelled like mothballs. Franklin hardly ate anything and, after fifteen minutes of cutting up his pancakes into smaller and smaller pieces, asked for a Styrofoam container to "take it home." Mary asked him where home was, and he just nodded at her, like he didn't understand English. Willy piped up and said they all lived in the "Seaview Hilton," which "has no sea view and ain't exactly a Hilton neither."

When Franklin got up to go to the men's room, Willy said, "Don't let him fool you none because he's so quiet. That guy's a real hero. His daughter showed me a newspaper article about him, all his medals. He was a belly gunner. You name the medal, he got it. And she told me, even after he'd finished his tour of duty, he volunteered to fly supplies over enemy lines. He could have gone home, and he stayed. Imagine that. I couldn't wait to get out of 'Nam. That place was a maze. We all got lost there." He paused. "One way or another."

The world looked washed and bright through the windows. Daniel watched Mary talk to a nurse seated on her other side. She was a thick-bodied woman with a permed helmet of blond hair and green flowered scrubs. She looked like a big, bunchy bouquet of daisies. She was a comforting type he saw a lot on the west coast of Florida: middle-aged, from the middle of the country, middle-class. Middle people were such nice people—underrated, he thought. They never got any attention in the world, just went about their business coaching local soccer teams, working at their jobs, mowing their lawns once a week, hanging their sheets out on the clothesline, volunteering at the firehouse. It was people who did all the bad stuff and people who had no talent at all that got all the attention. That was a funny thing about the world these days.

He looked at the clock. It was ten thirty already. Addie would be here by twelve. He didn't want to go back to the boat, but he'd have to get going soon. He looked at Mary. She met his eyes. He knew she knew what he was thinking. He didn't know how he knew, but he did. Then she looked down at Tripod, who was sitting on her feet. Tripod liked her. He kept licking her ankles.

"Stop," she kept saying, laughing.

"He must like the lotion you put on."

"He just likes me."

Daniel had to agree. And it was a shame. It was a damn shame the dog was leaving.

They drove back to the Low-Key Inn in silence. The sun streamed into his truck. He thought of his first girlfriend when he was in eleventh grade. Katie Barlow. He used to take her for rides in his truck. He had an old red Ford back then, and he'd say, "Do you want to practice driving a stick shift?"

And she'd say, "Yes, I do."

So she'd put her hand on his stick shift and he'd put his hand over hers, and he'd tell her when to pull the stick, when to push it.

"That right there is first gear. Can you feel it, how it wants to go into second? You can sense when it's ready to go, can't you?" he'd ask.

She nodded, but he could tell she wasn't really getting the feel of it.

That truck had a hole rusted out in the floor on the passenger side and one long front seat that was worn and soft and had tufts of foam sticking through, and it had an old wooden beam clamped on the front as the bumper. Every day they did this ride-around-and-learn-to-shift thing. Daniel would drive around town, carefully puttering up and down the streets. He didn't know any fancy places to take her. And she wanted to go to fancy places—he could just tell. She always wore a necklace with a pearl that sat right in the hollow of her collarbones like it expected something.

He didn't really know what to say to her, so they'd driven in silence. He'd never gotten any farther with her than that stick-shift thing. After a few weeks of driving around going nowhere with Daniel, she started going out with Tom Billet, who was on the track team and who had a white Toyota. An automatic.

Now Daniel put the truck into fourth gear. The gears ground a little bit. Daniel looked over at Mary's hands. He wondered how she'd be at driving a stick. He'd bet anything she didn't know how. He wondered if she'd like to learn.

He imagined her yelling at him the way she had in his boat, her hands waving around, her voice on the verge of laughter or tears or some combination of both, her hair sticking out, her hand pulling and pushing the stick this way and that, not listening to him at all, and him sitting in the passenger seat, watching her and smiling his fool head off, his hand cupped on top of hers on the stick, warm and cozy as a hat.

He pulled up to the Low-Key Inn and stared straight ahead at a pink hibiscus bush. Hibiscuses were such continual flowers, always a new bud opening up. You could count on them.

He felt Mary looking at him. She was nobody to count on. She was going to leave soon. People were always coming and going. That was the trouble with Florida. Every goddamn week, a new batch was leaving all sunburned, another batch was coming in with suitcases. *I hate Florida. Maybe I'll take the houseboat and go somewhere else. A staying kind of place. Ha. Where the hell is that? I don't hate Florida. It's the going part I hate.*

He felt her leaning toward him. She was going to kiss him. He knew it. He closed his eyes and turned to her.

OLLIE

It was morning, but Ollie was still tired. She hadn't gotten enough sleep. Al had stayed until after midnight, sitting on her front porch talking, then swinging silently, watching the rain. The whole time, they'd held hands. Not clamped tight, just lightly touching. They didn't acknowledge that they were holding hands. It was like a secret they were keeping even from themselves.

He'd fallen asleep at the end of the evening. His head bobbed once. Then he looked over at her.

"Past my bedtime," he said.

"Me too."

He got up and stretched. The rain had stopped but the trees were still dripping. The moon came out, and the gulf in the distance reflected a shimmering path. Once, when Ollie was a girl and her parents had taken her for a vacation at the lake, her mother had told her that the moon elves came down on rope ladders and walked along the path the moon made to come ashore. Ollie had asked her, "How can they walk on top of the water?"

"They are as weightless as the light itself," her mother told her.

Al said, "Let me get dressed and run along."

When he came out of her bathroom, he said, "Thank you for a wonderful Christmas Eve. I can't remember a better one."

"You napped through it," she said, tapping his shoulder.

"I did not."

"Thank you for the company."

"Thank you for the hospitality." He bowed toward her.

"Wine and salami are not exactly a Christmas feast."

"It was just what I needed."

She smiled at him, and he backed away, looking at her, and then he was gone, dissolving into the night.

She'd put the glasses and dishes in the dishwasher and gone to bed. But she couldn't sleep. She kept turning her pillow over to get to a cool place to put her cheek. She was uncomfortable on her back, on her side, on her stomach. She couldn't get the feel of his hand on hers out of her head. It took her hours to get to sleep, and then she slept fitfully and woke up late. She always woke at dawn. The birds called to her. And she loved the dawn. But today she'd missed it. It was almost ten o'clock.

She felt very weak. It was the no sleep. It must be.

What a night. Her body prickled all over like there were bees buzzing through her veins. She'd woken up humming "Jingle Bells." It was Christmas. She felt like a little girl. She felt like she herself was a present, all wrapped up, full of surprise.

Her birds were waiting for her. They were singing loudly.

"Stop complaining so much," she told them. "I have a life too."

They fluttered around her and landed on her shoulder. She loved to bend her cheek to them, feel the warmth of their heads. They sang their small songs to her. They almost broke her heart, these songs. Most people didn't even listen to them. If Ollie said, "Hear that?" they'd say, "What?" The birds were background noise. But if that noise ever went away, why, they'd hear the silence then. It would be like 9/11, when the planes were banned from the skies and everyone was suddenly aware of the emptiness, the vast clarity of the blue, the puffed-up undisturbed clouds.

After she fed the birds, she went for a walk on the beach like she did every day. She supposed she prayed, if she really even knew what prayer was. If it was noticing things and being thankful for them, then Ollie understood it because she liked to notice things—a distant red boat, the smell of seaweed drying in the sand, the footprints of the sandpipers, the way the sand was hard packed in spots and sank under her feet in others, the echoey sound of a gull calling, *ah*, *ah*, *ah*.

She walked one mile to the end and one mile back. She was determined to be ninety and still doing it.

Every dawn was different. Some days were bold, and the sun split the sky open. But some days were shy, the sun edging over the horizon and peeking before it showed itself. This day was already up and running, the sun's rays bouncing off the sand and the water. The gulf was a clear aqua, and a group of ibises walked in front of her, pecking at the sand. When she got too close, they rose in a white flurry and settled farther down the beach. A sand dollar washed up by her feet. A perfect one. It never ceased to amaze her how beautiful they were. It was things like sand dollars that made her believe in God—in a creative, gentle, nature-oriented God, not one of those Old Testament angry types. A kind of God who would think, *Hmm, let me make a sea creature that looks like a flower.*

She bent and tossed it gently back into the sea.

What would she do with herself today? What she did with herself every Christmas: sit on her porch, watch her birds. She hadn't had a present in years. Well, that was all right. Her birds were her presents every morning. The sea was too. She didn't want for anything. She didn't want for a blessed thing.

Except now.

She looked around. The beach was empty. Everyone was busy doing Christmas-morning activities, no doubt.

She got it in her head that she'd like to skip. She tried a few steps. She hadn't skipped in fifty years or more. But she wanted to now, with the day smiling all around her. She wanted to skip like a girl again. There. It was a strange hitchy gait, wasn't it? A little stutter, then a jump. She tried it again. A little stutter and then a jump. Her cotton dress bunched a bit as she moved. Was that her leg creaking like that? She hoped no one was watching her.

She skipped along the winding path through the mangroves. It felt nice to be in the dappled shade. She enjoyed the way the path twisted and turned, how she had to duck under branches in places. It was touching how people made paths like this through the wilderness. They were these winding affairs that went around obstacles and found their own snaky way through a maze, catching a nice view when they could, veering into a bit of sun, a bit of shade, taking the easy way, no, taking the hard. Each so human, so individual, so quirky.

She'd been tossing it around in her mind, and now she'd decided. Al was a businessman. She'd trusted him last night, and he'd trusted her. She'd tell him about the hotel, all the problems. She'd lay it out for him, ask him for help. Maybe he'd know something.

There was the hotel up ahead. It was bustling with activity. Someone was raking the beach—Joseph, that would be. She'd given him a job even though he'd done time. He'd stolen a car when he was twenty "for no good reason," he told her. "It wasn't even a good car." He went for a joy ride, except "there wasn't no joy in it. Just a lot of stupid." He was a good worker, steady and methodical, like he was trying to diligently stitch the bits and pieces of his life together. He looked a wreck, though. He was a white boy, but he had those dreadlocks sticking out of his head like he'd been struck by lightning, little shells—actual shells!—woven into the long cords. She wondered what would happen to him if the hotel went under. The Marriott wouldn't take him. No chance of that.

He'd already put out the cabanas and lounge chairs, pulled the kayaks down to the water's edge. Everything looked colorful and happy. She walked back to the reception desk to check on how Alice was doing. She was so young. And she needed a bit more overseeing. The other day she'd given out the wrong room key to someone and they'd walked right in on a couple sleeping. Thank goodness that's all they were doing. And the husband was forgiving. "Could have happened to anyone," he had said. The wife needed a bit more reassuring. Ollie had to offer her a free dinner, and then she was satisfied. Except she made a point of telling Ollie that she'd chain the door from here on out. Just in case. And the woman rolled her eyes.

Ollie walked behind the counter. Alice was combing her hair in long, luxurious strokes, staring at herself in her phone. Ollie told her, "Oh, Alice, do you have to do that here at the desk?" There were hairs sifting down everywhere. *Focus on something else besides yourself!* Ollie wanted to tell her. Kids and their phones and their selfies! Ollie remembered how it was being young and so unsure—*Am I pretty? Am I fat? Why is my nose this way?* How seductive and yet how torturous a mirror could be.

"Fine," Alice said, and stomped off toward the ladies' room. She had a bit of an attitude. Well, her mother was an alcoholic. Ollie knew that sometimes Alice came home from work and had to step over her mother's prone body. Ollie had to make allowances.

She skimmed through the computer screen register. So many people were checking out tomorrow! The hotel would be half-empty. She shook her head. The shadow fluttered over her eye like a bat's wing. She blinked hard but it was still there.

As she was looking at the screen, a name caught her eye. Emerson. Emerson? Yes, here it was—Emerson, Albert. Room 2. Albert?

She got a heavy feeling inside her. "No," she said aloud. A woman walking through the lobby in her bathing suit stopped a second, looked at Ollie, and then walked on.

Ollie stood very still. Her breath rasped hot in her throat. She rubbed her bad eye. She heard the clock ticking slowly. Was it slowing down? No, it couldn't be.

She bent over the computer. Her fingers shook as she googled him—Albert Emerson. Why hadn't she thought to do this before? Well, she wasn't much of a computer person, and you had to be these days. If you weren't, you were left out in the cold. *Like me,* she thought, and shivered.

There was a glossy ad. He was in a tight buttoned-up business suit. He didn't look like Al. But then again, he did. He was standing in front of a giant white high-rise. The plate glass windows reflected the sunlight. She read, "The Gold Institute—Retirement Living at the Top. Come live in the tallest condos in Florida—the ultimate in luxury—where every room feels like a penthouse and the world stretches out at your feet. You've earned it!"

"Where's your hat?" she asked the screen. "Where's your stupid hat?" Her voice screeched.

Stephen walked by her and stopped. "You okay?" he asked her.

She took a deep, trembly breath. The room breathed too. No. She shook her head. No. The computer screen was breathing with her, in and out—no, it was swimming. It was like she was in one of those lava lamps where everything melts into rising and descending blobs. She was aware that she was falling. *How could this be?* she thought. Then she crumpled to the floor. And it was dark.

DANIEL

Addie was here. A car pulled into the lot, and she got out the back. He was sitting on the deck with Tripod, a notepad on his lap. He'd made a list of what Tripod's brand of food was, how much to feed him, how many times he had to go out a day. What else could he write?

Love him.

He watched Addie get out of the car. She was a short woman and had always carried an extra ten pounds. She looked stouter now. The weight had squared her off, thickened her into a kind of box and blurred all her curves into straight lines. He watched her walk toward him. She went side to side, almost waddling. *Weebles wobble but they don't fall down,* he thought suddenly. And that was true of Addie. You could push her down, but she'd right herself. No matter what you did to her, she'd come back up at you.

This wasn't going to be good.

For days now, he'd thought about arguing with her, even begging her when he saw her. But all those scenarios went out the window as he watched her walk. He'd forgotten. She was like John Wayne entering a town that had gone all to hell. She was determined. Yes, he could see it in the set of her mouth.

He stood up, and Tripod got up too. Tripod leaned his body

against Daniel's leg. Lately he'd taken to doing this. Daniel supposed it eased the weight on his one back leg.

Addie waved to him as she walked. He lifted one hand. Tripod growled deep inside his chest. It was almost a hum. Daniel fought back a smile.

When Addie got to the boat, she said, "Ah. Look at this."

Daniel was suddenly aware of his houseboat, the black swath of paint on it, the worn canvas chair he sat on with the red fabric faded down to pink. He'd bought the boat furnished, but "furnished" wasn't quite an accurate word for it. Whatever was screwed down was left. And he'd kept it all just the way it was. Maybe he should have added to it. He thought suddenly of Al. Life-is-about-addition-not-just-subtraction Al. He thought, *That philosophy might be true, but not today, Al.* Today was going to be all about subtraction.

Addie's mouth was in an O. He knew she'd be surprised to see how spare he was living these days. When he and Addie lived together, he was always "doing up" their house. Although she called it "trashing it."

He'd taken a class in macramé at the adult school one winter. Addie had made fun of him—"You and your hippie friends tying knots together." He was the only man in the class. He'd hung the macramé holders in their windows, woven shells and branches into them, sometimes planted air plants in the shells.

He loved to go to flea markets and find old oil paintings that people had done. He'd bring home portraits of women with folded hands, men in straight-back chairs.

Addie never got it. "Who are these people?"

"I don't know," he'd say. "But they're interesting, aren't they? Look how telling their faces are."

She'd shake her head.

He brought home old furniture with peeling paint.

"Are you going to refinish that?" she'd ask.

"Refinish? It's perfect just the way it is. Look at the chips and the worn spots on this blue table. Someone probably sat for hours thinking and dreaming here. Why would I want to erase all that?"

Now he thought, *Yes, look at this indeed. Now I'm just bare bones.* But he didn't say anything.

"How was your flight?" he asked, giving her a hand onto the boat.

Her hand felt different than it used to, more fleshy. He let it go quickly as she stood on his deck.

Tripod was still growling. "Easy," Daniel said.

"Have you turned him into a recluse too?" Addie said.

"He likes who he likes."

She bent down. "Come here."

Tripod looked at Daniel.

Daniel shrugged.

Tripod took one hop toward Addie.

See? It will be fine. It will be okay. See how okay it is?

Daniel looked at the sky. It was very blue and went on and on forever. He wished she was leaving already. He wished they were both gone. *This is going to kill me*, he thought. Then he thought of last night. *No, probably not. I'm not that easy to kill.*

"Go, Tripod," Daniel said. His voice was gruff.

Tripod stood still, considering.

"On the way down, I was thinking of changing his name," Addie said.

"What do you mean?"

"That's a bad name. Timmy was always making a joke out of terrible things."

"So?"

"I just think I would always be reminded, you know, saying that name."

Daniel held his body really still. He was not a violent man, had never gotten into a fistfight in his life. He walked away from conflict. But now, it was all he could do not to shove her—not hurt her, really, just push her into the water, see her arms flail, her legs cartwheel, see her make an awkward big splash.

She said, "I think a dog should have a real name. Like a human name. Like Larry. Or Mike. Or maybe like a happy thing. What do you think of Seesaw?"

He shook his head.

"Merlot?"

"That's a wine."

"I know that's a wine, Daniel. I'm not an idiot. It sounds stately. Dignified. He's a war hero. He should have a better name."

"Like Mike?"

Addie looked at him and bit her lip.

"He has a name already," Daniel said.

"Well, he's going to get another one."

Daniel gritted his teeth and looked away. He knew it was going to be like this—he just knew it. Why couldn't she just not be so . . . her? Whatever. He'd have to let it go. Let her call the dog whatever she wanted. His heart felt like a fist.

They stood there looking at each other.

"I changed my return flight. I got an earlier one back," Addie said.

"Oh, really?"

"Yeah. I didn't see the point of staying. So, if you could just give me his stuff, we'll go. The Uber is waiting."

"You mean now?"

She nodded.

"Listen, Daniel, it's not like I don't know it's going to be hard for you. I imagine you've made a connection. It's not going to be easy for me either, though. I mean, I have a new place and, well, a lot is going on. It's going to be an inconvenience."

"There's a name for you. Why don't you just call him The Inconvenience?"

"Why do you have to be this way?"

"What way is that, Addie?"

"Impossible."

"I changed my name to that."

She stared at the deck. "Do you have his things?"

"All ready to roll." He bent and picked up a duffle bag. "You won't have to check it. It should fit into the overhead bin. And there's nothing in it that should set off the sensors. Just some things that he likes." His voice broke. His goddamn voice broke. He promised himself he wouldn't cry. He cleared his throat. He bent down to Tripod.

"You be a good dog, now. You listen to Addie. You take care of her, you hear?"

Addie climbed off the boat, and Daniel bent down and picked up Tripod. Tripod's thick body was shaking. He put Tripod down on the dock next to Addie, let his hand linger on Tripod's back, felt the straight line of his spine. He handed the leash to her.

"Goodbye, then," she said.

She pulled on his leash. Tripod didn't move. He dug his heels in and Addie kind of dragged him toward the waiting car.

Addie turned and over her shoulder said, "Daniel?"

He forced himself to look at her. At them both. Together.

"Merry Christmas," she said.

Daniel turned his back. He heard one sharp bark. It went into him like a BB, and he felt it lodge deep into his soft tissue. He knew it would be in him forever. It was just another one of those hard things that accumulated in a body over the course of a life, that a body couldn't digest or break down. Just another piece of the world.

MARY

She'd kissed Kipper. What had prompted that? Some mix of sexual something or other mingled with the longing smell of browning pancakes that lingered on both of them? Some idea about throwing herself off the cliff of herself—whatever edge she'd been toeing the last few days—and plummeting in a new direction?

She smiled.

He kissed so good.

She hurried back toward her room. She'd go over to Kipper's boat later. After Tripod was gone. He couldn't be left alone after that heartache. Or maybe Kipper would get some gumption and say no to Addie—"You can't take my dog."

Then maybe Mary and Kipper and Tripod would all go out on his boat. Maybe it would be sunset. Maybe she'd kiss him again.

The morning smelled green like sap, like sea salt and vaguely like pancakes. She turned the bend in the path and pulled up short. There was a man sitting on the porch of her igloo. He stood up. It was Ron. He looked like he hadn't slept in days. His perfect hair was mussed, and he had the shadow of a two-day beard. His eyes were red-rimmed.

Mary walked toward him slowly.

She stopped.

He said, "Will you marry me?"

Mary opened her mouth, but nothing came out. She felt a strange peacefulness descend on her. She'd dreamed of moments like this for all the years she'd known Ron—a time when he'd stop running away and he'd turn and come looking for her. She searched inside herself to see what she was feeling. Her anger was nowhere. It had dissipated like a cloud. And in its place was what? A muddle of feelings. Well, it didn't matter.

"No," she said.

"Please," he said.

"What are you doing here?" she asked.

"I had to find you."

"But how?"

"I looked on your computer at work." He shrugged. "I was desperate."

"You looked at my email?" She felt a hitch in her heart. Well, there it was. There *was* still anger in there.

"Mare, I know your password. You *told* me it."

"That didn't give you permission to look at my personal stuff."

"I didn't. I just looked at your travel plans."

It was true—although he did know her passwords, he always respected her privacy. She could trust him with that kind of thing. And he did know everything about her. She should have thought to change the password. But it didn't occur to her that he'd look. Or maybe a part of her wanted to be found?

She shook her head. "You shouldn't have."

"But I did. I had to. Listen, hear me out."

She could see him trembling. "I don't want to. I've heard it all before."

"This time is different. I was wrong. I've been wrong my whole life. Scared wrong. But your leaving threw me for a loop. I can't sleep, can't eat, can't live without you. I'll marry you right now. I mean, let's go find a preacher from the Church of the Palm Tree and get hitched. Or maybe everybody's off for Christmas, even the palm tree people. So, we'll get married tomorrow. Come back home with me. I'll marry you tomorrow, then we'll go buy ourselves a house. The first goddamn house we see. The biggest goddamn house in the world."

His arms were waving.

"I need us to be together," he said. "I need us to be a family."

"Where's Joanna?" Mary said.

"She's home. I told her I had to come down here and see you."

"You left her on Christmas?"

"She told me to come. She said you were good for me, that you made me happy. She said, 'What are you waiting for, Dad?'"

"Why did she say that? She doesn't really like me."

"Of course she does."

"What happened to Alexandra?"

"Alexandra called me from jail yesterday."

"What?"

"She stole three thousand dollars' worth of clothes from Bergdorf's. She told me she wanted me to come bail her out."

"Are you kidding?"

"She said she was buying Christmas presents for Joanna, and it was all a misunderstanding."

"What did you do?"

"I hung up on her."

Mary raised her eyebrows. "Really?"

"Then Joanna and I talked. She was like a grown-up for the first time in her life. I thought she was going to have a meltdown after the whole thing with Alexandra, but she didn't. She kept telling me to go get a life. 'Go to Florida, Dad. Go for it.' So, here I am."

"Um," Mary said. She looked at her igloo room. She didn't want to let him into the igloo. It seemed somehow too personal, too hers. Maybe he would make fun of it, and she couldn't bear that. So she said, "Let's walk."

They walked together down to the beach. He cuffed his pants up and rolled his sleeves and they waded away from the hotel. Mary was waiting for him to say something disparaging about the hotel, but he didn't say a thing. He said the beach was nice. He said the sun felt nice. Everything was nice, he said.

But she was trembling. Was it fear or excitement? It was too much, too fast. But that was Ron. When he decided he wanted something, he leaped into it full force. He always had with his work. Mary had been waiting years for him to commit like that to her.

She walked next to him, her body matching itself to his stride. *This is what I know*, she thought. *He's been my friend, my lover. I've memorized every inch of his body, the rhythms of his speech, the turns of his moods. I know him. I know this.* She felt her body relax. Like her muscles that she'd held so tight the last few days, maybe held tight for years, finally eased. Like her bones that had felt dislocated and wrong slid back into their rightful slots.

Three pelicans glided low over the water, so close their bellies almost skimmed the surface. Mary wondered how they managed it, such big, seemingly awkward birds but so capable of grace. She stopped to pick a white feather off the sand. Ollie had told Larkin that if you found a feather, that meant you could fly. Or something like that. Mary twirled the feather in her hand. She glanced at Ron.

Umbrellas were popping up on the beach, and people were sitting under them together. The sun was hot. She wished that she and Ron had an umbrella to sit under. She thought about the painting Ollie had done for her. People in the shelter of each other. Ron was offering her family, a home together—something she'd been longing for for so long.

They walked in silence. Usually, he wasn't good with silence. He tried to fill it in. He turned on a radio or a TV or some music, but this time, he just let the quiet be. Mary thought of going back to her condo. Her front door opening wide to her key. The view of her living room. The fireplace she'd never been able to light—something to do with the flue lining that had crumbled. So she'd arranged a few white birch logs in it like they were ready to burst into flames. But they'd sat unlit in the same spot for years. Maybe she and Ron would buy a home with a working fireplace.

He stopped suddenly. He said, "You haven't really looked at me yet."

She almost said, *I'm afraid to*, but she didn't. She forced herself to raise her face. There he was. The man she'd loved for years—from the moment she met him. She'd always been scared of the power of her feelings toward him. All her neurons seemed to fire at once when she was with him, sweep her along on their raging current like one of those log flume rides.

Now she held his gaze. Heat blazed through her like she was radioactive. If she were holding a light bulb in her hands, it would go on right now. She was sure of it. One hundred watts of glare.

She felt her body leaning. She wanted to fall into him. She was falling, and he was holding her and his arms were trembling. His whole body was trembling. He kissed her. The world blurred. She closed her eyes and let herself go.

A gull called, and another one answered from far away.

"Let's turn around," she whispered to him.

They walked back to her room. She fumbled for the key, then pushed the door open. Mary was blinded walking into the dark room from the brilliance of outside. And she was shaking. Was it the air-conditioning? Was it cold in here or too hot? She felt dizzy.

Ron went into the bathroom. As the door clicked shut, Mary

was hit with a memory. She was a child. She was in her nightgown and her nightgown was wet and the world was shaking. She was on a train. The train smelled like dirty metal and like electricity and rats and darkness. She shivered. She remembered now. It was after her parents died, and her uncle came to pick her up and take her back to his house. They went in a taxi to the city and then down, down into a dungeon place and her uncle said, "This is where the dragons live." Did he know how much those words scared her? Was this how he thought you were supposed to talk to children? But she believed him. She carried a little cloth suitcase that had zippered compartments, and she could only fit a few things in it. So she'd packed her favorite red skirt and yellow sweater, her favorite book—*The Secret Garden*—and a tiny box that her mother had given her that when you lifted the lid, a ballerina twirled to a theme from *Swan Lake*. She remembered it now, so vividly, the sound of the zippers as she zipped them up in her empty house, the echo of her footsteps leaving her bedroom.

They ate dinner in the train's club car. It was fancy. Pink cakes and chocolate cakes whirled around in glass cases like they were on a carousel. She couldn't eat her dinner. Her uncle showed her to her room. The bathroom was down the hall, he said. Then he left her. She went to sleep and it took her a long time because of all the bumping and clattering.

Then she woke up in the middle of the night and had to go to the bathroom. The hall was dark with glowing green lights. She couldn't find the bathroom. All the doors were locked. She went back to her room—3A. She remembered that! It was locked too. She must have hit the button on the knob going out. She didn't know where to go for help. She went through a door and was in between the cars, and the train was going fast, and she could see the ground and the dark trees going by, and it was loud but she didn't cry. There was another door and a car with seats in it, and people were sitting in the seats sleeping. One man in a suit was drooling and one of his eyes was wrong—shriveled up around the socket. She curled up in a corner on the floor. At some point in the night, she wet her underpants, and she was sitting in her puddle. She didn't know what to do. A porter found her in the morning and asked her where her room was, and she said 3A, and he took her there, and the door really wasn't locked at all and she went inside and threw her nightgown away and put on her red skirt and yellow sweater and then her uncle knocked on her door and took her to breakfast in the club car and she never said anything about it. Ever. And, until this day, hadn't even thought of it.

Mary swallowed. She couldn't believe she remembered all of this now. Was this at the heart of all of her sleepwalking? Looking for that door back into her room? The door that was really always open and never locked at all?

Ron came out of the bathroom. He stood next to Mary in the dim igloo room. The bedside clock ticked. He pulled a box from his pocket. He opened it. "Please marry me, Mary Louise Valley," he said to her.

She stared at the ring. A big diamond glinted in a bed of black velvet. He knew she didn't like diamonds.

"I know it's big," he said.

"You know I don't need big."

"You deserve big."

But I don't want big, she almost told him.

"I want everyone to know that you belong to me."

The world "belong" was like kryptonite for her. It buckled her at her knees.

He said, "I bought us two tickets back home this afternoon, so you're going to have to say yes or no right away." He smiled.

He had a crooked smile. His eyes were denim blue and crinkled up at the edges. His face looked weary but hopeful. She could see the little boy in him. Ron had told her that he used to get beaten up by his father for no other reason than that crinkly smile of his—because that smile was his mother's smile. And his father hated his mother because she'd left him for another man right after Ron was born. Ron's father used to say to Ron, "You're probably not even mine."

Mary held her breath. She had an image of a shadowy man, a kind of tree-man in the back of her mind, a three-legged dog, both watching her. But she shook her head. They were just strangers to her, really. Figments of a vacation dream. And this new self that she'd found down here. Why, that was just a vacation dream-self too.

Ron got down on one knee. He stared up at her. Tears were in his eyes. They ran down his face. She'd never seen him cry before.

"Don't cry," she said.

"Remember . . ." He struggled to compose himself. He swallowed, wiped at his face with his arm. "Remember how it used to be? How much fun we had?"

"I know, but that's not now. Now it's a complicated mess, and everything gets in the way of us."

"We won't let it. We can't let it."

"But we did."

"That was my fault. I was afraid."

He bowed his head. His shoulders were shaking, he was crying so hard. "Please give me another chance."

She touched his head, ran her finger along the part of his hair. That little vulnerable path. She remembered how it was with them at the beginning. Yes, she did remember.

"Oh, Ron," she said. "Okay. I mean, yes."

OLLIE

Ollie woke up in a white room. She thought she was dead. Except there were tubes coming out of her arm and a monitor that beeped, and she was in an awful hospital gown with little blue triangles on it and a sheet was pulled around her bed. A nurse was bending over, adjusting her arm. "What happened to me?" Ollie asked.

"You had a spell, dearie," the nurse said. She had a soft, lilting Caribbean accent. Her hair was buzzed short and dyed blond at the tips. She looked at Ollie, and her eyes softened. "You're in the ER. We're giving you some fluids."

Ollie liked the way she said the word "fluids." It was so, well, fluid. She closed her eyes. "Is . . . ?" Ollie asked.

"Do you want to see the person who came with you?"

Ollie nodded and opened her eyes. She heard murmuring voices, then footsteps.

Al pulled the curtain back with a whoosh. "You scared me to death," he told Ollie.

"I . . ." Ollie said. *I just forgot to stand up*, Ollie almost said. Her brain felt muzzy and soft. *I forgot to be me.* Al reached down and patted her shoulder under the thin blanket. Why were blankets so thin in hospitals? They barely existed. They were like a cocoon skin. Which made her a butterfly. No, she was a person. It was very confusing. She was so tired. Al had his hand still on Ollie's shoulder. *Leave it there*, Ollie wanted to say. *It's so warm and your fingers feel like feathers*, and she maybe said it, because Al did just that.

But then she remembered that she was mad at him. She closed her eyes.

She must have slept. She heard the beeping of machines, and people murmuring behind the sheet that blocked her from the next bed. Someone said, "Why can't they stop the pain? When is it going to stop?"

Oh, that wasn't good.

She didn't have any pain. That was someone else. She just had this muffled feeling. She opened her eyes, and Al was sitting in the chair smiling at her.

"What happened?" she said. She was surprised she could talk. Her voice sounded just like herself.

"I was walking through the lobby. The waiter was calling 911. Your receptionist was screaming. You passed flat out."

"Oh," she said. Her insides felt hollow and cold, and fear was bouncing around in there like a rubber ball. She felt herself blushing with embarrassment. *I don't want to be frail. I don't want to be old.*

"Everyone is worried," he said.

"I'm fine."

"You just rest. It's okay."

She shook her head. No, it wasn't. She wanted to be young again, not some person in a hospital bed who passed out.

"You'll be fine," he said.

"But I wanted . . ." She stopped.

Something clicked in her brain. Al was Mr. Emerson. He'd lied to her. She struggled to sit up.

"Hold your horses there," Al said.

"You are . . . You are . . ." She didn't know what to say. She felt like Dorothy talking to the Wizard of Oz—*I think you are a very bad man*. But she couldn't say that. Her brain felt like a crumb bun, powdery and breaking to pieces.

She said, "You didn't tell me the truth. You were here to scope out my hotel so that you could put up high-rise condos." Her mouth kind of faltered on the word "condos." She really kind of said "conkos." But he got her point. She could see in his face by the way his smile faded to something wistful and then was gone.

She gathered herself. "I trusted you and opened up to you. Oh, what a fool I was. And you were just trying to take advantage of me, weren't you? Indisposed Mr. Emerson. Really? Did you tell your secretary to lie to me, the poor woman?"

He shook his head.

"How could you have?" Well, that was an awkward sentence. But everything was awkward right now. She wanted to reach out and punch his arm. She wanted to cry. She wanted him to say, *No, no—you've got it all wrong. I'm not Mr. Emerson. Not* that *Mr. Emerson*. But he didn't.

"All that talk of opening doors . . ." she said.

"I suppose it looks like that," he said.

"And I look like a fool. An old fool. Yabba dabba doo, I ask you. All you were trying to do was get over on me." That was a weird phrase, but it just popped out. It sounded kind of sexy and inappropriate. She had a sudden image of him rolling on top of her in her hospital bed. Why couldn't she focus here? And why wasn't he saying anything?

"You wanted to build one of your high-rise, ultra-luxury, whoop-de-do 'Gold Institute' experiences, right?" She couldn't remember the exact words. Something about seeing life laid out at your feet.

Like her and all her wildlife. She could see the bulldozers already pushing her igloos to the ground.

"You're no better than the Marriott," she said.

"I knew it was delicate," he said.

"Delicate?"

"We were prepared to offer you a life residency. You could have stayed there for the rest of your life."

"Where? On the thirty-fifth floor?"

He shook his head. "I could tell when I came that it wouldn't work."

"But you continued on anyway."

"It wasn't like that. I came to do two things: come back on Christmas Eve to the house where . . ."

Oh, she didn't want to hear another word out of him. "Killing two birds with one stone, so to speak. And what? You found that you still had a heart under all that concrete you've erected?"

He hung his head.

She felt her body suddenly give out. She was like a balloon that she'd let go of, and it was whizzing around the room like mad, and now she felt like a shriveled skin of a thing slumped in her bed.

"Was it all an act?" she managed to say.

He said, "I can see that I didn't handle this well."

"Handle? People are not supposed to be handled."

He looked toward her monitors. She heard the blip of some machine.

"I should let you get some sleep," he said.

"Running away again, Mr. Emerson?" She felt mean saying it, but she was tired. And now there was no hope at all. Her blood felt so hot running through her veins. She was surprised steam wasn't coming out of her mouth with every word. "You've spent your whole life running," she said. Oh so meanly.

He got up. He looked slumped and old. His bucket hat was in his hands and his hair was like blond fuzz on top. *Like a pelican*, she thought. And then she thought, *My birds*. Her mouth hardened into a line.

"For what it's worth, I'm sorry," he told her.

She looked away, then out the window toward the far, blurry horizon. No, that was her eyes that were blurry. A tear fell, *plop*, onto her hand. She turned to him, but he was gone.

DANIEL

Daniel didn't realize before how empty his houseboat was. His footsteps echoed on the deck. He sat in his chair, the chair he always sat in under the awning, but it didn't feel like his chair today. Too big, too hard, too strange.

He didn't want to think about Tripod, but he thought of him anyway. He imagined the dog in his red service vest hopping across the airport floor. Tripod hated shiny floors. Sometimes Daniel carried him when the floor was slippery, although Tripod didn't like being carried. He'd stiffen like it was the end of the world to be held whenever Daniel picked him up. He couldn't yield to it in any way. Well, Daniel understood that. It was best to hold yourself hard. That way you didn't get broken.

He'd been telling himself that for a year now, anyway. He'd gotten off track these last few days. Mary and Larkin and now Tripod. Well, it was Christmas that was screwing everything up. Once it was over, he could be back to normal.

He looked at the sky. Blue with streaky clouds. A plane cut a white swath through it. When he was a kid, planes used to loop around doing skywriting with their white plumes. Daniel would watch as every letter was formed, and then he'd wait to see the letters blur until it all became just sky again, and the plane was gone.

What was that whiteness made of? Where did it go when it went? It was weird how things just disappeared—like sounds, for example. Where did words go? When he was a kid, he used to think that they just floated up into the atmosphere until they eventually accumulated into clouds. He'd thought rain was just old words coming down.

He was going to drive himself crazy thinking about the sky, the sky that might have a plane in it carrying his wife and a dog maybe named "Merlot" by now.

He couldn't just sit here.

Why are you just letting your life happen to you? Why don't you do something? But what? If the boat is sinking, you do something, anything you can think of, right?

But was his boat really sinking? No, it wasn't. It was under him steady, a heartbeat, *lap*, *lap*, *rock*, *rock*. It wasn't going anywhere. His life was going on.

He realized his cheeks were wet. He was crying again. A slow, steady leak. Jesus.

~~~

He must've fallen asleep in his chair. A dog was barking and he sat up fast and looked around. The world came back to him clear and empty. It was his phone, his stupid ringtone. His heart was pounding.

Daniel answered his phone. It was Sleep. "Merry Christmas, man," Sleep said.

"You too." He had to clear his throat. It was all froggy.

"You all right?"

"Hanging in. You?"

"My mom's not good," Sleep said. "I had to bring her home from the hospital. The cancer spread. I had to put her on hospice.
~~~

I mean, they told me to at the hospital, that it would be easier that way. But I feel like I'm giving up on her."

"That's hard."

"So I have to stay here, stick it out with her, take care of things. My sister's coming too. The doctor said she has maybe six months. Maybe more. They don't know anything."

"Good that your sister's coming."

"She can only stay for a little while. She'll go back and forth. She's an hour and a half away. She's got kids in high school still. Her husband can help, but she can't be here to stay. That's on me."

Daniel nodded. It was stupid to nod on a phone, but he couldn't think of what to say.

"Can you keep an eye on things for me, water my cactus?" Sleep said.

He had one prickly little cactus. It looked like a porcupine in a pot. It didn't even look alive.

"Sure," Daniel told him. "No problem."

"I need your help," Sleep said.

"Whatever you need."

"I have to rent my boat out. I could be up here a year. I could use the money. My mom doesn't have much. Just Medicare. And that's not going to cut it."

"You want me to put up a for-rent sign?"

"Nah. I don't really want a stranger. Maybe you know someone?"

"Not really."

"You can spread the word around the docks."

"Okay."

"It's driving me crazy, being here, already. I got nothing to do except sit around and think and worry and watch my mom go downhill."

"Downhill," Daniel said. The word hung in the air even after they'd quit talking. Daniel sat staring at the dusty parking lot, the thick vegetation beyond. It was getting hot. The palms shimmered and a buzzing rose up from them.

Downhill.

When Timmy was a toddler, they had a hill nearby that they went sledding on in winter. One summer, Timmy wanted to go sledding. He couldn't understand why there wasn't snow anymore or why the sled wouldn't work on grass. So Daniel took him to the top of the hill and they both lay down with their arms tucked into their chests, and they rolled down the hill like logs. Timmy got up at the bottom of the hill with grass clinging to his cheek, his knees smudged, his smile wide.

"Da," he said. That's what he called Daniel back then.

Yeah. Daniel remembered that day. They'd held hands and climbed the hill again and again. They'd made the world spin.

MARY

Mary hurried, tossing all her clothes into her bag. Ron hadn't given them much leeway with travel plans. *He didn't leave a lot of room for discussion, did he? Just "yes" or "no."* But they'd had enough discussions over the years, enough time to think it all through. Now it was time for action. She thought of what she'd told Kipper about wasting so much of her life getting ready. Now she thought, *There's no such thing as ready, and there's no more time to waste.*

She pulled Larkin's presents out from under the bed. They wouldn't fit in her checked bag, so she packed them in her carry-on. When would she have a chance to give them to her? *I can't think about that.*

She looked around the empty igloo one last time. Someone else would be living in here soon. It wouldn't be her room anymore. She placed the key on the bureau with a big tip for the housekeeper. Ron had taken her credit card to go pay her bill because she didn't want to go into the lobby, see Alice or Stephen or Ollie. No, not Ollie. Mary didn't want to have to explain herself to Ollie. She imagined Ollie's eyes assessing her. *She would be disappointed in me*, Mary thought.

But you can't just hurry out without saying goodbye. That's so wrong.

When Ron came back, he took her bag and walked out of the

room. She hung back for a moment. Took one last look, then closed the front door behind her. The sound of the door clicking shut made her want to cry. It was so final. Yet things seemed so, well, unfinal. So in the middle. She tried not to look at the flowers lining the path as Ron dragged her bag along. She focused on the ground and the sound of the rolling wheels of her suitcase. She didn't allow herself to look back at the pool. The dolphin fountain.

I won't cry.

She did force herself to open the lobby door to see if Ollie was there. *I can't be rude to that lovely woman.* But the office was empty. The phone was ringing, but no one was there to answer it.

Mary drove back to the airport with Ron next to her. He was busy on his phone the whole time. Texting Joanna. Evidently Alexandra had been trying to contact her. Ron kept sighing. Mary didn't ask what it was all about.

The Florida landscape swept by. Small houses with scruffy lawns, large Spanish-style houses with tiled roofs, people in pastel outfits bicycling on the sidewalks, medians lined with palm trees, then the bridge arching over the bay, boats carving through the water leaving white wakes, the endless vista of mangrove islands. Mary focused on the road and the traffic—landscapers' trucks, convertibles, SUVs. Heat shimmered off the road. Cows stood in a field. High walls surrounded a gated community. She felt like she was in a chute rocketing forward into the future.

They were on a highway. Then they were exiting, funneling through the winding roads for rental car returns. She parked the car, handed in the paperwork, and they trudged silently through the exhaust-laden heat, entered the bustle of the airport, got their boarding passes, made their way through security, sat down on plastic-molded seats at the gate. They'd barely spoken a word.

Mary opened the book she was reading. She read the same line five times. She wasn't taking it in.

Ron bought a thick, glossy home magazine. He started flipping through it.

"I have to see what the competition is up to," he said.

Mary could smell the ink wafting from the pages. She glanced over. He was reading an article about a house that looked like it was made of stainless steel.

"Look at this," he said, pointing. "So cool."

The windows were narrow slit openings in shiny walls.

"It looks like a toaster flipped on its side," she said.

"Huh," he said.

The interior was vaulted and cavernous and the furniture was clustered in the center of the rooms as if huddling for warmth. *Where are the toaster heating coils?* Mary half smiled to herself. A huge Christmas tree loomed in the living room surrounded by ornately wrapped white-and-gold boxes that Mary knew were empty. Outside the French doors, lines of boxwoods were trimmed into topiaries.

Kipper would hate that, Mary thought.

She'd texted him before she left the hotel. She'd snuck into the bathroom with her phone, so Ron didn't see her. She wasn't planning on saying a word about Kipper to Ron. He'd be jealous. He'd be raving. She'd kissed Kipper. She'd actually kissed another man. She'd liked it too. She felt a shiver run up the back of her neck.

That was her secret, and she'd keep it close.

She'd texted—Had to leave early. Thank you for everything. I loved it all.

Yes, she had.

Ron patted her knee, left his hand there.

She fumbled in her carry-on bag for a mint, but she couldn't find one. Her fingers hit the pad Ollie had given her. She felt a stab of sadness. She'd miss Ollie. And Mary wouldn't get to write more of her letters today like she had planned to or do her storyboard. Well, she'd do a storyboard when she got home—for her and Ron's new house! She took out the pad and a pen. Maybe she'd scribble some ideas down now.

"What are you doing?" Ron said.

"Planning the future. Dreaming," Mary said. Although "dreaming" didn't seem like quite the right word for it.

"Sweet," he said. He went back to his article.

Her hand rested on the pad. She couldn't think of a thing to write. It was all suddenly so confusing when she thought of the choices ahead. Did she want white kitchen cabinets? Subway tile or sea glass tile? Neutrals or colors? Patterns or solids? She couldn't picture any of it. The only thing that was in her head was the toaster house.

Don't think about that.

She thought of the piece of art that Ollie had given her. It was pressed into the back pages of this pad along with the feather. She wanted to pull it out and look at it, but she couldn't. *Who's that guy?* Ron would say, pointing at Kipper.

What could she tell him? *A fisherman. A guide who took us places. A man who makes butterfly gardens.*

The memories will fade, she told herself. *Just keep going. One step at a time, you'll find your way back to yourself and your real life.*

What would she do with Ollie's painting, though? Nothing. She'd leave it hidden where it was.

She closed the pad. She looked out the vast windows at the tarmac and the palm trees waving in the blue sky and listened to the airport speakers crank out orchestral Christmas carols. She felt some movement in the seats across the aisle from her. She looked over. It was a woman with a dog on a leash. The woman was sitting down. The dog was looking at her. His tail wagged.

"Tripod," she said.

The woman looked at her.

"You must be Addie," Mary said.

Addie frowned. Ron looked up from his magazine.

"I know your husband." The word "husband" sounded odd. This woman didn't look like what Mary had expected. Mary had envisioned a wispy type of woman with big blue eyes, kind of floating and ethereal. That was ridiculous. Addie was a solid middle-aged woman in cuffed jeans, sneakers, and a sweatshirt that said NIKE.

"Ah." Addie considered Mary, her eyes narrowed. Mary realized that she was wondering if Mary was Kipper's girlfriend.

"My granddaughter and I went out on a fishing trip with him," Mary explained. "My granddaughter fell in love with Tripod. Your husband was very good to her. He let her play with Tripod. It made her vacation." She was hurrying to explain her relationship with Kipper so that Ron didn't get jealous. She realized, too, that Ron didn't even know that CC and Larkin were with her in Florida. He didn't know anything, and he hadn't asked. Well, to be fair to him, there just hadn't been time.

"Daniel was always good with kids," Addie said.

"He listens well," Mary said.

"He always had more patience than me."

"This is Ron," Mary said, gesturing toward him. She was going to say *my fiancé* but didn't. Addie and Ron nodded at each other. A stiffness had come over Ron. His magazine had been open to one page for a while.

Mary knew she should shut up, but she kept talking. It felt good to talk about Kipper. "I barely know my granddaughter, so it really helped to have Tripod around. It kind of broke the ice."

"Oh, that's a shame."

"They live far away. Well, not that far. It's just complicated."

Why am I telling this to a perfect stranger?

"My daughter is, well, she's difficult," Mary said. "No, that's not it. I think I've been a disappointment to her. She wants me to be more myself in life. And I guess I want her to be more herself. So it's hard." It didn't sound hard, though, as she was saying it. It seemed to make perfect sense.

She could feel Ron listening.

"I mean, I miss how it was between us when she was young. We used to sing that Winnie the Pooh song about being friends forever."

Mary was talking like she was in a daze, rattling on. But she kind of felt like she knew Addie. Because she knew Kipper? That was weird thinking, but why else was she opening up?

"I sang that with my son too," Addie said.

"I thought that she would never stop loving me. We seemed like we were in it together for life. Then she grew up." Mary stopped. "Now she and my granddaughter cut their vacation short with me to go to Disney for some Star Wars ride," she said. She sighed.

"That's too bad," Addie said.

"I figure I'll get another chance. Life keeps giving us second chances, doesn't it?"

Addie looked down.

"Oh," Mary said. She shouldn't have said that. Timmy was gone, and Addie had no second chance with him. Now looking at Addie's bowed head, Mary saw a little bit of gray in her roots. She wanted to say something else, but what?

Addie looked up at her then and smiled. A tired smile. But brave, Mary thought. *This woman is brave.*

Mary wished then that she could have a second chance at Christmas Eve. She could have sat down next to CC, touched her arm, maybe even given her a hug, talked about Winnie the Pooh. Something. Anything different from what she had done.

Addie reached out to pat Tripod's head, but Tripod winced away.

"Tripod is such a good dog," Mary told her.

"His name is Winston now."

"Winston?"

"After Churchill."

"Well, I figured. There aren't too many other Winstons around."

"At least I think it's Winston. I was also thinking Ulysses. Or maybe Merlot. I keep coming back to that."

Tripod was pulling to come see Mary, and Addie was holding his leash short so he couldn't go. Mary was aware of Ron sitting back in his chair. He was allergic to dogs. His body shifted away as he flipped a page in the magazine. Another room. A master bedroom.

Mary thought of how, when she and Ron got their new house, they'd go buy a bed together. Ron liked firm and she liked soft. They'd talked about getting the kind of bed that had those separate controls on it. The bed in the picture was massive with pillars on each corner. It looked like a castle. Tons of pillows crowded the bed. *Fluffocating*, she thought, and smiled. Where was Larkin now? Mary missed her so much already.

She glanced at Ron. He had his tortoiseshell reading glasses on. They made him look intellectual and sexy. His legs were crossed. He could look dressed up even in jeans. His long fingers were splayed across the page. She wondered what he was thinking about, looking at that bed. She felt the air-conditioning in the terminal blowing cold. A woman announced on the PA system that someone had parked their car in the wrong place and was going to get towed if they didn't move it.

Addie let Tripod's leash slack a bit, and Tripod rushed over to Mary. Mary touched his head, his sweet face. "Oh, Tripod," she said. "Hello."

Ron jerked away and brushed a hair off his pants. "Don't," he said, pushing Tripod with his leg. Tripod fell backward and scrambled back to his feet. *Oh*, Mary thought.

"It's okay," Mary said to Tripod, but Tripod looked embarrassed.

"Don't let it . . ." Ron pointed at Tripod.

A bit of spit came out of Ron's mouth and landed on Mary's pant leg. She froze for a second. Then she wiped the spot over and over as Addie pulled Tripod away.

Tripod barked. He was trying to get closer to Mary again. His bark was high-pitched and sharp and it echoed in the building.

"I hope he doesn't do this a lot. There's going to be no barking allowed," Addie said. "Winston, stop this instant." She pointed at him with her finger. Tripod kept it up.

Ron shook his head. "Maybe you should get a crate," he said. "They say it's good to crate your dog."

"Oh, I don't like cages," Mary said.

Addie looked down. "I thought the dog . . . Well, I didn't know, but I somehow thought the dog would make me feel like I had my son back. He was my son's dog. But he's just a dog, isn't he?"

"I don't think he is to your husband."

"Maybe he's more of a dog person than me." Addie said it kind of like a question to Mary.

Tripod was barking so hard that every time he barked his three paws lifted off the ground. It was almost funny, almost made Mary want to cry.

Tripod was pulling on the leash now, running in one direction and then the other. Mary could tell he didn't know which way to run. He just wanted to run. If he got free, Mary thought, he'd be through the airport like a shot, out the door, and then he'd be one of those dogs on the side of the highway sniffing the ground, running frantically, trying to figure out which way was home. Her breath caught. *Don't think about that.*

The loudspeaker announcement came on to warn people that unattended bags would be confiscated.

"Let me try holding him for a minute," Mary said. Tripod hopped over to Mary. He sniffed her pocketbook, pushing it with his nose. Ron angled his body away.

"What?" Mary asked Tripod.

But Tripod was snuffling and snorting. He pawed at the bag, then he tried to dig around it, his paws slipping and sliding on the linoleum. He whined.

"Maybe he smells food in there?" Addie said.

Mary shook her head. "I don't have any," she said.

She unzipped her bag, and Tripod's head disappeared into it. His tail quivered. His head emerged from the bag, the fur on it mussed, his one ear flapped back. Blanket was in his mouth.

"Oh," Mary said. Her eyes filled with tears.

"He shouldn't," Addie said. But both women just watched him as he put Blanket between his paws and lay down, his head resting on the stuffed animal like it was the best pillow on earth.

The airline attendant came on the loudspeaker and started calling for people who needed assistance and people with small children to board.

"Can you hold him a bit longer while I hit the restroom?" Addie asked Mary.

"Sure."

Mary held the leash tight. Addie walked away. Mary watched her walk. There was a downtroddenness to her shoes. She wore them out on the inside more than the outsides. Her shoulders were slumped.

Mary was aware of Ron staring at her.

She wondered what he was seeing. *The whole of me?* She thought suddenly of her mother's face. She only had a few memories of her mother. Mary's mother's face used to crinkle up whenever she smiled. "Like a piece of paper," her mother used to tell Mary. "I'm like a story with all the words laid right smack out on it. Every single one true." What would Mary's life have been like if her mother had lived? Who would she have turned out to be if she were raised by a woman like that? And what would CC's life be like if she had a grandmother like that? Or a mother like that. Was it too late for Mary to be that kind of woman?

Mary wondered what story was on her own face now. She looked at Tripod, and Tripod looked up at her. He was very quiet, very still. His eyes were dark with one gold star speckle in his right eye. Like a bit of sunshine pie.

Ron stood up. Mary looked at him. He said, "I'll go get us a place in line." He always liked to be ahead of people. Although they were all going to the same place at the same time. Why rush?

Mary sat holding Tripod's leash. She could almost feel the leash quivering with emotion.

"Go ahead," she told Ron. "There's something I have to do."

"What?" he said. He got his things together.

"Something I have to try, anyway," she said. It was a risk. Of course it was. What wasn't? *And what's the point of my life if I don't put my heart on the line?* she thought. *I've been trying to live safe for a long time now, and what has it gotten me?*

She felt the leash tug in her hand. Tripod was standing up, looking right and left. Searching for something. *Addie? No*, Mary thought. *Not Addie.*

Mary looked at all the people milling about, standing in line, waiting. All of them traveling places, some of them going home. She could see Tripod's whole body shaking. He was scared. She could tell. Well, she was scared too.

"I'm not coming with you," Mary told Ron. Her voice came out measured and calm, but her heart was leaping in her chest.

"What?"

"I'm not angry at you," Mary said.

"What are you talking about?"

She pulled the diamond ring off her finger. She stood up and put it into his hand. His palm felt soft, and she thought for a moment, *What are you doing?* but then she said, "I'm not going to marry you, Ron."

Tripod looked up at her. She looked down at the dog. She swore Tripod was smiling.

"Mare?" Ron said.

She looked at him. He was so handsome. Her heart felt like it was bouncing off the wall of her chest. He glanced behind him. They were calling his boarding group. She looked at Ron, right into his denim-blue eyes. "Go," she said. *Go live your life*, she thought. *And I'll live mine.*

He shook his head. "Mary, don't pull one of these."

She felt like the floor was tilting. Everything looked blurry. Was the world opening up like a chasm? No, she was still standing. She shook her head.

"What's gotten into you?" he said.

She smiled at him sadly. She felt a deep ache like a bruise on her heart. The Ron bruise. It would always be there. She knew it. Some bruises stayed with you. Even years from now, if she touched it, she would feel it, she would flinch. But everyone had those.

She thought of Zelda. She thought of her mother. She thought, *This is the true story of me*. She suddenly had a buoyant feeling, like she was breathing helium instead of air, in and out, lifting off the floor.

"You're going to regret this," he said. "You know you will."

She bit her lip and said nothing.

He turned and went then. She watched how he held his shoulders firm and walked with purposeful steps. He didn't look back. She realized she was holding her breath. She watched him move forward one step after another in the line. She watched him disappear into the tunnel.

I made this happen, she thought. Yes, that was true. She was someone who made things happen in her life.

Mary walked toward the restroom, Tripod hopping alongside her. He had Blanket held in his mouth. She wanted to run, make a break for the front door, but she forced herself to walk. Addie was just coming out. They stood together at the doorway looking at each other. People were going in and out of the door. It smelled like disinfectant, like Cinnabons. Mary wanted to be outside breathing the fresh salt air.

Mary said, "You don't really want him." She didn't say it as a question.

DANIEL

Daniel was sitting on his deck chair staring at nothing. He had a charter booked for tomorrow morning. That was good. He'd go check on his boat, get it gassed up. He'd neaten up his tackle box. Maybe he'd put new line on the poles. He could use up a couple of hours anyway. That's how he'd have to do it from now on. Just fill up the days. Otherwise, he'd drift. He saw it happening to people down here all the time. Soon they were sitting at the bar stool at nine o'clock in the morning with a Bud in front of them. Pissing the years away.

He'd work. That's what he'd do. And maybe he'd go back to the VFW. The pancake thing was good today. Funny how giving made him feel fuller. That didn't really make sense. It should make you feel emptier, shouldn't it? But it didn't. He'd have to give some more. He thought of that guy he'd read about, somebody's grandfather, who went into hospitals just to help out holding the babies. And the people who went into schools with their dogs and helped the kids who were too shy to read or had trouble reading, but they would read to the dogs, and the dogs would lie there and listen. Tripod would have loved to be read to. And Daniel might have liked it too. Although it might have been hard to face those kids.

But what are you going to do—flinch away from hard for the rest of your life? You should have turned in the direction of the skid more, he thought now. *You should have turned right into the pain instead of turning away.* That's how you stop a skid. Anybody knew that. It was a law of something—wasn't it?

He shifted in his chair. He looked up at the blue sky, the palm trees swaying. The world looked crisp and focused. Every leaf was outlined against the blue sky. He looked down at his phone that he'd been holding in his lap. He reread Mary's text.

How could she just leave? Not even a goodbye. Something must have happened. He'd never see her again. He was suddenly aware of his heart as a pump, just a mechanical pump he had to keep going. A rusting, ageing thing. For the past few days, it had felt like more. A soft, electrical something or other. *I wish I had Tripod back. Try-Hard. I should have tried harder.* His heart pounded. The damn pump. No, the damn electrical thing. Whatever it was, it felt like it took up his whole chest.

Addie would be boarding now. Or was she already gone? Gone. That was a bad word. His hands moved on his phone. He was scrolling. He was pressing Addie's name. *What am I doing?* Her phone was ringing. His hands were shaking. He would ask her to let the dog stay. He'd beg her. He'd drive up to the airport right now. He'd pay for her to get another flight. What had he been thinking letting that dog go?

The phone rang two times. Three. Four. Then it went to her voicemail, saying, "Please leave me a message."

He dialed again. Same thing. And again.

His body felt wooden. Like he'd turned into one of his driftwood people. *Go on now with your life*, he told himself. *You blew your chance.*

He drove to his fishing boat and spent an hour cleaning it, although it was already clean. The chrome was shining. The fiberglass gleamed. He really worked at it. His fingers were raw. *Good job*, he told himself. *Give yourself a reward now.* He'd go back to the houseboat and have a beer. Just one. He'd make it last. Maybe he'd get his old harmonica out. He hadn't taken that thing out in a year. He was just starting to teach Timmy to play when Timmy left. God, he wondered if he remembered anything. If his lips remembered.

He thought about kissing Mary. His lips remembered how to do that.

He drove back to the houseboat. There was that black swath he'd painted. It seemed like he'd done that a long time ago, but it was just days. He didn't think he really wanted to paint the whole boat black anymore. *Maybe I'll paint it aqua. Something wild.* Well, he'd go look at color swatches tomorrow. That guy behind the counter would laugh at him again. Daniel didn't care. It would be good to have a project. He liked the idea of painting slowly, carefully, each stroke a layer of clean and new.

He sat on his chair. He kept his eyes on the horizon. He sipped his beer. It was cold and beaded with sweat. He'd squeezed a slice of lime into it, and he liked the tang of sour that touched his lips and then the peaty, dark taste of the beer. He focused on that. One sip. Then two. He licked a tiny piece of lime off his lips. He thought about Mary, a life with her in it. That wouldn't happen. Probably she'd gone back to the asshole boyfriend. He'd never know. She would always be in his brain as one of those idea-only people. A maybe girl.

Sleep had told him that he named his boat that because he'd once had a maybe girl, and he'd "chickened out on her." He'd always regretted it. "I wanted her to stay an idea. I kept her at a distance. I thought reality would be a downner, the end of a dream." And so, he'd let her go. Well, people did that. Probably that's what Sleep had spent his life running away from. But when Sleep came down here, he'd bought the boat and that boat had become his maybe girl. At least Sleep had made *that* dream come true.

Daniel thought about Mary. She was a person who didn't even know how interesting she was. She probably had miles of trails in her leading to fields, to clearings, to forests. He thought of walking down those sunny trails. The sweet smell of trees. He'd never been haunted by any woman. Never really dreamed of one. All he'd ever known was Addie.

He put his beer down on an old coaster leftover from the people who used to own the boat. It said, WE ARE BEACH PEOPLE. He should go to the beach, become a beach person. Maybe tomorrow evening. He liked to go at sunset. He'd bring his book and settle into a beach chair, wear his straw hat that made him feel like an old salt, his faded blue bathing suit.

Maybe I'll cut loose this houseboat one of these days, go see some of the world. Now, that was an interesting idea. He'd never been the traveling kind. Always liked his own backyard. But he'd come to love how changeable the sea was. How one day there'd be a hundred pelicans on the beach, but the next day, they'd be gone. Some days, dolphins played around his boat. Then other days, the sea was deserted. One day, the wind chopped up the waves and another day, knocked them down. Change was a thing here. You could count on it more than sameness.

He got up and went inside and pulled out the drawer in the kitchen. There was the carving of Timmy's face. He caught his breath. He held it in his palms. He placed the carving where he could see it, right there on his shelf, looking out on the interior of the boat. *Watch over me.*

He went into his bedroom. He found his harmonica tucked

away in the closet. It was in a blue velvet bag closed with a pull string. He got it out. Maybe he'd teach himself something new. He went out on the deck again and sat back down. He started poking around at notes, breathing in some sounds, breathing out. Moving it slowly around his lips. He closed his eyes. Yes, he remembered. It was almost like kissing. He thought of Mary. The metal felt cool against his lips.

He was making a tune. *You are my sunshine*, he heard. *You are my sunshine, my only sunshine.* Those yearning notes. *You make me happy.* Nope—he got that high note wrong. He felt around with his mouth for the right note. Yes, there it was. *Happy.* He heard a car, the pop of a car door. No, it was the note piercing the sky. No, it was a high-pitched howl. Someone had a dog.

He opened his eyes. Someone was walking toward him. He blinked. He pulled the harmonica down from his lips and looked at it in his lap. This was weird. Had he conjured something up playing that song? Was this a mirage? His heart thumped. He didn't want to look up and see the empty lot, no cars, no people, no nothing.

MARY

Mary stood on the dock with Tripod.

"Are you real?" Kipper said.

"Winston was not happy. And neither was Merlot," Mary said.

Kipper cocked his head.

She said, "This dog is named Tripod and that's all there is to it. He's your dog. And you're his person. And Addie, well, she's a good woman. I think she still loves you."

He bit his lip.

"Is it okay?" Mary asked. "I mean, I took a chance."

"Thank you," he said, looking at her, then looking at the dog.

He put down the ramp he'd made for Tripod to get on the houseboat from the dock, and Tripod trotted down it.

"No trampoline for this boat?" Mary asked.

"He doesn't need it. This boat rides so high in the water."

He rubbed Tripod's ears. Tripod rolled over on his back and Kipper ran his hand over his belly, then he reached out to Mary and helped her onto the boat.

"I think the look on your face was the best Christmas gift I ever got," she told him. He still looked like he was lit up from the inside.

He nodded once. "I owe you. How about I buy you a beer?"

She smiled.

He went below and got her a bottle. She sat on his other deck chair and took a long sip. "Good," she said. "Great, actually."

They sat in silence. There was all that was unsaid between them. Mary didn't want to explain about Ron, what she had done. She didn't want to think about it now. She looked at the dock, the seaweed clinging to the pilings. She smelled drying fish and creosote. She watched a gull turn into the breeze. She breathed.

Tripod snored gently. He was worn-out.

The boat rocked. The sun was starting to slant, and the light was getting that golden cast to it.

"What does that mean, 'The Maybe Girl'?" Mary said, staring at the side of Sleep's boat.

"It's about what's possible."

"Oh, is that all?"

She met his eyes, and they both smiled shyly. He told her then about Sleep's mom and how Sleep wanted to rent out the boat.

Mary looked at the boat as it sat in its slip. It looked like a fairy-tale house, so small and compact, bobbing gently, a faded blue flag waving off its back. Or stern or whatever you were supposed to call it.

"If I lived there," Mary said, "I'd have to learn boat language. Like port is left. I always have to think first—'port' has four letters and so does 'left.' I'd have to memorize things like that. At least it isn't a sailboat. That's so confusing with all the names for the different sails. I don't think I could ever learn that."

"You'd be surprised," he said.

They both sat there considering the boat.

"What's the difference between 'bow' and 'prow'?" Mary asked.

"The bow is the whole front. The prow is the very front edge."

"If I lived there, I'd put a hammock on the bow."

"Oh yeah?"

"One of those macramé beige ones with the fringe."

"Uh-huh."

"And some plants in pots all around it for a sense of enclosure, so you'd kind of feel like you were in a secret spot. Maybe use those tropical plants with the big leaves that look like hands. And that plant with the purple flowers."

"Bougainvillea." He looked at her.

"And maybe hang one of those sailcloth doohickies over it to give it some nice shade. What are those called?"

"I don't know. Sailcloth doohickies?"

Mary smiled at him. He smiled back at her.

"I wonder if I'd like to live there," she said.

"Are you serious?" he asked.

"I don't want to go home." When had she decided this? But she must've, because she said it like she meant it. She'd felt so free leaving the airport, not getting on that plane. "All my clothes are flying to New York right now, which is making me so happy I can't even tell you. I really do have to start from scratch now. I don't even have a toothbrush. Why not start here?" She pointed at the houseboat.

Do I really want to live on a boat? Why not? She felt a thrill of excitement run through her.

Kipper was looking at her, listening hard. "I thought you didn't like to go up and down," he said. "I thought you wanted a solid foundation under you and something to look out at from your kitchen window. Besides all this nothing." He swept his hand around.

"Well, it wasn't so bad on your boat last night. I didn't get seasick even with that storm."

"No."

"I would probably get used to it."

"Uh-huh."

"And all this is not really nothing, is it?"

He smiled. "Do you want to go look at it?" he asked her.

She looked at the cut over his eye. It was starting to heal in a crusty, jagged way. He'd probably always have a scar, a pale path through his eyebrow. She wondered if he minded. Some scars you don't. Some you grow attached to.

She nodded. They got up. She said, "You told me there was no such thing as safe."

"I think I did."

"And that's not so terrible, is it?"

He looked at her. "It has its moments."

He went inside and got the key, and then she followed him. They all walked over to *The Maybe Girl*, Kipper carrying the dog ramp. He put it down for Tripod, and Tripod hopped onto it and made his way up it.

A wounded dog and his wounded guy, Mary thought. *Not too wounded to find a way, though.*

Kipper got onto the boat and then stretched out his hand to help her on. She felt the warmth of his hand, the calluses. Did he hold on to her hand an extra second?

The back deck of the boat had two wooden chairs and a little table. *Fine,* she thought. Maybe an outdoor rug? A simple strand of shells hanging next to the door with a little sign that said BEACH HOUSE DOORBELL? Yes, she could collect the shells herself on the beach, the ones with holes in them. Then she could tie them into a kind of chime. She could see it.

He took a key out of his pocket.

She said, "Can I?"

He stopped. "Sure, if you want to." He held out the key to her.

"I think I need to," she said. Her voice was shaking. What was this? She held the key in her hand and looked at it. It was a silver key with a cork at the end of it.

"It'll float if you drop it in the water," he said.

"That's good," she said, and opened the door.

It was decidedly a guy place. Knotty pine cabinets lined one wall. Jimmy Buffett CDs were stacked next to an old black radio. Some yellow-raincoated sailor figurines were lined up on a shelf. One was obviously hand carved. Mary went over and touched it. She smiled when she discovered Sleep had glued it down so it wouldn't tip. A lifeboat ring hung on the wall. It said AHOY.

Nothing matched. The seat cushions on the benches around Sleep's kitchen table were covered in beige gingham checks. The curtains were sprinkled with images of red utensils. The living area had a couch upholstered with fabric that was a melee of green palm fronds. The master bedroom had a black-and-white geometric quilt.

There were two small bedrooms. One had bunk beds. *Oh*, Mary thought, *Larkin will love this.*

Light streamed through the boat windows.

She'd have some sprucing up to do.

"This will be fun," she told Kipper, a kind of merriness in her throat, a giddiness in her heart.

OLLIE

It was the day after Christmas, the day when all the shoppers were returning sweaters and foot massagers and eating leftover turkey sandwiches. Ollie woke to a doctor prodding her. She read his name tag—DR. PLEASURE. Of all names. He looked like a penguin. But he told her she could go home, which filled her eyes with tears.

They were worried she'd had a stroke, but now they thought she'd just been dehydrated.

"Are you taking care of yourself?" Dr. Pleasure asked.

Ollie shrugged.

"How's your stress level?"

"Ha," she said.

"I want you to go see an eye specialist about that shadow. Here's a name of someone," he scribbled something on a pad, ripped the sheet out, and gave it to her. "It could be nothing. Floaters happen when we age. But I want you to get checked out."

She nodded.

"Drink a lot of water. Put your feet up. Relax." And he was gone.

Ollie rubbed the age spot on her wrist, the one that looked like an upside-down smile. It hurt a little how hard she was pressing, but she wanted to feel pain right now, the grate of skin on bone, the hard push of her stiff finger. She couldn't allow herself to relax. *My life is going to be bulldozed.* She could hear the grind of the gears starting up, the ground being turned over and peeled back, the raw gape of roots and black dirt and rocks. She'd be in there with the earth and the worms, getting crushed by the big tread wheels and shoved into a pile, the trees cracking, the roots upheaved.

Oh, the birds would be yelling at her. She couldn't bear it. *Just plow me under too, Al*, she wanted to yell. *Build your concrete building on my bones.*

Her heart pounded. She had to relax.

I wish I'd had children, she thought like a stab in her chest. It was a wish she never voiced now. Wilson hadn't wanted any, and she'd argued and begged and he'd started sleeping in the other bed then. They hadn't touched in years and years. How many? Oh, her children would be in their forties now. Grown-up people who could have taken over for her. *Ma*, she could almost hear her son saying, *we need to upgrade.* He would have looked like John-John Kennedy with that shock of dark hair and his face breaking into laugh lines. Both her children would have had her laugh lines. Her daughter would have had fine hands. Maybe she would have played the piano.

But all Ollie had were her birds. Her stomach ached, or was that her womb? That was a weird word. What did it look like, her unused womb? A helpless sac that could never be filled. She'd spent her life loving a hotel. Well, that wasn't a wasted life, was it? She'd fed others, sheltered them, shown them a bit of nature. She'd watched them smile, heard them laugh. She'd made her tiny piece of the world a beautiful place. That was the whole point, wasn't it?

She wondered if Mr. Emerson ever felt alone. If he built over his aloneness, condo after condo. Didn't he feel lonely, too, in the Gold Institute?

Which gave her an idea.

Ollie's friend Frances came to pick her up from the hospital. Frances helped Ollie into her old Buick. The thing was bouncy and drove as heavy as a cruise ship. Frances had to sit on a pillow to see over the steering wheel. Not even a thin pillow. One of those thick cushions you put on patio furniture. She barely paid attention to the road when she drove. Ollie hated to ride with her. Ollie was constantly pushing the floorboards to brake, or saying, "I think, up ahead, that might be a red light. You might want to . . ." Frances believed that stop signs really didn't apply to her. "They're for people with slow reactions."

Now Frances said, "I fed your birds last night."

"Oh?" Ollie said. "Well, thank you."

Frances was usually skittish around her birds. She kept her distance. Ollie felt that Frances was a bit jealous of them, of Ollie's intimacy with them. Frances actually was a generous person but gruff about showing emotion. "How do you *do* that?" she'd ask about getting the birds to land on Ollie's shoulder.

"I'll teach you," Ollie would say, and Frances would always say, "Another time."

"They were worried about you not being there," Frances said, staring blankly out at the road ahead.

Ollie looked over at her. Frances was biting her lip.

"I find that if I move slowly and maybe hum a little tune, they relax. Sometimes it takes them a while to trust," Ollie said.

"Oh, Ollie," Frances said. Frances's voice was suddenly strained, and she clutched the steering wheel so hard the knobs of her knuckles were standing out white.

Ollie had felt the prickliness of Frances since she came to pick her up. Frances was overly brusque, harsh even, with the way she'd tossed Ollie's bag of fresh clothes she'd brought onto the bed.

I'm sorry I got old, Ollie wanted to tell her. She and Frances were the same age. "I'll be okay," she told her instead. Even though she was thinking, *Oh my, why is my body giving out? And what if I DO have a stroke, and I become paralyzed or have half my face drooping down and can never smile again except only a half smile and I can't use my right side at all and I won't be able to draw or hold a paintbrush? I'll have to do weird abstract drawings with my left hand or just give up altogether and watch daytime TV all day, and I'll have to walk with a walker, and what if I can only eat Jell-O for the rest of my life? Or what if I go blind and I have to learn braille and get a Seeing Eye dog and tap around with a cane? Oh, I can't think about all that now. I have to manage my stress levels. But I have to think about Mr. Emerson too. Mr. Lying Emerson.*

Frances glanced over at her and smiled a thin smile, a kind of apology, Ollie thought.

They passed a Piggly Wiggly, then a McDonald's, then a urology clinic. Frances meandered slowly in and out of traffic. Some kid in a black Mustang beeped at them, yelled something out his window and whizzed past.

In a park, people were strolling around pop-up tents.

"Oh look, a farmers' market!" Ollie said. She loved farmers' markets—the stacks of lumpy breads, the peppery bunches of arugula. She suddenly realized how hungry she was.

"Let's pull in," she said.

"I think we should get you home."

Ollie eyes filled up with sudden tears. *Over a farmers' market?*

"But we'll never have this chance again," she told Frances. "I mean, this particular day." She meant this just-getting-out-of-the-hospital day. She wanted to clutch the moment. The tents looked so fragile, like they could lift up and fly away with a big gust of wind, all the bushel baskets of daisies tipping and the blossoms taking off into the clouds. "Just for a minute?" Ollie asked.

"Oh, all right." Frances made a hard right and they jounced into a dusty lot. They sat for a moment after they parked, the air-conditioning blowing mildly.

"Are you sure you're up for this?" Frances asked.

"I was lying in that hospital bed thinking that I should have grown raspberry bushes," Ollie said. "Do you think they'd grow at the hotel? Isn't it amazing how prickly the stalks are and how tender and bruisy those little clusters of berries are? Like the bush has to protect the fruit. I love raspberries, and I only buy them on special occasions. Why do I do that?"

Frances looked at her. "You're right, Ol. Let's go buy us some raspberries. We can eat them warm right out of the little carton."

The line was long at the key lime milkshake truck. A man was playing a guitar and singing Tom Petty. *Gonna keep this world from draggin' me down. Gonna stand my ground.*

Ollie hadn't told Frances anything about Al. Well, she hadn't had time to. It had all happened so fast. But that wasn't entirely true, was it? She'd kept it from Frances because she thought Frances would feel jealous. They had been united in their aloneness. Frances's husband had died ten years ago. Frances "dated," if you could call it that. She did ballroom dancing with her friend Alonzo, who had a waxed mustache and adored her, but she said, "I just string him along to have a dance partner."

"Who could kiss a man like that?" she asked Ollie. "His walk is more like a cha-cha than anything else."

Then she mimicked his walk like a hurried waddle with her butt sticking out and they laughed and laughed. And then there was Herbie. "The Love Bug," she called him. She cooked him a meal once a week. Then they watched something from Netflix on her couch. He was comfy, she said, to lean against. When he kissed her, he made a humming noise, *mmm*, *mmm*, *mmm*. Frances could only kiss him so long before she got the giggles.

"Let's sit down," Ollie said. There was an empty tent with folding chairs. A few other people were eating ice-cream cones.

"That shade feels good," Frances said. She took out the box of raspberries they'd bought from the little organic stand, the girl so cute with no makeup and her sweet round face under her green handkerchief, a sprig of something—was it parsley?—woven into a braid in her brown hair.

Frances held the box out to Ollie. "Age before beauty," she said. Frances was exactly one month younger than Ollie, and she never let Ollie forget it.

Ollie smiled at her, took a couple gently, put them in her palm, and put one on her tongue. "It tastes like summertime. Like dreams of summertime."

"Yes," Frances agreed.

Ollie said, "How was your Christmas?"

"Oh, my niece had her boyfriend and his son over. The boyfriend is a stripper!"

"No!"

"One of those Chipper men."

"Chippendale men?"

"Uh-huh. I tell you, Ol, I was tempted to ask him to do a little dance after dinner. That man is rippled."

"I think they say 'ripped.'"

"Ripped. Rippled. Same thing. He ate half the turkey. He said he only ate protein. I think I might start eating more protein myself."

Ollie laughed. She ate a few more berries, savoring them. Frances's face looked tired. She looked like she'd been worrying hard about Ollie and now was relaxing a little.

"Remember Mr. Emerson? Well, I met him," Ollie told her.

"What? How? When?"

"He was staying at the hotel, masquerading as a guest. A nice guest. He builds high-rise condos."

"Oh no," Frances said. "Oh, I'm so sorry, Ol."

"Me too. I thought he was nice. He took me out on a cat boat."

"Really? You?"

"Yes, me. What do you think—I can't have fun?"

"Of course I don't. I just didn't think you would like something like that. Did you?"

"It was something."

"You liked him, didn't you?"

"It doesn't matter."

"He didn't tell you who he was?"

"He came to visit me at the hospital. He said he handled it wrong."

"Men can be so silly."

"So there goes my whole life." Her hand clutched her pocketbook strap.

"That doesn't mean your life is over. Come on. Did he check out?"

"I'm sure he did. There's nothing for him here."

"Maybe he didn't."

"So?"

"So maybe you should talk to him some more. When you're not so vulnerable with an IV in your arm in a hospital gown with your ass hanging out."

"It wasn't hanging out."

"You know what I mean."

"So I should put on my power business suit and go talk to him?"

"You have one?"

"Of course not."

"Put on that nice blue top that makes your eyes look like a swimming pool and go get him. Tell him what you want. Don't back down . . ." she sang.

"Come on," Frances said, and they got up and walked toward the car. Ollie stumbled once and Frances slipped her arm through hers. And left it there. It felt so odd to be walking arm in arm. Frances's arm was bony and warm and it was crimped at a stiff angle, but she held it there, and Ollie leaned lightly against it and smiled to herself.

When they pulled into the Low-Key Inn parking lot, Ollie's eyes filled up with tears. "Oh," she said to her familiar world.

"Toughen up, old girl," Frances told her. "No time to get mushy."

They walked together along the path to Ollie's igloo. The world looked lovely and green. The little geckos scuttled quicker than a blink, bustling about their business. The hibiscus flowers yawned open lazily. Their insides were so yellow with pollen the bees inside of them came out rolled in gold.

When they got to Ollie's yard, the birds started calling to her. Her heart pounded. One little fellow swooped and landed on her shoulder.

"They are so happy to see you," Frances said, a bit of wistfulness in her voice.

"They would come to trust you too," Ollie said.

"Really?" she said quickly, like she'd been waiting for permission.

"Why not?" Ollie spread her arms out in a sweeping gesture. The world looked like it was overflowing, the buds bursting into bloom. Ollie's small garden fountain burbled. Birds splashed each other in the basin.

Frances stopped walking suddenly, and Ollie looked toward her door. Someone was sitting on her porch swing.

"Oh no. It's Al," Ollie whispered.

Frances nodded. "Go get him."

"I can't."

"Yes, you can. Go be yourself. Your strong, wonderful self."

"Thank you," she said. She hugged Frances, watched as Frances walked away. Then she took a deep breath and turned toward her porch.

Al stood up as she walked toward him. "They told me they were letting you out. I called the hospital," he said.

She stared at him.

"Let's sit out here," he said, looking at the porch swing.

"Okay," she said, and put her bag on the ground.

She felt fragile, like all her bones were made of twigs. She wanted to go take a shower, wash the hospital smells off her. She sat down next to him. "I don't like you right now," she said.

"I don't like me much either. But, Ollie . . ."

He rubbed his knees with his hands. His knees stuck out of his plaid shorts. He had white socks on that had slumped around his ankles. One looked whiter than the other, like it wasn't a true match. Ollie didn't want to feel kindly toward him, but she still did. He was such a bad dresser.

"I am sorry," he said.

She shook her head.

"These last few days, coming back to where I started, to where I used to live, walking down these old paths, I didn't realize . . ." He looked down. "I'm ashamed to be me right now. What have I really done with my life? I tell you what means more to me than all those high-rise condos I've built—that I gave that old house to the VFW. And I tell you what. I didn't even do it for the right reasons.

I just wanted out of it after my family was lost there. I didn't want anything to remind me. The army straightened me out when I was a kid going the wrong way, so I figured I owed them something back."

"You never told me how you lost your family," Ollie said gently.

"There was an electrical fire. I wasn't home. I was busy traveling for business. I was always too busy." He stops. "I just wasn't there for them."

"I'm so sorry."

"Yes, well, I didn't want the house. I gave the insurance money to the VFW, and they rebuilt."

"That was kind. That was generous," Ollie said.

"No. It was nothing. It was long-distance. Giving money doesn't make you feel much of anything. Especially if you have money."

"But you gave them a place. Sometimes that's all that people need."

"They did something good with it. They *turned* it into something. They have meetings there. They help people heal. That's the key, Ollie. You have to convert things into other things. What is that law of energy? It can never be created or destroyed. It can only change shape. All I've done with my energy is build big buildings for the wealthy."

Ollie sat there quietly. She wanted to reach out and touch his shoulder, but she didn't. She heard voices in the distance, splashes in the pool, a gull calling. She heard the blender going at the tiki bar. It smelled like gardenias. A bee hummed around the porch, then went on its way.

"You know, the seventies are back in," she told Al.

"I'd heard that." He looked up at her and raised one eyebrow.

"*The Brady Bunch*, the Monkees."

"I remember."

"What would you think about turning this place into a seventies retro hotel? I mean, it already is. But exaggerating it. Making it more itself. A mod version of itself."

"I *did* always like the seventies. They were so jaunty, so smiley faced, so hopeful," Al said.

"People are longing for that now."

"Mod?"

"Hope."

"You can't sell hope, Ollie," he said, looking down at his feet.

"Oh, no?"

He looked into her face.

She hurried to say, "Think of it as a destination event-place. For weddings, maybe. This has always been a good place for love. And maybe creativity events like workshops. Maybe a learning center where people, I don't know, study mind-body things—self-healing, self-awareness." She could picture it. The hotel becoming more than it was now, becoming a kind of sanctuary where people gathered to grow. She felt a surge of excitement and—what was it?—pride. Yes. The little hotel where dreams could be realized. She imagined people strolling around the grounds, studying. She imagined the flowers, tended and nurtured, bursting into blossom.

"But it would have some market strength as just a hotel too," Ollie said. She couldn't turn away from the hotel's essence. It had always been a refuge, and it would have to stay that. A place people came back to for vacation. There was a kind of magic in that simplicity.

She paused.

He stared at her.

She'd been rattling on. Did he think she was crazy? She was actually pretty proud of using that term, "market strength." *I almost sound like I know what I'm proposing. I might as well keep on going,* she decided. *I have nothing left to lose.*

"It wouldn't be the Gold Institute, and it wouldn't be the Low-Key Inn," she said. "But maybe we could combine our two ideas." She interlocked her fingers. "We could call it the Institute of Low-Key Living."

He smiled.

"It would need a lot of work. Renovation. Some of that changing-shape energy."

"Ah," he said. His eyes looked interested.

"Of course, we'd keep the birds and the gardens." She looked pointedly at him. "Nature is the heart of it all."

"Hmm."

"Don't make a decision based on the fact that I just got out of the hospital and you feel sorry for me."

"I don't feel sorry for you, Ollie. I feel sorry for me. You were right. I *have* spent my life running away. When I look at the buildings I've built, they look like mausoleums to me now. Big tombstones. Maybe that's what I've been building all along—my own cemetery."

"Maybe it's time to get out of the cemetery."

She waited.

He said, "There's that whole magazine full of things I'd still like to do. Manatee-watching tours and shell collecting and exploring the mangrove tunnels. And, of course, kayaking with alligators!"

She raised her eyebrows.

"Would you consider joining me?" he said.

"First things first," she said.

"What would that be?"

"I have to feed the birds."

"Can I help?"

She got up and went to her bucket of birdseed, opened the top, and took a scoop. "Come over here and make your hands into a cup."

MARY

Mary had heard about Ollie's trip to the hospital. The whole hotel had. There was a big WELCOME HOME, OLLIE poster in the lobby with a bouquet of flowers gathered from her garden. A lot of people had signed their names to the poster and written her a little note. Mary wrote, *Love and healing wishes from Mary, CC, and Larkin*. Forget James-Walter.

She went to the gift shop and bought herself a bathing suit. A two-piece, navy blue stripes. *Nautical*, she thought. *Because I'm going to be living on a boat.*

She couldn't really believe herself.

She walked out to the beach carrying her backpack. All it had in it was her phone now. She'd unpacked Larkin's presents in the room, along with Ollie's sketch pad and paints. *I have virtually nothing*, she thought. The fluttering in her chest was part fear, part excitement.

The air smelled fresh. She waded into the clear water and turned on her back and floated. She looked at the wisps of clouds, felt the water moving around her, buoying her. Then she got out and started walking along the hard wet sand. She'd let the air dry her skin.

A few people were collecting shells, but mostly the beach was empty. She walked all the way to where the inlet cut in, and the boats were chugging through on their way to one adventure or another. Sandpipers fluttered ahead of her as she walked. Tiny wavelets whooshed against the sand. *Lightning whelk*, she said to herself. *Fighting conch*. She was proud that she'd learned some names of shells. She'd have to learn more.

Ollie had told her that she walked every day on the beach. *I'll do that too*, Mary thought. *Maybe I'll walk with Ollie. I would like Ollie as a friend.*

Mary looked out over the gulf. Little fish were jumping clear out of the water. Mullet, Kipper had told her. Kipper. She smiled. Then she thought of Ron, and it was like a chasm opening inside of her. She took a deep breath. *Don't go there.* She thought of CC and Larkin instead. She hadn't heard from CC at all. But she'd call them later, she decided, reach out to see how they were, to hear their voices, to say she loved them. Gestures, she thought, could turn into steps, and steps could turn into paths, and paths could turn into roads. Maybe that's how it could be done.

She sat down on the sand under a palm tree. The shade and sun dappled the ground. She called Joelle, told her about Ron, about the houseboat.

Mary said, "I'll fly back to get my condo ready to sell, and I'll bring some of my things back here, but I don't want much. I'll sell all the rest."

"Can I have your orange throw pillows?"

"Of course."

Mary thought about her closet. The clothes arranged, button-downs, then scoop necks, then tees, her sweaters folded in cubbies. All the blacks and grays. The closet of the shadow Mary.

"I'm giving away all my clothes," she told Joelle.

"Good," Joelle said.

"I want to live without anything for a while. Maybe then I'll know what I really want."

Joelle asked, "What do you feel about moving so far away from CC and Larkin?"

"CC hates me anyway," Mary said.

"Oh, Mary," Joelle said. "She loves you. She's just figuring out how to be. You both love Larkin. You have that in common."

"They're different kinds of love."

"Not really."

Joelle knew CC pretty well. CC called Joelle sometimes just to talk. She confided in Joelle the way she didn't with Mary. It made Mary a bit jealous but also happy that her friend and her daughter were close.

Mary said, "Maybe CC will come down and visit me and bring Larkin. Now that I'm living at the beach, I'll probably be a lot more popular."

"If you have a beach house, they will come," Joelle said.

Mary said, "What if she brings James-Walter?"

"You'll deal with it."

"He can sleep in the dinghy."

"I can see you in the night cutting the lines, sending him out to sea."

"That sounds like fun."

"CC has to be the one to cut the line, Mary."

"I know, I know."

"Let it play itself out."

"I will."

"Do you think walks on the beach can heal us?" Mary said.

"Yes."

"I think I'll stop whatever I'm doing every day to watch the sunset."

"I think I want to rent a houseboat too."

"Maybe you'll come visit me?"

"I can't wait."

She walked back toward the hotel. She wound around the tiki bar and the pool and back to her igloo. Her funny little igloo. It hadn't been a problem checking back into the same one. Kipper said Sleep was going to email her a rental contract to sign for *The Maybe Girl*. Then she could move in there.

She thought she heard something as she walked up the steps. A laugh. Coming from inside? Her heart stuttered. The door opened. CC was standing there.

"They gave us the key," CC said.

Mary stared at her.

Larkin ran out carrying Blanket, threw herself at Mary, and clutched her legs. Mary put her hand on Larkin's head. "Oh good, you found Blanket. He was waiting for you," Mary said to her.

Tripod had carried Blanket in his mouth all the way from the airport, so Blanket was a little worse for wear. His nose was a bit chewed. But Tripod had put Blanket down after he saw Kipper, and Mary had put Blanket in her carry-on and brought him back to the hotel.

"First thing she did when we walked in the door was look for that stuffed animal," CC said.

"You gave her a haircut?" Mary asked CC.

"We had all of Christmas Day in a Motel 6 with nothing else to do. We watched Christmas movies and I did the haircut with a tiny pair of scissors I had in my makeup bag. It took forever."

Mary raised her eyebrows. *No Disney? No James-Walter?* CC shook her head.

Mary looked at Larkin. "You look like your mommy now," she said, stooping to give her a hug.

"We brought you a present," Larkin said, pulling on Mary's hand and dragging her toward the door.

"Really?" Mary asked, looking at CC.

CC shrugged, smiling. "Larkin insisted."

Larkin said, "We went to the Quicky-Mart."

"There wasn't much to choose from on the highway," CC said. "We could have gotten you some Slim Jims. That's about all they had. Who knew Slim Jims came in so many different flavors?"

Larkin was holding out a small wrinkled-up package to Mary. "I wrapped it," she said.

"Beautiful," Mary said.

She sat down on the bed. They both sat with her. She undid the paper. "Oh," she said.

"Do you like it?" Larkin asked, hopping up and down.

"Yes. Of course. Who doesn't love bubbles?" Mary said.

"Let's play with them, Gramma."

Mary looked at CC, and CC grinned at her.

"Let's see," Mary said, taking the plastic wrapping off the bubble pipe. She poured some bubble solution into it and blew. Bubbles frothed up, and one broke off and floated away. Larkin jumped up on the bed and popped it. "Do more," she said. "More."

Mary blew again. Larkin chased the bubbles around the room. Mary and CC looked at each other.

"Mommy, you do some," Larkin said.

CC took the pipe from Mary. Their fingers touched. CC blew bubbles. The air was full of iridescent little globes. Larkin jumped back on the bed and bounced on it, laughing.

Mary said, "Santa left presents for you, Larkin." Larkin's eyes lit up. She unwrapped each one carefully. "I love this," she said to each one. She put the pink mask right on and started doing her puzzle on the floor.

CC looked at Mary and silently mouthed, "Thank you."

Mary bowed her head. "Can I ask what happened?" she said to CC.

"We ditched him," CC said.

Mary almost laughed but held it in. Then she thought, *Oh my, what if I had left with Ron and they came back to my not being here? Well, it didn't happen. Somehow CC and I both left but found our way back. Maybe this hotel pulled us back.*

CC said, "When Larkin realized that we'd left Blanket behind, she had a meltdown. I said we had to go back to get him, and James-Walter said he wouldn't turn around just for a stupid stuffed animal. It was a big fight," she kind of whispered. But Larkin wasn't listening. She was humming to herself and doing the puzzle, Blanket by her side.

"He gets all puffed up when he gets angry," CC said. "'Can you say aaangrrrry,'" she said, mimicking him, "'verrrry sloooowllly?'" She rolled her eyes.

Mary laughed.

CC laughed too. One of those hysterical laughs that has anxiety and fear in it as well as release. Mary laughed harder. She snorted, and they both were suddenly swept up in a laughing fit. Mary couldn't breathe. "St-aah-op," Mary said. And they both collapsed into another bout of laughter. Tears were running down Mary's face. She hiccupped.

Both of them lay back on the bed and stared at the ceiling. Their laughing slowly subsided into occasional trills.

"I'm exhausted," CC said.

Larkin lay down on her back on the bed next to CC. She stretched her arms and legs up and down, up and down in swoops.

"What are you doing, Larky-Loo?" CC asked her.

"I'm making a snow angel. Except it's a bed angel. You make one too."

So Mary and CC both lay on the beds while Larkin got up and watched. Mary closed her eyes and let her arms and legs open, then close. She felt the soft nubs of the blanket.

"I feel like a butterfly," Mary said.

"Me too," CC said.

Larkin said, "I'm a hungry, hungry butterfly."

Mary sat up and said, "Let's go eat. What are you hungry for?"

"Mr. Chip pancakes!" Larkin said.

CC stood up and rolled her eyes. Mary waited.

"Okay," CC said. "Just for today."

Just for today was a good place to start, Mary thought.

Larkin skipped ahead of them as they walked to the dining room. CC was looking down.

"You okay?" Mary said.

"I can't believe he just left us. I mean, I told him to go, but he actually drove away and left us nowhere. Basically standing at a rest stop."

Mary held her breath. "You must have felt so alone," she said.

In that moment, all the years flowed together in Mary's mind, her childhood of aloneness and all the men who'd made her feel alone after that. CC knew about abandonment too.

But they were here together now.

Mary touched CC's arm. CC turned to her so quickly Mary was startled. "Oh, Cee," Mary said. CC leaned into Mary, and Mary held her. CC's body shook. Mary breathed slowly. Then Mary was aware of Larkin walking back toward them and stretching her arms around both of them. Mary put her hand on Larkin's head.

Mary knew it was just a moment. But it was a good moment.

AFTER

It was three days after Christmas, and it was happy hour. People were laughing and talking at the tiki bar. Mary was sitting at a table near the pool having an iced tea with Ollie and Al. Somebody had taken the Santa hat off the dolphin fountain and put a sparkly New Year's hat on it.

Mary asked Ollie, "So, you really are going to renovate?" Rumors were flying about the hotel's future. Was the hotel getting knocked down to build a golf course? High-rise condos? Was it being converted into a nature preserve?

Ollie smiled. She looked beautiful in a soft white linen shirt with her blue eyes and white hair. *Sprightly*, Mary thought.

Ollie said, "Yes. We have a general plan. It's just working out the details." Ollie told her the vision she had for the Institute of Low-Key Living.

"So much is in the details," Al said.

"We'd like to keep the seventies vibe of the rooms and the simplicity but update it all," Ollie said. "Build a meeting center. Renovate the kitchen and dining area and gardens. I'd love to make the restaurant garden bigger and serve all organic, grow a lot of our own food or locally source it!"

"Oh, I can see it," Mary said, so happy that the hotel's essence was going to be preserved.

"It's going to need a lot of work," Ollie said.

"I've got that part covered," Al said.

"And a lot of love," Ollie said.

"Ollie's got that part," Al said.

Al and Ollie looked at each other and nodded.

Ollie said to Mary, "We'd like to have you on our design team."

Mary sat very still. She and Ollie had talked yesterday, and Mary had wondered why Ollie was asking all the questions about her work flipping houses, and her time at Oskar's and at Ron's magazines, why Ollie was asking her about her philosophy of architecture and design.

Ollie's eyes twinkled as she looked at Mary.

Mary leaped out of her seat and hugged Ollie. "I couldn't think of anything I'd love more," Mary said.

Her thoughts were running already to fabrics and textures and colors. *Bamboo*, she thought. *Sea colors. Soft white. The texture of raw wood.* She realized she'd been thinking these things ever since she got here. *Maybe I can convince Kipper to help too*, she thought. *I'm sure Ollie would love to have him.*

The last few days, he'd been too busy with charters to visit them. She couldn't wait to tell him about this. Tell CC. Tell Joelle.

She almost ran down to the beach. CC was sitting on the sand with Larkin. That nice young man, Paul, was sitting with them. They were building a dribble castle. Larkin had her pink diving mask perched on her forehead and was sitting in a pool of water. Paul was busy building a wall around the castle. CC was decorating the wall with dribbling sand. *Hmm*, Mary thought. *Isn't that interesting?*

Just let it be, she thought. *You're getting way ahead of yourself, Mary Valley. If you had your way, CC would be married off to Paul already, and she'd be moving down here, getting a job in Ollie's organic kitchen. Larkin would be living close by!*

One step at a time, Mary thought, but her heart and mind were bolting like horses set free in a field, running, almost flying.

Mary sat down next to the castle. She let the wet sand drip through her fingers. She built a tippy tower that went up and up, reaching toward the sky. She held the secret of her new job within her like a little sun. There would be time to tell CC later. Right now, she just wanted to sit with them and build the castle.

They'd all extended their vacation a few more days to be together. And although Mary and CC were very careful around each other, they eased up when they played with Larkin. Every walk they took, every bubble they blew, something seemed to grow between them all. A slender vine tying them all together. They were really so much alike.

Of course, they still had their issues. They tiptoed around certain things, but both of them seemed to relax their rigid stances some. They managed to have whole conversations without fighting. Mary put a lot of energy into forcing herself to listen rather than comment, to nod rather than criticize, to do what Zelda had advised and lean toward CC when CC was talking, open up her body language. It made a difference.

Plus, Mary tried to respect CC's rules as best she could. And CC relaxed some of the rules herself. About Larkin's clothes, CC still favored dresses over shorts and tees, but she'd softened some when it came to fabrics. And though they were back to following CC's weird diet, every once in a while, CC allowed a treat to slip by, and Mary pretended not to notice.

They'd painted shells and made a wind chime out of the sticks and shells they'd found on the beach. They went exploring in town and found a funky little shop where Mary bought everyone a few new clothes—colorful, flowy things. They poked around consignment shops and talked about furnishing the houseboat. CC took a real interest in the boat, couldn't wait to go see it. "The floating space," she called it. They were both thrilled to find a great hammock for hardly any money. A retail coup!

Mary talked to CC about how she didn't want to fill up the houseboat with stuff, just leave it sparely decorated with natural things she found on the beach, and CC agreed. CC and Larkin found a big weathered branch and dragged it back down the beach for Mary's "houseboat-warming present." They were so proud of it. CC said Mary could use it as a hat rack, but Mary said it was a work of art, and it would stand unadorned and be her most prized possession.

When Mary had told CC she thought she'd get a different kind of job eventually, not writing, CC had told her that she might get another job herself, one where she could be home more for Larkin.

"I wish you would let me help you babysit," Mary said.

"How? You'll be so far away," CC said. Did she say it a little sadly, or was Mary imagining it?

"Wouldn't you like to live on the houseboat with me?" Mary said to her, laughing.

CC smiled and shrugged.

Mary thought, *Well, at least she didn't say no.*

CC said, "I'm not sure what I want, but it will all become clear."

It will all become clear became CC and Mary's new mantra for everything. What's the weather? It will all become clear. What do you want to do today? It will all become clear. Even, how do you feel? It will all become clear. And it was funny how, when they just let things be and become, life did seem to get a lot clearer.

She knew she'd like to volunteer doing something in her new

life. Help save the gopher tortoises. Or help the veterans somehow. She even thought about maybe rescuing a dog of her own.

In these last few days, Mary tried not to think about the future at all, tried to just stick with the present. Making Zelda proud! But she found herself daydreaming about having Kipper for a neighbor. She thought she'd like to invite him over for a beer in the evening to watch the sunset. She thought she'd like to have him teach her about the mangrove islands and how to navigate a boat through them. Teach her the names of seabirds. She thought about kissing him again, or maybe they'd just end up being friends. *It will all become clear*, she told herself.

Mary found herself writing a lot in her journal these last few days. Letters to Zelda. But weren't they really letters to herself? Maybe, she thought, she didn't really need Zelda anymore. And she was hopeful that she wouldn't even walk in her sleep anymore either. The fear that she'd had about wandering away from her life, well, that had already happened. And she hadn't drowned or gotten lost or anything tragic. She'd actually found herself in a good place. And maybe that thing she'd been looking for sleepwalking and opening all her cabinets, well, it wasn't really a thing she'd been searching for after all.

It was just her all along.

Now Mary watched CC and Larkin and Paul working busily on their castle. She breathed deep the salty, sweet air. She looked back toward the faded pink hotel. It looked like it was glowing in this light. She thought of *The Maybe Girl* and all her possibilities. She could see Ollie and Al sitting together. Were they holding hands? She smiled. A few pelicans flew over the hotel. Heading somewhere. She shaded her eyes with her hand and saw there, walking steadily toward them across the beach, a man and his three-legged dog.

ACKNOWLEDGMENTS

Big thank-you to Meg Ruley for believing in me (and for falling in love with Larkin). To Monique Patterson for giving my book a chance. To the smartest and sweetest first readers of this book, Sarah Tantillo and Barb Daniel. To Stephen Dunn and Peter Murphy, my best teachers, for all the years of workshops, and for helping me find my voice. To Jess Errera for being such a smart and sweet part of my team. And to my family for loving me.

ABOUT THE AUTHOR

Ryan Johnson

SANDY GINGRAS is the author and illustrator of twenty-five gift books. She's also published fiction, poetry, and narrative nonfiction, and she won the Debut Dagger Award for mystery writing in 2012. She's designed hundreds of products for national stationery companies and owns two retail stores. She lives on an island six miles out to sea in a happy cottage on the bay with her husband and a dog named Turtle.